PRETTY LIKE A DEVIL

EDEN O'NEILL

PRETTY LIKE A DEVIL

COURT LEGACY: BOOK SIX

EDEN O'NEILL

Court High

They The Pretty Stars

Illusions That May

Court Kept

We The Pretty Stars

Court University

Brutal Heir

Kingpin

Beautiful Brute

Lover

Court Legacy

Dirty Wicked Prince

Savage Little Lies

Tiny Dark Deeds

Eat You Alive

Eat Your Heart Out

Pretty Like A Devil

CONTENT WARNINGS:

PRETTY LIKE A DEVIL is a dark new adult college romance recommended for readers 18+. Please see the author's website at www.edenoneill.com for all the book's content warnings.

PROLOGUE

Aspen - age 12

I held my legs, shaking.

Oh, please. Oh, please. Oh, please.

My eyes shut tight, "Jupiter" by Mozart playing in my head. Symphony No. 41 was always my favorite. It always helped. This entire summer it helped.

Please. Please. Please.

My nails bit into my legs, my fear a white-hot current. He wouldn't hurt me. He didn't hurt me.

But he did chase me.

The last time he was here he did, and when the leaves crunched outside the cabin, I hid my face in my lap. I cried. I sobbed. I just wanted my mama. I wanted my—

The door crept open, and I couldn't even look. The fear overtook me, and I pressed myself so hard into the corner. I didn't know what I'd do if he chased me again. I wouldn't run again. I promised him I wouldn't run.

I won't run. I won't run. I won't run.

I rocked while I thought it. I rocked while I said it. I knew

I was saying it. Over and over, I was saying it out loud, but I wasn't sure if he could even hear me. I was crying too loud, my wails too loud.

He'll get mad.

I tried to silence myself, but as the floorboards of the small cabin creaked beneath me, I wasn't sure I could. He was getting closer. He was…

"Please. I won't run. I won't run. I won't—"

I jumped when a hand touched me, my voice instantly cutting off. In fact, I slammed into the wall so hard a searing pain shot into my shoulder. I groaned, gripping my arm, but even still, I couldn't look at him. I just sobbed.

"Aspen…"

My head shot up. It wasn't *his* voice but someone else's. That someone else was my mama, and I leaped from the floor, my body shaking.

Mom grabbed me, burying me in the ruffles of her dress. She was crying too, and she didn't cry.

"Baby girl. My baby." Tear trails ran down her dark cheeks, her hands gripping me, my locs. My mama was crying, really crying.

She fell to the floor, me in her arms like I was five instead of twelve.

"Baby girl, did he hurt you?" she asked me, and I gasped.

She knew about him. She knew about what *he'd done.*

I couldn't say anything. Well, I did say something, but it was just her name over and over. I kept saying *mama.* That was all I could hear in my head. That and "Jupiter." "Jupiter" saved me. It kept me from crying most nights being here, screaming.

"Mama." I absolutely shook in my mom's arms, and I wasn't aware when she finally got me up off the floor. Once we did, we moved steadfast, her directing me, holding me.

We weren't alone.

There were lights outside, flashing lights, cop cars. I saw

so many, their lights blinding me in a forest of trees and cabins.

So many cabins.

The one I had been in was one of many, vast, and I was sure that was why he'd chosen it. No one would find me out here, not when the new cabins were being used on the other side of the campgrounds.

I buried my face in my mama's chest. My mama didn't have a lot of body to hug, but she held me so hard. She kept me *safe*, and I hid my face from all the cop cars. I hid my face from all the campers. I saw them too, boys of various ages both older than me and younger in shorts and T-shirts. They all watched my mama and me alongside camp counselors.

Everyone was out of bed for this.

I couldn't stop shaking, and it was only when I was in the back of a cop car with my mom's arms and a blanket around me that I finally looked up. I looked up just in time to see another cop car pulling away. Someone was in the back of that car too, but he was alone.

My physical nightmare was by himself.

He looked so unusual back there, a kid like me. He glanced over his shoulder at me, the car putting distance between us, and as soon as he made eye contact, I pressed my face back into my mom's shoulder. I couldn't look at those cold blue eyes. I'd stared at them every day for an entire summer, and I couldn't look at them again.

Instead, I let fear take me again because I only glanced up after his own cop car took him away. I saw nothing but a head of dark hair while a boy no older than me was driven into the night. The other campers saw him too. They saw *what he did too*. Thatcher Reed was a monster.

And now everyone else knew it.

CHAPTER
ONE

Aspen - the present

"Excuse me. Are you incompetent? My daughter's dresses go in her closet. Not on her coffee table, honestly."

Eugena Davis spun on her red-bottom heels. The middle-aged black woman directed her staff with a firm hand while she questioned their intelligence. She waved at another, her expression terse, frustrated. "And you definitely be careful with that. One string on that cello matters more than your life. I assure you."

Jesus Christ.

"Mom," I gritted. One would think after so many years of hearing my mother speak to people as if they were below her wouldn't faze me, but I could honestly say the opposite. I cringed. "Please."

She was embarrassing herself and me. I didn't want people to think I was above them. Never had. Even with all the attention my career had gotten in the past few years.

My mama grunted, twisting in my direction. She popped her curled fists on her designer jeans, seemingly ready to tell *me* off. That was until someone came into the room with another one of my cellos and set it on the couch of all places.

I had to rub my temple when she told them what an idiot they were, how accidents could happen and someone could sit on it. Again, the cello itself mattered more than his life. At least to my mama, and what was sad was I knew she believed that.

Instead of losing my fucking mind, I sat on the couch next to the cello case. I continued to let my mother direct bags upon bags into my new dorm room like I was some royal princess. She'd had our staff pack up my entire life.

She glared at a man with hat boxes. "You set those down gently. The pearls on that…"

"Matter more than his life." I was smart enough to keep the quip under my breath, but I got the attention of Franklin Jones. He was surveying the room like he was supposed to, his suit polished, professional. The guy was jacked and looked like he belonged elbows deep in dirt while he dragged himself through trenches. Actually, that was how I'd first come across his work, a war film.

Keeping that thought to myself, I watched Franklin's eyes flare wide when my mom literally grabbed something out of someone's hands. She once again called them incompetent, and I palmed my face.

Not long now and she'll be gone.

I'd be counting the minutes. I had been counting the minutes and long before the decision was made for me to go to college this semester. I'd always planned to go to school, but life had different plans for me.

I didn't think either my mom or I thought those cello lessons she'd invested in for me when I was five would amount to anything. Most kids got involved with music at a young age, but I'd taken really well to it. In fact, so well that people now paid me to perform. This little dream my mom and I'd had turned into a career and a lifestyle I certainly hadn't been ready for. My life had seemingly changed overnight in a matter of years. The cover of music magazines. Award shows and sold-out arenas…

I'd actually gone on tour with some of the biggest hip-hop artists in the game. I played with people I'd grown up watching, and now, people paid to see just me. It was crazy, overwhelming.

My mouth dry, I continued to study my mom's frustrations. People said we looked alike, but I thought I resembled more old photos of my dad. Not that I could compare since he dipped when I was a kid. A judge, he had another life and apparently Mama and me didn't fit into it. He actually only started calling when he saw me at an award show, which was honestly just embarrassing. He had another family too, according to the tabloids, and I couldn't help feeling sorry for them.

I wished I looked more like my mother. She was that classic American beauty featured in jeans ads in the nineties. Literally, she used to do modeling before she put everything on hold for me and my career. We also both had locs and people compared us, said we looked more like sisters on red carpets than mom and daughter. This was also the reason she was rail thin, and though I didn't get those genes, I was happy with my curves. They were modest, and I wasn't anything more than a C-cup, but I liked to eat and wasn't willing to sacrifice them. If things were up to my mom, though, that would be different. I had to look a certain way with this life, cameras and all that.

"You can go. In fact, please go," my mom said, and I could breathe now that all my stuff was finally in the room. All my mom's dictating was doing was stressing me the fuck out. Everyone but Franklin left the room, and once they had, Mom got out her phone. "I'm obviously going to have to look into hiring some new help when I get back to LA. Honestly, we'll be lucky if they didn't break anything."

These people *were* new, and that was due to the staff's choice. No one wanted to work for us since my mom was so strict. She liked things a certain way and was the epitome of a momanager.

"Everything looks fine," I said, pretending to look and appease my mom.

I got a *look* from Franklin along the way, the man doing his own pretending. I had to say he'd done a lot of research for his role. He actually looked like a bodyguard over there with the way he studied the windows and peered outside at college students like he was making mental notes about them.

I guess that's why you're paying him.

That was why I was paying him, and he kept his mouth shut when my mom came over and asked him if he saw anything out of the ordinary outside. He probably wasn't seeing much, which was the point, of course. Queenstown Village was a college town, and that was what was down there on Pembroke University's quad. People were studying and listening to music below down on the grass while others played Frisbee nearby. It was a typical fall semester in the Midwest. At least, I believed it was typical. I'd only seen college on TV before this.

One thing the TV got right was how quiet things were, how normal. It all was the complete opposite of the busy and often frantic lifestyle I normally led in the music industry. I literally felt my body seep free of stress when I'd gotten here, and it'd been nice.

So nice.

This was another comment I kept to myself, and when Franklin gave my mother canned answers about the lay of the land outside, I breathed another sigh of relief. He was doing his job very well.

"Everything looks on the up-and-up, ma'am," Franklin said before dismissing himself. My mom had worked out a two-bedroom dorm so my hired security could have a room nearby. He was to stay with me all semester while I was here.

Little did my mother know that room wouldn't be needed. She needed to believe I needed it, though.

Mom allowed Franklin to leave. He stated he was going to analyze the perimeter again. It felt like he'd said he had already done that a few times, but I wasn't going to out his lies.

Play it cool.

Mom joined me on the couch. "So I've spoken to the chancellor personally," she said, her tone serious. She was serious, and I knew she was. She frowned. "He's kept the details of you being here on the low. Not even any of the professors know. You'll be able to attend classes like everyone else as long as you remain discreet."

I'd already been told about that. I was to keep to myself and not draw attention. No one was supposed to know I was here. I was to blend in.

Mom touched my shoulder, her fingers twisting one of my locs. "You'll be safe, Aspen, and we will get to the bottom of those threats."

A pang of tightness hit my stomach, the threats the reason I was actually here and blending in as a student this term. I was at Pembroke-U to go to school, but I wouldn't be going to school if what happened at Carnegie Hall hadn't occurred. I'd been playing the biggest concert of my life, my literal dream. I'd done a lot in my career, but the opportunity to play Carnegie Hall hadn't come right away. It eventually had, and it proved to be the worst night of my life.

My mouth dried as my mother studied my face, actual concern there, and I knew she had it. I mean, if my daughter's life had been threatened on the biggest night of her career, I'd be unnerved too, and this wasn't the first time I'd put her through the wringer. I'd been kidnapped once. She almost lost me once.

Of course, that was a long time ago, but neither of us forgot. I mean, how could we, how could I? My mother and her overbearing nature kicked into overdrive after the summer I turned twelve. She'd already been that way since it had just been us for so long. I was my mom's life, and I knew that.

She moved a few of my lengthy locs over my shoulder. "Now, mind Franklin. You can have fun but be responsible about it."

Be responsible meant blending in. I was to wear a disguise at all times. Again, no one was supposed to know I was here. I nodded. "I will."

"And of course, stay militant about your practice schedule. Your music isn't your focus here, but we don't want you getting loosey goosey and obliterating everything you've worked for," she continued.

No, we wouldn't want me getting loosey goosey, which was why she'd arranged for my teacher, Deborah Hays, to send me weekly emails of all the rigorous sheet music she wanted me to perfect while I was here. They ranged in difficulty, but knowing Deborah, they'd be challenging. I was also to keep up on my workout schedule and various appointments with my trainer, which would be conducted via Zoom now that I was here instead of in LA.

"The Peloton is in your room," Mom informed, the perfect place for it to stare me down when I didn't feel like doing it. She studied me in my jeans and tube top. "We wouldn't want you gaining the freshman fifteen while you're here, and dear God, don't eat anything you can't pronounce or that has additives. Basically, stay out of that cafeteria. That's why we got you a meal delivery service. You don't need to get fat just because you're here."

Franklin came back in right around the time Mom said that, and though his attention averted to the room, that didn't mean he failed to hear Mom's comment.

God.

"Then there's your medications, Aspen. You have a lot of responsibility being here on your own, and we don't want you having a—"

"I'll be fine." I stood, adjusting my shirt, adjusting *every-thing*. She made me feel so fucking self-conscious sometimes and like a child more often than not. Between the schedules and the appointments, it was just too fucking much.

Calm down.

I focused on the positive thoughts that soon my mother and her habits would be gone. She'd leave me alone, and she'd look into those threats.

She'd leave.

That was when the guilt hit, sharp, and it always did when I got frustrated with her. I knew she was only this way because she cared.

Because of that, I didn't fight her hug before she finally left. She told me she loved me, and I truly believed she wanted me to have fun. Her delivery was just crap some-times, and she mentioned for me to have a good time again before she left. She told me not to worry about anything and that she would find out who'd threatened me that night at Carnegie Hall. There'd been letters. Ones she'd found…

"Your fee as promise," I said to Franklin, who'd waited after my mom departed. We made sure she had before I got my purse. I nodded at the check. "And there's extra there. For your discretion?"

He'd already signed an NDA, but he'd had to deal with a lot in the few days he'd been with Mom and me. My mom could be a lot, and I got that.

The white man's eyes flashed. I assumed at the amount. It was worth it if he kept our agreement on the low.

Opening his jacket, he pocketed the check. "No problem. Though, I'm confused why you wouldn't actually hire secu-rity for yourself."

I was sure he was. The whole world had heard about those threats I'd gotten. It'd been a few letters. The words on them had been cut out from magazines and pasted on the paper like something out of a psycho killer film. The threats had also been graphic about what the person would do to me if they found me.

My throat got thick all of a sudden, my heart racing. I was scared, but I was sure not for the reason Franklin believed. "I appreciate your concern, but I'll be fine."

Gratefully for me, Franklin wasn't being paid for his opinions, and I was sure he didn't care enough to make any more. He took his money. He left, and I was also grateful for something else after he did. I was grateful my mom didn't have time to watch movies. More specifically, war films like the ones Franklin, the actor I'd just paid, starred in. It'd definitely set off red flags for her.

And she'd probably question the same thing Franklin did before exiting my life.

CHAPTER
TWO

Thatcher

I tossed my head back, smoke billowing into the air. I was high as shit and barely cognizant of my phone buzzing in my pocket.

Wells: Whatcha doing?

Getting high as shit, and when I told my friend that, his second text came quick.

Wells: Where are you at? I'll come to you.

I gazed around, under the protection of strobe lights and *lots* of easy ass. Some chicks were even topless, these underground raves something else. My frat put them on, and they traveled to allow for anonymity. Tonight's was at an abandoned warehouse.

People could do whatever they wanted at these things, and there were no witnesses to tell them different. That was the point and another reason I came.

Me: Nah, I'm good.

If Wells came here, he'd put an ice bucket on my shit.

Normally, my best friend was up for a good time and doing whatever the fuck we wanted and *to whomever* the fuck we wanted. The stories he and I had were legendary, and that was just from high school.

Things had changed, though. They were recent, and though I knew they weren't his fault…

Wells: Come on, man. Don't be like that.

I would be like that. I would if he continued to be weird every time he fucking saw me. Between him and our other best friends Dorian, Wolf, and Bru, I was completely over it. They were acting different. Different around me, and I couldn't stand that shit.

Me: Just let me have my good time. I'll sound the alarm if I need something.

I did and the cavalry would come running, aka the other guys. I noticed none of them were texting me or texting anything in our group chat. They knew when I got like this only Wells could get through. We were the closest. Dorian and Wolf were slightly older, and Bru was new to our clique. We all were boys for life, but Wells and I had a different bond since we were a little younger. We got up to our own juvenile shit over the years and never took life too seriously.

Things were getting too serious lately. At least, for me, and my friends were picking up on that.

Wells: Fine. Just be safe.

Another thing Wells would never say to me. Be safe? Really? This fucker went to sex parties on the regular, and I was getting the "be safe" like he was my mom trying to check on me. I mean, I went to parties too, but not on the reg. It was usually when I was bored or something, but it wasn't my religion or anything.

I didn't even bother texting Wells a response. I'd say some shit I would regret no doubt.

Fuck was I high…

It was bad tonight. Even for me. The heavy bass from the music sped up my heart, and I was glad I wasn't on any other drugs besides weed.

I grabbed the hips of a ready and willing chick under the strobe lights, but pushed her off when she got too handsy, too possessive. I belonged to no one. Least of all some bitch that smelled like cotton candy body spray and wore too much body glitter.

"Get a fucking life," I growled when she grabbed for my cock, and though she pouted her pearl-pink lips at me, I had a feeling all I had to do was bend that ass over to have it. Even if I wasn't a Reed, I was me and could get anything I wanted. I'd gotten something of a rep since coming to Pembroke University. I got into whatever the hell I felt like, and my family donating obscene amounts of cash to this university had nothing to do with that.

I really shouldn't mix booze with the weed, but I did. I was just taking my second swig when a flash of white caught my eye. It followed up by something silver, and I lowered my bottle.

A girl danced over by one of the neon towers, a black girl with warm brown skin and hips that knew what to do with that music. She had her fingers pushed into a blonde wig, the flash of white I saw, but there was nothing blonde about it. It was Marilyn Monroe style, but it was stark white like the dye job my buddy Wells did. His roots were dark, but everything else was platinum.

A small crowd had formed around the girl and rightly so. She swiveled those hips in a way that had my cock at full mast, and the territorial fucker in me couldn't help but clear the floor around her. Some guys had wet their lips like they wanted a taste, and when they started to take their cell phones out (I assumed to record her), I quickly made sure it was just this girl and me on the floor.

All it took was a look.

It probably would have taken less had they seen me coming. Though, I didn't know it was possible for me to enter a room period without being noticed. I was a big enough fucker for people to know about me, whether I wore full black tonight or not.

Fuck was I hard.

This girl made it easy, all that beautiful flesh glowing under the neon lights. Her thick thighs exposed every gyration she made to the music, but because she danced with her back to me, I couldn't see her face. I wanted to, though, and angled with my bottle in my hand. I may have approached her and erased the five or so feet between us, but then, I saw her.

No fucking way.

The beer was forgotten about. I handed it off quick and sobered the fuck up. I also put more distance between us, and right away, I tugged my skull neck gaiter up over my mouth. It was cool tonight, but I wore it sometimes to fuck around with no names. Girls could be clingy bitches at these raves.

Between my neck gaiter and my backwards hat, I was nothing but an anonymous face in the crowd, but the girl in front of me wasn't.

She was fucking famous.

It'd been *years* since I'd seen this girl in person, but a dude had to be living under a rock not to know who Aspen Davis was. The chick went on tour with people like Beyoncé and had topped some charts just herself with her cello. She mostly did hip-hop in classical style, and everyone knew who she was.

You know who she is.

I did and well. Gone was her baby face, but then again, so was mine. I resembled nothing of that snot-faced twelve-year-old who had changed both of our lives.

Mostly hers.

I was aware of that, again keeping my distance. It was easy to do since I'd cleared the floor, and with no one looking, I took advantage. Still stunning, Aspen Davis was always a pretty girl. She was a pretty woman now, her lips full, glossed and pouty. Again, she'd lost her baby face and nothing was left now but large brown eyes, a pert button nose, and a body with generous if not copious amounts of tits and ass. Said tits currently swelled above her glittery, silver dress and caught all the light around her, that warm brown skin like dark honey.

What are you doing here, snowflake?

She hated that name. I saw her wince every time I said it, but I couldn't help it back then. It was relevant at the time and kept her from being a person to me. She couldn't be a person back then. She was just a girl and...

Full hips swayed in front of me about the time I caught the whiff of peppermint and cocoa. This girl smelled like Christmas, sweet, savory...

"What are you supposed to be?"

I got too close, fucked up. I knew because the smell of peppermint bark was right in front of me and so were deep dark eyes that narrowed harshly, questioningly. Aspen Davis wanted to know why some dude was all up on her.

I followed her.

Like an innocent to the Pied Piper, I'd literally followed this girl behind the neon towers. We were basically by ourselves now, but the thing was, I wasn't looking like the innocent one in this scenario. I was like three of this girl between my height and general bodily dimensions. I crushed dudes on the football field *weekly*. My friends and I played for Pembroke's team, and it was lucky if I didn't leave guys in body bags after I was done with them. Then there was the fact I was wearing a mask in front of this girl.

Nah, I wasn't looking innocent, but at least masks weren't

much of a thing on the dance floor. A few guys were wearing them tonight.

Aspen approached, all that chocolate sugar in my nose again. I had to say she was brave stepping up to me. Especially since she didn't know me, and something flashed in my mind that I had seen her face lately. Though, obviously not in person. She'd been in the news recently.

She'd been threatened at one of her concerts.

She wasn't acting threatened, her head tilted as I assumed she waited for answers from me. She asked me a question, and I hadn't answered. The tone of her wig brought out the vibrancy in her eyes as well as the few crystals she wore to the side of them. They were flecks of silver just like the material of her dress. "Well?"

So, I wasn't going to answer her. My voice had changed just like the rest of me during those nine years since we'd seen each other, but I wasn't taking any chances. Aspen Davis definitely didn't want to know who she'd approached at some random rave in the Midwest.

Especially if she'd been threatened.

I said nothing, and apparently, she found that funny. Her glossed lips lifted a little, which did nothing to help the state of my cock. The fucker was still at full mast, which was just wrong on so many levels. Being attracted to Aspen Davis was fine, but wanting to fuck her?

Yeah, so fucking wrong.

It was because of our history, and I needed to get out of here and this situation asap. I didn't know why Aspen was here, but our raves were legendary. She could have honestly just been passing through town, and she'd clearly wanted anonymity herself with her wig.

"You're The Punisher, then?" she questioned, her voice momentarily distracting me. It was rich just like her music. She pointed at my neck gaiter. "Your mask?"

Her next move was to touch it, touch me, but I angled my

head. Even if I didn't want her to see my face, no touching was happening. At least from her end. *I did the touching only.*

The maneuver brought that smile back to Aspen's mouth. She wasn't hurt or put off like some girls would be and actually bumped a small laugh after. Like I was beneath her, and when she moved to give me her back, I got her wrist. She wanted to touch me? Well, she'd get fucking touched.

What are you doing?

Well, probably something considered fucking stupid. I was sure my friends would think that and certainly my father. He'd had to do some damage control last time I was in the same space as this girl, so pulling her into a deep dark corner to dance with her probably wasn't smart.

It didn't stop me from doing it, though, and I brought Aspen's thick hips right up against my swollen cock. The fucker definitely wasn't trying to be discreet, and at the first feel of it, her breath hiked.

"Someone's excited," she said, trying to face me, but I didn't let her. The more anonymity I had on this girl the better. She wouldn't want me touching her, not if she knew who I was.

You should let go.

My hands and Aspen's tight little body spun a different tale. She swayed her hips to the bump and rhythm of the music. She ground into me, and at one point, I had her bent over. I drove my cock in a slow thrust against her. The only thing keeping us separated was our goddamn clothes.

Fuck.

This was *bad.* So goddamn bad, but I couldn't stop when Aspen lifted and let me fondle her tits. This girl had some freak shit in her that called to my dark shit. It was deep, *primal,* and the freaky fuck only got off more because I knew for a fact she didn't know anything about me. I was some guy at a rave in a fucking mask.

Snowflake…

She was being bad, but then again, so was I. This kind of shit wasn't foreign to me. I fucked more than one girl at these raves, but Aspen Davis was a good girl. I'd seen her goodness on social media. Followed her…

She was following me at this point, letting me touch her. She spun, and the next thing I knew, she was grabbing my cross necklace. It matched the sharp ones in my ears, the ends pointed, deadly.

I didn't wear a ton of jewelry, but I never usually left the house without something in my ears or around my neck. I also wore a thick gorilla ring, something symbolic from home, and the metal of it heated on Aspen's back when she brought herself closer to me. She did that via my chain, and when she popped up on her toes, she only got as high as my chin. She wasn't a short girl. I was just fucking big. Her gloss lips lifted. "You want to fuck me, Punisher?"

She shouldn't be saying such things. Not here, and why the fuck was she here? She was being foolish. If she'd been threatened like the internet said, she was being an idiot.

She let go when I got her neck.

My thick fingers swallowed her delicate throat, forcing her to back off and stop being reckless regarding her safety. A slight flick fluttered behind my palm via her neck. It was quick, nervous.

Exhilarated.

I saw that completely behind her dark eyes. Something wild ringed around them, like the very prospect that I'd do something to her did something *for her*. That deep primal shit came to the surface again, and I had thoughts of chasing her, pinning her down and taking her.

That really was inappropriate, and the thoughts freaked me out enough that I let go. I did only for her to grab for me. She went for my belt loops and would have gotten a hold of them and something else if I let her. No one fucking touched me unless I wanted it, but I touched her when I got her by the pussy.

Breath instantly gone, her breath, and the area got really dark when I drowned us further in the shadows. I backed her right up against the wall, that hot heat of her snatch in my hand, and all thoughts escaped me in the next moment. I knew because I pushed my neck gaiter up.

I knew because I kissed her.

The taste… was maddening. A jolt to the system by a fucking jumper cable shocked less, and I groaned, forgetting about everything. I *forgot* about how stupid this was, and how I definitely shouldn't be kissing the girl I'd kidnapped when I was twelve. I'd kept her in that cabin for weeks.

Months.

Time had stopped passing eventually back then. It became a distant memory to motive and goals. Aspen Davis was an accomplishment. She was a code I needed to hack, and I was a good fucking hacker. I was taught by the best. My dad was a computer genius, and he'd passed that shit down.

Let. Go. Of. Her.

I gripped her throat harder, our tongues flicking, dancing. I couldn't really see her or even myself in the dark, but that didn't matter. We devoured each other's mouths on pure instinct, adrenaline, and the lack of air made us both gasp. All the while, I held her pussy, making her grind against me, feel me.

"Fuck…" she rasped, biting me. She bit so hard something metallic hit my tongue, and I growled.

We're too exposed.

I didn't care how dark this corner was. We were still out in the open for anyone to come across, and I wasn't letting anyone see what I was about to do to this girl. Fuck, I wasn't letting anyone *see her*, and I picked her up by her thighs.

A short *yip* left her throat, followed by a surprised laugh.

It sounded like wind chimes and shit and kicked something weird in my heart.

I need inside her. Now.

Aspen wrapped those wonderfully thick legs around me during my strides, her tight thighs hugging me like a bear cub, and I didn't break the kiss while I took her away. I didn't let her do anything but kiss me.

"So The Punisher does want to play," she said, once we were literally both behind a wall. It was all I could find. The best I could do, and it was even darker over here.

I didn't let her talk anymore, my tongue down her throat now. Her silence made it easier to taste her and tuck away my guilt about doing this with her.

My neck gaiter was down around my neck now, the thing completely forgotten, but with as dark as it was, she couldn't see me. She'd stop if she could.

God, this is fucked.

So fucking fucked, but I didn't stop. Aspen didn't either. She continued to kiss me right back and let some anonymous guy drive his tongue down her throat. She let me gather her dress and finally feel that wet pussy.

Shit, she's not wearing any panties.

Aspen Davis had come to play, and the TV obviously didn't reveal this girl's kinks. She was a celebrity, but she clearly wasn't past having a good time. She was doing what most people did around here. A rave put on by my frat was a great place to release inhibitions, to just have a good fucking time with whoever one wanted to do it with. Aspen Davis was letting her hair down like the rest of us, and the fact that she could be doing this with any guy had me gripping that pussy harder. She wasn't doing this shit with any other guy, and the startled cry that ripped from her throat only summoned more action into my hand. She dripped into my palm, so wet for me.

It's not too late to stop.

But it was. It was the moment she let me have a taste. I got another when I moved to her neck. Immediately surrounded by cocoa, I tasted that sweet skin, and Aspen bucked when my fingers tunneled inside her pussy. She rocked against my fist, and when she tried to shove her hand under my shirt, I got her wrist. I forced it above her head, and another wind-chime laugh fluttered from her throat into my mouth.

"Controlling much?" she gasped, the question cut off when I bit her neck *hard*. She moaned, clearly forgetting about her line of questioning.

She didn't know the half about my control, and she appeared to enjoy the benefits of the domination. She allowed me to take both of her hands and pin them above her, a maneuver I did while I got a condom out of my jeans. I made sure she knew what I was doing even if she couldn't really see. I ripped the foil open with my teeth, then sheathed myself.

She really should stop me. Hell, I really should stop me, but I was too far gone, and she literally had her naked wet pussy hovering above my cock. Her thighs around me kept her aerial, and I wouldn't let her fall.

At least not until she was on my cock.

I slid right in with an easy thrust, the noise we both made feral, untamed. I physically bit that shit down and ended up using her shoulder to do it.

"Christ," she ground out, her hand gripping her breast, squeezing. I could feel that shit between us, and that made me pick up the pace like an animal. I wanted that breast in my mouth, to see if her nipples tasted as good as her tongue.

I didn't dare, already mad, and she was the only one talking and eventually… screaming. The harsh beats of the rave were the only thing that masked her sounds, but I kept my shit on lock. I didn't say a damn word and wouldn't. I physically was drawing blood by biting the inside of my cheek but I couldn't reveal myself. I couldn't risk her finding out who I was, and I knew how fucked up that was. I knew how shitty this was.

But she felt so fucking good.

I considered myself a bit of an aficionado when it came to sex. I had a lot of goddamn sex. Fucked a lot of goddamn girls but being inside this chick hit different. Why was it different?

You know why.

Probably because I shouldn't be. As far as she and I were considered, Aspen Davis was the Garden of Eden and her pussy the forbidden fucking fruit.

That certainly didn't stop me from deep-diving in it, the muscles in my thighs burning from the intensity of my thrusts and that said something. I did suicides on the football field that left me feeling less labored.

"Yes. Yes. Yes." Aspen got my shoulders, fucking me right back, and the heat of her hands drove me faster, harder. "Fuck, yes."

I found I wanted her praise. I found I wanted her hands on me, and I didn't reject her when she reached for my face this time. Her hands touched my cheeks, deepening our kiss.

Fuck.

This girl was a drug, both heaven and hell wrapped into one. The kissing managed to intensify the fucking, and when her pussy clamped around my cock, I knew she was close. Her thighs hugged my hips, and our mouths separated when she came. Her back bowed, her hands falling away from my face, and I physically felt the absence.

Shit.

I held on to her while I came myself, letting her use the wall and me to bring herself back down from her high. She twitched in my arms, and I thought I'd die I flooded the condom between us so hard. Roaring, I milked her for every-thing she had. I didn't want to leave this girl's pussy. I refused.

But I had to.

Eventually, there wasn't anything left to take from her, and I knew what that made me look like. I knew *what this* looked like. I took advantage of a situation, and I wasn't a goddamn saint by any stretch of the word, but I did have a moral compass. The fact of the matter was, Aspen Davis wouldn't have done this at all if she'd known who she did this with.

Exhaustion combined with my guilt, both of us exhausted. Aspen sagged against me, and I slumped against her.

"Punisher?"

The prompt was for me to lift my head, to kiss her, and I let her touch me again. Her hands returned to my face, and if I had my hat off, I knew I'd let her touch my hair. I'd allow her to put her hands all up in that shit. I wanted her touch *everywhere.*

But when the kiss ended, my actions told the opposite. I tugged my neck gaiter back up, then returned Aspen's feet to the ground. As soon as her heels were on the floor, I backed up, giving her some space. I even turned around so she could adjust her clothing, giving her some privacy even though we couldn't see each other for shit behind the wall. While she did, I removed the condom, then tucked my dick away.

"Well… that was fun." She nearly sounded shy behind me when she hadn't been moments ago. I didn't think I got the read on this girl wrong even though I'd only seen her through social media through the years. She gave off a good-girl image even if she was sexy as sin.

Which she was.

I couldn't really see her in the dark area, but I had my hands on her, tasted her. I turned around and got little more than her outline.

Her steps brought her closer, and my heart kicked a beat when her hands slid up the hard panes of my chest. She wasn't shy about it, harsh heat gliding across my chest before she wrapped her arms around me.

Back away.

Every instinct within me wanted to, gongs firing off in my head and my body tensing, tightening. Aspen clearly hadn't noticed because she pressed her warm tits against me, and for some reason, I let her. For some reason, I allowed her to meld into me, and as soon as she did, my shoulders eased away from my ears. I actually ended up holding her back, my fingers gathered in the material of her dress.

God, this girl was dangerous.

For both of us and I didn't need the distraction. I already had enough addictions in my life. I was already *avoiding life.* At least, when I could.

Aspen's outline shifted. "You going to tell me who you are now or what?"

It'd be natural for me to, wouldn't it? I mean, we had fucked. In fact, this probably could have become something if it wasn't her or me. But the thing was, she was her, and because I was me, I got a hold of her, my hand cupping her ass when I removed the last bit of space between us. Her staggered breath sounded in my ear, and it hiked when I moved to hers.

"Anarchy," I whispered, and if I could see her, I knew I'd see her tremble. I could feel it in her hot little body, her curves quaking in my hands. "You asked what the mask was. What I am? And that's pure and unadulterated anarchy..." I drew in closer. "Snowflake."

I physically felt the moment shift.

Again, she was in my hands.

Aspen's body locked up almost instantly, and right away, her heat left my hands. In fact, she recoiled so fast a breeze hit me, and when shouts started blaring above the rave's noise, I placed more distance.

Someone yelled, "cops," and Aspen moved toward the

voices into the rave's neon lights. The strobe lights hit her blonde, Marilyn Monroe wig as soon as she got from behind the wall, and I think she only headed that way on instinct because the next time I saw her, she was looking back behind her. She scanned the dark corner where we'd fucked moments ago, but I'd already faded deeper into the darkness.

Move on, snowflake.

Sometimes the cops crashed these events. It was a big reason why they moved. The fuckers could hit their quotas for years with the amount of drugs and illegal betting that went on here, but the threat of that wasn't enough to make Aspen Davis move. She kept looking behind her until the crowd forced her to physically move.

I followed. Of course I did because I was a dumb fuck. I wanted to make sure she got out of here, and she shouldn't have been here in the first place.

I stayed with the crowd, and even fought a dude when I noticed him shove her. She just about fell to the floor, but she stabilized herself.

Keep going, snowflake.

She kept turning back, something new in her eyes that hadn't been there when she first saw me and we'd been dancing. I knew this girl's fear. I'd seen it every day I visited that cabin so many summers ago.

Run, little one.

She finally did. She wised up to the warning of cops. She followed the crowd, and I stayed with her until she got outside into a rideshare. She must have sent for one during her run, and I finally wised up myself and let her go. The car got her out of there, and she escaped the area and the trees flashing with red and blue lights. The cops were quickly surrounding the place, and I turned my back to it all. I followed the crowd in the opposite direction, not feeling like dealing with the police myself tonight.

Maybe Aspen Davis was just moving through town. Like

stated, these raves were popular, and she probably just got word.

That better be the case.

I wouldn't let my thoughts entertain anything else. I had enough on my fucking plate as it was.

And the last thing I needed was another vice to tempt me to dodge the shit life was currently throwing me.

CHAPTER
THREE

Aspen

Why the fuck did I drink so much coffee?

I groaned before dodging out of my lecture. My very first one and I was already missing shit. I'd been distracted, and now, I had to pee.

Christ.

I found the bathroom after I bumbled my way out of class. No one really paid too much attention in the giant lecture hall that sat a few hundred, and I was pretty sure my disguise worked. I didn't consider myself crazy famous. I was a performer, but my industry was pretty niche since I did classical music. In the right circles, people definitely knew who I was, though. Especially if one followed hip-hop.

Dark shades over my eyes and ball cap on my braided locs, I washed my hands after using the bathroom. I could barely see shit since my sunglasses were so dark, but I resisted taking them off. The light would burn into my tired eyes. Hence the need for so much coffee this morning.

I… couldn't sleep.

For several reasons, I had issues last night, but the biggest one was the reason I was currently washing my hands raw instead of going back to class.

What the fuck was that last night?

What the fuck was *he* or, I guess, who the fuck was he? The guy in the skull mask last night had fucked me like a god, a beautiful *sinful* god who hit my shit in all the right places. I hadn't gone to that rave with the intent of fucking anyone. Quite the contrary, I'd actually wanted to just go and get out of my head for a little bit, to blend in and have some fucking fun for once in my life.

It'd been nice.

It'd been *freeing*, and even more so after I met that guy. He'd been a big dude in black jeans, a cutoff tee, and huge arms. Everything about him oozed sex appeal from his dark boots to his flashy cross to the sharp earrings in his ears. He'd been a white guy who had swagger for fucking days, and I wasn't usually that much of an easy lay. Actually, it was the opposite because of the industry I was in. Guys in entertainment could be the worst, cocky, and frankly, because the guy hadn't been very verbose before we got going, that'd been a big part of his appeal.

That and his mask.

I didn't realize I was into any kind of kink, but the fact that he wore one basically melted the panties off me. That and all his jewelry, and the fact that he smelled like the fucking ocean. He also knew what to do with his jewelry. He had on this gorilla ring at the rave and buried it deep into my pussy before taking me…

God, why did you fuck a stranger?

It'd been a mistake, and how I knew it was a mistake was because of what hooking up with that random guy last night had done. It sent me into a tailspin of nightmares and memories I'd spent years (and therapy) trying to flush out of my system.

I was still washing my hands.

I turned off the water, letting my hands drip in the sink. I hadn't forgotten the memories, of course. I mean, how could I? I'd been *kidnapped*.

Go back to class.

Making myself, I forced the images of a dark-haired boy out of my head. Thatcher Reed had been crazy, and the guy wearing a Punisher skull mask calling me the nickname that psycho creep had given me (while holding me against my will) had been a coincidence.

It had to be.

I was stressed out. That was all this was. With everything with the threats, I was stressed, the concert…

Swallowing, I forced all that bullshit out of my head. I'd ruined my own night last night. Not some crazy fuck from the past. Things had been great with the guy in the Punisher mask before that. Again, he'd fucked like *a god* and got me completely out of my head.

At least, for a little while.

I really was some kind of damaged, and shaking my head, I started to leave the bathroom. I only made it a step before I realized I'd left my purse in the freaking stall.

Get your shit together.

The whole point of me being here at school and not in my real life was to *not* do this. I wasn't supposed to be freaking out, panicking…

I shoved my purse over my arm, then turned around. I nearly ran into someone, but that was only because they were taking up so much space by the sinks.

I dropped my purse. It hit the floor and literally everything inside it spilled out. My lipsticks went everywhere, pens, my cell phone… gone, but I couldn't really focus on any of that.

I was too busy staring at the guy with his arms crossed in front of me.

Dark, unruly hair ran every which way. Like he tossed his fingers through it often, and it happened to rest perfectly despite the tousle. His hair was borderline black it was so dark, but his eyes weren't.

Those eyes…

A glacial, sapphire blue, and a stark contrast to everything else about him. He wore black down to his high-tops. Even a few of his fingernails were painted black, but it was his eyes that gave me pause.

And his chain.

I'd had that very chain in my hands last night. I'd tugged on that shit while he'd fucked me into an oblivion. I recognized those and his sharp earrings. They were crosses that were sharpened at the ends.

The guy pushed off the sink, and I backed up, instinctual, and the opposite of what I'd done last night. I hadn't backed up at all. In fact, I'd thrown myself at him.

No way.

It was the eyes… those *eyes* that I recognized the most, and the fact that he really hadn't changed much. His facial features were damn near the same. Just older, and if I'd been able to see them with those irises last night…

"Hey, snowflake." The word shot through me just like it had last night, those eyes holding a familiar twinkle.

Mischief.

I'd seen it the day he'd chased me in the woods. It'd been that day that ultimately saved my life, even though I hadn't gotten away. Before that, his eyes had been nothing but vacant. A tried-and-true sociopath. Thatcher Reed was fucking insane.

And he was currently smiling at me.

Thatcher

She left, of course, after savagely grabbing her things off the floor, and I knew she would.

Don't make me chase you, snowflake.

Aspen Davis didn't have many places to go, and damn near none where I wouldn't find her. My buddies and I owned this fucking campus.

I followed Aspen's little backside into her class, her acid-washed jeans hugging her ass, but I tried not to make a show of my arrival. My friends and I were known as Legacy at this university. Everyone knew us because of our bloodlines and the amount of money our families had been sending to the school for generations. That went triple for mine. The Reeds were one of the oldest families to attend here, so naturally I got attention.

I wasn't trying to get it today and managed to avoid it since Aspen's class was in an auditorium. The entrance was at the back of one of the larger lecture halls, and Aspen herself was trying to lie low as well. She kept her head down, her hand bent over the bill of her hat, but she passed several glances behind her as she made quick steps.

Yeah, I'm still here, snowflake.

Perhaps, she thought moving into a random aisle and sitting between a couple of people would keep me from her.

I showed her different.

I was like a fucking peacock in this bitch with the way I got attention. Needless to say, I didn't have to do much when I hovered over one of the guys she decided to sit between. She gave herself a few seats' berth between the guys, but one still blocked my path to get to her.

The guy I loomed largely over bristled, and when I jerked my chin, he got up and literally climbed over the seats. I smirked, but Aspen didn't. Her jaw dropped beneath a set of dark Ray-Bans before her supple lips pursed tight. I'd licked the gloss off those lips just last night, and they were still too fucking tempting.

Yeah, that's not why you stalked her into her class.

I'd been doing lots of stupid shit when it came to her, and apparently, I was taking up a goddamn tally. I sat right next to her *close*, and she jolted just like she'd done last night. As this reaction was normal, I didn't call attention to it. I leaned closer. "Snowflake?"

Aspen gauged her situation. She was caught between me and a guy a few seats down, and the one who dodged me sat right in front of her. She was trapped, and because she was, all she decided to do was hunker down in her seat. Her hand gripped her ball cap, adjusting it further over her head. She obviously wasn't wearing her wig today and had her long hair in a single braid over her shoulder. Her tresses were thick with length and reminded me of that actress from the new *Little Mermaid* movie. I knew all about that chick for, um, reasons. Aspen's low-sitting jeans and tube top were giving the vibe of that singer Aaliyah from the nineties, though. The outfit showed off her pert navel as well as gave ample views of the outline of her tits.

And I wasn't the only dude to notice.

The guy next to her may have been a few seats down, but he wasn't being subtle about looking at her chest.

That was until I growled.

He pulled the same maneuver as his friend as he scaled the seats, and I'd laugh at that shit if I were trying to catch attention.

Snowflake took an opportunity with the seats next to her vacant. There were still too many people in the aisle for her to escape, but she didn't have to sit next to me anymore. She moved, giving us a few seats' berth, but sighing, I got up too. She really was going to make me chase her.

I sat right next to her *again*, and this time, she gazed around. It was like she was looking for backup, but after I growled at the fucker earlier, no one was looking at her.

That's right, snowflake. It's just you and me.

That was how it should be, what I wanted, and why the fuck was this girl at my school?

I said her nickname again, low, and Aspen chose to further ignore my ass when she pulled a notebook out of her purse. Perhaps, she thought she'd actually get some notes in during her lecture and the well over two hundred pounds of Pembroke football player beside her would just disa-fucking-ppear. I was underweight as far as I was concerned, but I'd been stressed and hadn't gotten in the gym as much as I wanted to lately.

Pushing that out of my head, I draped an arm behind Aspen's chair. "So you'll fuck me but won't talk to me?"

The look she shot me was deadly, fearless. She'd had fear last night, and even some in the bathroom just now. Actually, there'd been a lot of fear then.

But not now. Now, she just looked like she wanted to take

that pen of hers and shove it directly into my goddamn chest. Her jaw clenched. "You're deranged."

And she was bold. I pressed against her. "Deranged is fucking some random guy at a rave after you've been publicly threatened."

Her head shot my way again, and if I could see her eyes behind her aviators, I bet I'd see the return of that fear. She now knew I was up in her life a bit, but I didn't give a single fuck.

"You really are a stalker," she gritted, and I could see why she'd think that. I mean, I had locked her away for an entire summer, and that required some planning, stalking. There were details of her life I had to take note of in order to execute what had gone down, and all that had been found out after her location had been discovered...

And I'd been arrested.

That wasn't the case today, though. Well, kinda. I'd been naturally curious after seeing her last night and instinct told me to check Pembroke-U's records. The hacker in me couldn't help myself, and it didn't take long for me to discover she was a new student here.

I may have done a little stalking for that detail, but finding out she was threatened recently had nothing to do with that. I wet my lips. "I just have a cell phone and the ability to scroll my social media feed."

She had been threatened, got some fucked-up letters, and now, here she was at a very public place. Private university or not, Pembroke had a lot of people on its fucking campus. In fact, because it was Ivy League, it had a lot of people.

Aspen restlessly messed with the braid over her shoulder, and her outfit looked a bit like she was trying to blend in *kinda*. Ball caps and sunglasses were actually pretty common in a world where folks showed up lazy and hungover for class, but enrolling in college after one clearly had a threat on her life didn't seem like the best idea. I heard of being hungry for knowledge, but what the fucking shit? She released her braid. "Kind of sounds like you're the one who sent the threats."

"Nice try, snowflake. You came to my campus."

"So what? You could have found out. Followed me." She gazed around again, but this time, it didn't appear for aid. She kept her voice down and stayed low like she was trying to keep this conversation between us. Her dark eyebrows narrowed. "How do I know it wasn't you who threatened me?"

Again, it made sense she'd come to this conclusion. A lot had come out after what happened between us, all the information I had on her day-to-day during that time. The pictures I had of her and the notes I'd taken…

Once more, I pressed my chest against her arm, which effectively pinned her in place. Right away, she jutted her shoulder, but she was a petite little thing, and I, well, wasn't.

I grinned.

"You'd know if I was after you, snowflake," I said, noticing the tremor in her full lips, but also the tremble in her body. A slight flush bloomed beneath her brown skin, the rose tint warmly coloring her cheeks, her chest. My grin widened. "And something tells me you might not mind that."

If last night was any indicator, that was true, and her lack of response for a beat only backed that up. It was like she was in a haze before she blinked, but then, she was shoving at me.

"You're unhinged," she growled about the same time I grabbed her hands. Instinct once again had her gazing around for a social connection, but she was getting no resources from the folks around her. People bent to me here. My friends and I were kings and queens, and she was far away from her world of paparazzi and privilege. Here, I reigned supreme. Period.

I think Aspen quickly discovered that. Her brow jumped half the width of her face when eyes averted from us. Aspen

Davis was realizing where exactly she'd placed herself. She was in the belly of the beast here at Pembroke University.

And I was the lion.

She forgot about her lack of help when I used her hands to pull her toward me. Her breath expelled, our hands between us, and something told me this little snowflake was all bark and no bite.

"I think your crazy matches mine, snowflake," I said, watching the tremble wrack through her body for a second time. I got close to her cheek, that flush. "And I think we both know you proved that last night."

She had fucked me, and she one hundred percent didn't know me. I wasn't going to let her forget that, and before she could respond and tell me off, I flicked my tongue across her cheek. I got a full drag down that flush, unable to help it. She looked so sweet and smelled even sweeter.

I was always a sucker for candy.

The sharp taste was worth the sock in the chest the maneuver got me. Aspen Davis was sweet as far as my cock and tongue were concerned, but everywhere else she was hellcat. She socked me in the chest (twice) before I let go, and the only reason I did was because I was too busy laughing. I physically had to fight the sound down as to not draw attention. My cell phone also happened to buzz in my pocket, and I fell out of my laughter enough to pull it out and see who was getting at me.

"You're a creep, and I'm calling the cops," Aspen said, threatening me, and I wished she'd try. There was no police precinct in the area where she could actually get assistance. My family's name meant something around here. No matter who the fuck she was outside of this place. She snarled. "I'm fucking serious. As soon as I get out of class..."

Her voice was lost, and this was fortunate for her because I didn't have to threaten her after what she said to me.

Gram: Can you bring some milk when you come home, darling? We're out in the fridge. *smile emoji*

My finger hovered over my device, the text. I'd make sure my grandmother got her milk. I'd do anything.

I swallowed.

Me: Actually, it's going to be a little while before I get home. I'll make sure you get the milk, though. Nurse is always happy to help, and I'm sure she can get you some.

Nurse was my mother and the one who spent the most time at the house. My mom used to have a career, but now, she was a stay-at-home mom. She was even though both her kids were out of the house and at college.

My jaw shifted, knowing the reason for that, and Aspen was still barking at me. Well, it was more like a muted rant considering where we both were, and somewhere in the far-off spaces of my mind, I heard her continued threats about the cops. She obviously didn't know why I wasn't responding and taking her seriously.

I wasn't right now, focusing on the text message bubble on my cell phone.

Gram: You treat me so wonderfully. Take your time, Nighty. I'll see you when I see you and love you.

I loved her too, and that was the only part of her message I responded to. It was the only thing I could that didn't leave my chest searing, locking.

After I told Gram I loved her back, Aspen became more audible.

She huffed. "I'm not joking, Thatcher. I swear to God. I'll get a restraining order on your ass."

Aspen's family had tried that before. Again, after it all went down with the kidnapping. It hadn't worked then, and it wouldn't now. It really didn't matter what kind of clout and fame she'd acquired since then. She would never be able to stand toe-to-toe with me. My family held too much power.

Whatever she'd been about to say next escaped from her

glossed lips. Shifting, I pressed my body right against her. A quick gasp left her full mouth. Her throat jumped, but she was once again saved from a response from me when I noticed my phone. The text message bubble popped up on my phone once more.

I directed my attention away from it but only for the time being to handle Snowflake. I studied her quivering throat, her mouth. "There's no cop in this town that would hear you, snowflake. Again, if I wanted you, I'd have you, and no fucking cops would keep me from you."

Her dark lashes flashed, and that rose tint from before fired hot across her face. Her honeyed skin glowed, and it may have fired hotter, but I was forced to draw back. My phone buzzed again, another text about the milk. My gram asked for it as if she never had, and she called me by the same nickname.

Nighty.

The locking sensation in my chest intensified, and it kicked into high gear noticing Aspen. She'd visibly shrunk in her seat, and where she'd been bold and confident before, she wasn't now. In fact, all confidence had wiped away from her dark eyes, and the only thing there was something chillingly familiar. Again, I knew this girl's fear.

I'd seen it every day for an entire summer.

"Remember that in case you want to start getting ideas," I said to her, wondering why I fucking cared that she was scared of me. She should be, and maybe if she was, she'd wise the fuck up about some things. She shouldn't be here *at all*. I pointed at her. "And if you're going to be here, going to school here, get some fucking security."

She needed someone to watch her back. There were plenty of fuckers around here who'd want a piece of her, and that was outside of the fact she'd actually been threatened.

Aspen jolted. A surprise flashed across her pretty face that didn't at all surprise me. I threatened her, then told her to get security in the next breath. That was probably very confusing for her, but that was in the realm of normalcy for me. My relationship with Aspen Davis was hella fucking confusing and always had been.

Another text came in, the same text, and instead of waiting for Aspen's response, I left. I didn't have time to deal with anything else right now. My gram needed me, and I was skipping the rest of my classes today to drive back to my hometown.

I had milk to buy.

CHAPTER
FIVE

Aspen

Unknown: Told you, you'd know if I was after you, snowflake. It was too easy to get access to you. In fact, it was as easy as blinking for me.

    Unknown: Now, get some security. I'm serious.

The texts came two days after I saw Thatcher Reed and didn't make good on my threat about calling the cops on him.

I should have. This was apparent because I currently sat in my dorm room watching the video that came with the unknown texts. It was at night. Last night. I knew because of what I wore.

He was in my room.

Sickness swirled as I watched a video of me wriggle beneath my sheets. I tossed and turned in my silk bonnet and oversize T-shirt, but it wasn't hard to figure out what I was doing under the bedding.

I was… getting off. My hand hit the sheets in quick time, and it didn't matter I had no memories of this. I didn't recall fingering myself into oblivion. I'd been sleeping.

Oh, God.

I watched myself through squinted eyes, my moans quiet but so obviously escaping my trembling lips. I knew they trembled because he got up close.

Air escaped my lungs, my heart threatening to beat out of my fucking chest. I almost threw my phone, unable to look at this anymore…

But then the finale came. Ironically enough, it did when I had. One solitary word left my lips as my hips rose and my body locked. The word was soft, aroused.

"Thatcher…"

I threw my phone then. Hot bile threatened to charge up my throat, and it took all I had to keep it down. There was no way I said what was in the video. There was *no way*.

But the evidence was there.

Thatcher Reed had captured it. I mean, that was *me* in this room.

Holy fuck.

The only explanation for my behavior I could come up with was that my subconscious thoughts obviously held on to him. We'd had great fucking sex, and my body remembered that.

That was all.

I wasn't insane like him, and with trembling hands, I grabbed for my phone. I nearly called my mother, but stopped.

I can't call her.

In fact, it was impossible for me to. So much shit would come up if I did, shit I couldn't explain, and the fact that I didn't have security would only be the tip of the iceberg.

"If I wanted you, I'd have you, and no fucking cops would keep me from you…"

He'd been right, of course, when he'd said that. I didn't know why I'd bristled after he did. Like I'd care if his crazy ass wanted me, but he had something there. Even if I or my mother attempted any ramifications against him for the video or anything else, there probably wouldn't be a point. There hadn't been back when he'd kidnapped me.

God.

Back then, Thatcher had literally told the cops the reason he'd done what he had… stalked me, then kidnapped me was because he liked me. He *liked me* and did the wrong thing.

I couldn't make this stuff up.

It'd been the thing of nightmares, and I'd been the victim. My mom had come for his family, but she had nothing and neither had the guy she'd been with at the time. She'd actually been engaged to Thatcher's football coach.

Everything was ruined after that summer. It was like the kidnapping had been a catalyst, and Thatcher frickin' Reed had been responsible. He'd ruined so many lives, and there'd been zero consequences. He walked away completely unscathed, and I had a feeling coming for him now would result in nothing but the same.

I felt truly dizzy, locked from action with my cell phone in hand, and I really wanted to believe Thatcher was stalking me. I mean, he'd done so before, but he kept telling me to get security. Why would he do that?

Because he's crazy.

This all felt like a game, a dark and twisted game, and Thatcher Reed made the rules. He did like he had the summer when I was twelve, but I'd been a kid back then. I'd been scared, powerless.

I was still scared, but I wasn't fucking powerless. Thatcher wasn't going to win this time, and he was definitely right that I needed security. I needed it to protect me from him, and I knew exactly who to call after a Google search.

"Reed Corp. How can I connect you?" a woman chirped into the line, and there was no hesitation. My Google search came up with some surprising information. I'd merely looked for contact information. I needed the number of someone

Thatcher would listen to and probably the only person who could stop him. He would to avoid the PR nightmare that was his son, but then I saw his name linked to a security firm both online and otherwise. Knight Reed, *Thatcher's father*, had the means and resources in which to keep people safe.

Just like he obviously had for his son.

CHAPTER
SIX

Thatcher

I was surprised to get the text from my dad about lunch for a few reasons. One was because he didn't text. It wasn't that he couldn't. He just didn't. For the most part, his secretary, Jonathan, set meetings up.

The other was because it'd been a while since I'd seen him. I was in school, yeah, but he worked a lot.

I dressed nice for lunch. My dad booked one of our favorite places to eat on campus, a fancy Italian restaurant few people outside of a Reed could get a reservation at last minute. My family had roots in Italy, and my dad had a favorite table at this particular restaurant. Pembroke-U was his alma mater, and I was excited to see my dad. Again, I didn't see him a lot.

I tried not to fidget in my pleated pants and dark button-up. I didn't mind the country club shit, but I was more used to jeans and cutoff tees. I greeted the maître d', and he spritely headed me back toward my dad's table after calling me sir.

This dude had known me since I was a kid, so that was always fucking weird.

He was cool as shit, though, and I shook his hand with a snap after he left me to head behind the wall to see my father. My dad had a private table, and I was glad I got to talk to the maître d' a bit before he left. He helped me get out some of my nerves.

I loved my dad and was really happy to fucking see him, but things had been kind of tense lately. Awkward.

I shook that shit out. I wouldn't let him see my fucking nerves and stopped acting like a bitch when I rounded the wall.

Dad wasn't alone.

"Ah. There he is," Dad said, rising from the table. He dwarfed that shit since he was big as fuck like me, and across from him sat a girl.

A snowflake.

What. The. Entire. Fuck.

Aspen had her fingers laced, innocently glancing up and up until she made eye contact with me. She stood too, sans sunglasses and hat today, in a peach-toned dress that hugged her body too good and heels that showed off her pert little toes. They were painted red just like her lips and fuck had I thought lip gloss brought out that full mouth. Her lips were entirely fuckable right now, and I was tempted with the expression she was giving me. It was a smug expression, a cocky expression, and set off red flags like a son of a bitch.

The fuck you doing, snowflake?

Dad wasn't surprised to see her. I mean, he was fucking sitting with her in a three-piece suit with his business face on. In fact, he looked like he was conducting business. He had a portfolio out and only waters on the table. No drinking was done at client meetings. He wanted the people he met with to know the terms and have complete clarity regarding what they were signing.

No fucking way.

But that was exactly what this looked like, my dad here with Aspen. He placed his hand on my shoulder. "Glad you could make it, and you know Miss Davis. She said you referred her for my services. It seems Aspen is in need of security while she's here attending school, and she said you sent her my way."

Fuuuck.

I swung my attention over to Aspen, her smug expression quirking her lips right, her smile high. It brought out a twinkle in her dark eyes, and if my father wasn't here, I knew I'd wring her little neck.

Or fuck her.

Fucking her sounded way more fun. Especially after that little video I shot of her. She talked a lot of shit, but clearly, she thought about me. I was in her dreams. Between her legs…

Thoughts of taking her while she fought me got me hard, which was kind of sick, but so was whatever this shit she was trying to play.

"We're actually just finishing up, and thank you for trusting my firm with your safety, Aspen," Dad said. "I'll be in contact as soon as we have someone for you. Should be less than twenty-four hours."

Dad shook Aspen's hand, and it basically ate hers. He had baseball mitts for hands like me, and they came in handy on the football field. I wasn't focused on football as much as I should be lately, my thoughts on Aspen and her "bright" decision to be here during what was clearly a turbulent time in her life. I'd had practice just this morning, and my mind had been fucked. She'd completely taken over my thoughts.

That and other things.

Those things I pushed out of my head at the moment. I could only handle things one at a fucking time. Dad smiled. "I was surprised to hear from you considering your history with my son, but I'm glad you two have been able to over-come that. I'm sure Thatcher is very grateful for that, right, son?"

My nod was stiff, and Aspen pasted on a smile that gave my fake shit a run for its money. It was red carpet ready and only something someone who'd dealt with cameras on the regular would know how to use.

Damn, she was good, but then again, so was I. Aspen shrugged. "It was a long time ago, and we're both adults now." Aspen faced me. "Right, Thatcher?"

Her smug expression managed to get more cocky, which was ironic as fuck considering how freaked out she'd been the last time we were together. Well, I guess that wasn't the *last* time we'd been together. She'd been asleep the last time. I smirked. "Right."

I couldn't say any more than that. Not in front of my dad. He was rather good at spotting my bullshit. Probably because he was my dad. Nah, in this instance I thought keeping my mouth shut and not giving any tells was the best way to deal with this.

She better hope he didn't figure me out.

Dad didn't need this shit right now, and though I didn't either, I was going to keep... whatever this shit was off his radar. Again, he didn't have the time to deal with it. No one in my family did, but especially not him.

So instead of letting him, I smiled as Dad told me all about how Aspen had reached out to his office. He tended to meet with high-profile clients like Aspen personally. Reed Corp., my family's business, had many different facets. Real estate and online security were the biggest, but recently, Dad had been branching out. He had lots of connections, which was how his other security firm had developed. He took every part of the business seriously, and he wanted his clients to feel like he cared. Especially if they were high priority.

Aspen's threats clearly placed her in that category, and

apparently, she'd listened to me when I told her ass to get some protection.

She thought she was cute.

I'd show her different if my dad wasn't here, and I realized now my lunch with my dad may have been one of convenience. He was clearly meeting with Aspen today, and since his son went to Pembroke, it made sense that he'd want to meet with me. I was already here.

Of course.

That was fine, and I didn't care. Again, I wanted to see my dad, and I'd see him in any way that made sense for him. Like stated, I didn't want to stress him out or be his stress right now.

Aspen and our… history would cause him stress. I'd been a headache for my entire family so many years ago when things with Aspen and me went down, and if Dad knew the hatchet between us wasn't really fucking buried, he wouldn't be happy.

"Oh. I have to take this," Dad said, his hand on my shoulder. He currently studied his cell phone, the device ringing in his hand, but he didn't answer it. He wouldn't in front of a client or me. One thing my dad was very good at was separating his business from his home life. He never took calls in front of my mom or my sister, Bow, and me growing up. He prioritized his family always.

I admired my dad so much and wanted to be like him when I eventually got involved in our family businesses.

He gave Aspen's hand one final shake before excusing himself and taking his call privately. He told me we'd start our lunch after he returned. He and Aspen had just met for the meeting as I had suspected.

No sooner had my dad cut around the wall than I got Aspen's arm. She twitched, wriggling, but I got a firm hold of her and brought her close to my chest. I was immediately assaulted by the smell of Christmas and candy, but I ignored that shit. I grinned. "You think you're cute, huh? Getting my dad's firm for your fucking security."

She obviously was trying to throw what I told her to do in my face. She shoved at my chest. "Let *fucking* go."

Nah, I definitely wasn't doing that. She'd have to fucking make me, and I'd more than love the struggle. My head cocked. "A word of advice, sweetheart. I'm the last person you want to make your enemy. Now, I gave you some advice the other day, and I have to say, you're shitting on it."

I pressed against her tight little body, and my hand would be all up in that peach outfit of hers if we were alone.

Perhaps, Aspen felt that *and me* when I tucked my cock up against her. Her eyes flashed, and she attempted to knee me in my shit, but I was quick. I lifted her away as if she was little more than a rag doll, and her irises blazed like hot coals in my direction.

"You're insane, and you did this to your fucking self." She managed to work her arm away and me when she shoved at my chest again. I went willingly, but it was cute she thought she could move me. She put a polished nail in my chest. "You *will* back the fuck off or your dad will know all about what a stalker you clearly still are. I gave him a nice little spiel about how you helped me out with that referral, but I can turn that shit on its head in two seconds."

She thought she'd found my Achilles heel by getting my dad involved, and that made sense. I'd made a lot of drama for my dad to fix back when Aspen and I were kids, and anyone with eyes today could see I respected my father. I'd do anything not to create a headache for him.

What a smart little snowflake.

That was where her smarts ended. My dad wouldn't always be here to keep me in check. I got her by the hip. "Better hide all up behind my dad's security, darling. It'd be dumb to find yourself alone anytime soon, and I'm not referring to your threatening fucking letters."

Her eyes flashed again, a familiar flare especially when I got that ass of hers in my hand. I gripped a nice full squeeze, and I chuckled when her next move was to dig a stiletto into my patent leather shoe. Yeah, that shit hurt a little bit, but the satisfying growl she made before shoving me off her dulled the pain.

"I have your dad's company on speed dial, asshole," she said, ramming her little shoulder into me. I think this was supposed to get me to move out of her way, and when I didn't, I chuckled at the red tint that flushed her brown cheeks. Her jaw shifted. "Stay the fuck away from me."

That sounded like nothing but an invitation as far as I was concerned. I pouted my lips at her, a promise when I kissed the air at her.

Her look of disgust barked more laughter out of me, but I allowed both it and her to leave since I was waiting for my dad.

"Sorry about that, son," Dad said upon his return, and I waved him off.

"It's fine, sir. Completely." It was. I knew he'd rather be here than dealing with any kind of business. My dad could be kind of a hard-ass and extremely tough on my ass in particular, but I always gave him a reason.

Again, I was trying not to do that today, and his obvious questions came barely after the bread hit the table.

"So Aspen Davis," he said, eyeing me across the table, and my heart kicked up its beats. Dad rested his hands on the tablecloth. "I really was surprised to hear from her, and even more surprised when she said the referral came from you. She said you two ran into each other at school."

As I didn't know exactly what snowflake told him, I kept my cool, making myself. I sat back. "Yeah. It was crazy."

"Crazy?"

I nodded. "I mean, it was awkward, but all that was a long time ago."

"It was, but I'm sure you'd understand why she'd still want nothing to do with you. You were a kid and made a mistake, but..." His dark eyes were intense. They were my sister's eyes despite the color, but also mine. Bow and I both got my mom's color, but that was as far as that went. When people looked at her and me, they saw my dad. Especially me since my dad and I could be twins. "You two really have moved forward? I'm glad if that's the case, but still I am surprised to hear it."

He should be surprised because Aspen Davis and I were still very much on opposite sides of the proverbial battle line. My father couldn't know that though.

"We're cool," I said, making it harder for my father to spot bullshit when my answers were less than three words.

"And this won't be a problem for you? You and her going to the same school together?" Dad leaned forward. "You can see why I'm a little concerned considering your reasons back then for doing what you did."

The general consensus had been that I liked Aspen, and I did so much that I'd done some stupid shit. I stalked her, then went extra psycho and kidnapped her. I had miles and miles of therapy notes that detailed those very facts, and I had no intention of creating any revisions to the notes.

"I was a kid, Dad," I said, passing that shit off too. "I had a crush. Nothing more."

I wasn't sure if my dad believed me, but he also wasn't great about getting deeply involved with my personal life. He loved me. I knew that, but needless to say, I went to my mom for all the heavy conversations growing up.

"Your gram asked about you today," Dad said, only proving my point that he and I didn't do heavy talks. My chest squeezed, and he fidgeted. He cleared his throat. "She said you came to see her recently."

I had and driven over two hours to do it. My hometown,

Maywood Heights, wasn't an easy trek, but I did it. She needed me.

I peered above my Coke. "Don't you mean she asked about you?"

I didn't know why I said that. It wasn't helpful and certainly not making things easy for my old man. I was going through shit, but he was going through mega shit.

I mean, this was his mom.

Dad studied the fibers in the tablecloth. "Thatcher—"

I didn't know what my dad was about to say, or what I hoped for him to say. I just knew things felt shitty for both of us, and it wouldn't be bad to just sit in it for a second. We were the only two who could relate to the issue in this particular way. It affected us both, my gram's health, and I just... I don't know, wanted to talk to him about it.

"It's a client. I." Dad paused, studying his device. My dad didn't generally do texts, but he was studying his screen after a buzz came in. He faced me. "It's unfortunately an urgent matter I can't ignore. It requires me to head back to the office."

Which meant our lunch was done, and of course, I wouldn't stop him. He wouldn't have ended our lunch for anything trivial, and I knew that.

My hand gripped my Coke glass, and I studied the bread as my dad wrapped up the meal and motioned our server. There was still steam on the bread, but that was okay I didn't get to taste it.

I had a feeling it wouldn't taste right in my mouth anyway.

CHAPTER
SEVEN

Aspen

Sunglasses obviously weren't a good enough fucking disguise outside of that Italian restaurant.

Especially since he'd already seen me.

Thatcher and his dad immediately spotted me on the bench I occupied when they exited the restaurant, and my stomach dropped into my ass. The swirl of nausea only increased when the father-and-son pair pivoted in my direction, the two like dual colossal trucks, and my butt was out here like a sitting fucking duck.

Shit.

Telling Thatcher off had felt like a better idea when I'd been inside, and well, around other people. He'd proved in the past he didn't generally give a shit about that, but he did give a shit about his father being around. That had completely rolled off him today inside the restaurant. He stood straighter in front of his father and delicately chose his words. He cared what his father thought, and I banked on that.

I mean, that was why I'd brought Mr. Reed in.

It was the only thing I could think of to keep his son in check, and I guess Thatcher and I had something in common. I was very aware of the things I said around my mother as well and certainly how I acted. That was about where my similarities with a certain Punisher ended, and I was forced to acknowledge both Thatcher and his father when they headed my way.

"Miss Davis?" Mr. Reed questioned, striding toward me. His son flanked him, and Thatcher's expression was smug to his father's right. He had his hands tucked firmly in the pockets of pleated pants that hugged his gargantuan thighs, and needless to say, they were a sharp contrast from his tattered jeans at the rave. Also different was the dress shirt he wore. His thick pecs and broad shoulders expanded the shirt to the brink of its seams. In fact, the button holes stretched every stride he took beside his father, and his ability to code-switch was quite frankly alarming as fuck. He had dirty, rave fuckboy and dashing, country-club playboy *down*, and there wasn't one part he played better than the other. They were both well-versed. Dangerous.

That danger highlighted his glacial eyes and locked my stomach the hell up. I didn't like how much fear he put in me, but at least fear was normal. He'd hurt me, then fucked me knowing he'd hurt me. Being scared of this tool was completely normal. What wasn't was observing what he wore down to his fucking patent leather shoes, or wondering if his ability to code-switch stopped at his clothing choices. If he was more playboy or fuckboy behind closed doors and which one did he use more to get himself (and a partner) off...

No, that wasn't normal. My stomach locked for a different reason, and it was like Thatcher's ass knew my fucking thoughts. A dark gleam hit his eyes standing in front of me, and I focused away from that to his dad. From the far-off spaces of my mind, I heard Mr. Reed ask me if everything was all right.

Oh, right.

I supposed it was unusual I was sitting here… on a bench. I'd been sitting for about twenty minutes waiting for a car to pick me up. I lifted my phone. "I'm waiting for a rideshare, but it keeps getting canceled."

I didn't know if some event was going on or what, but every time I got assigned a driver, they'd cancel.

Mr. Reed's head lifted upon my explanation, and I was surprised to see them both out here. I'd figured they'd be ordering lunch or something. Not that someone couldn't eat lunch in twenty minutes, but that seemed fast.

I asked Mr. Reed if lunch was okay, and his son bristled for some reason. In fact, Thatcher's entire demeanor changed. His attention hit the passing cars on the street, and Mr. Reed faced him.

"Had to cut things short today, I'm afraid," Mr. Reed explained before smiling pleasantly at me. It was kind of crazy how two people could look so similar but come off completely different. Mr. Reed has his own intimidation factor, but he didn't come across as evil like his son did. Just intense. He placed a hand on Thatcher's shoulder. "Work. But we will reschedule."

Thatcher's nod was subtle, and during his silence, Mr. Reed asked if I needed a car called. I started to take him up on the offer…

"Actually, Dad. I can take Aspen home. We both stay near campus."

My head swung in Thatcher's direction, and that dark flare in his eyes was back again. It'd been devious-looking in our previous interactions, but it felt different now.

It felt cold.

He had a vacancy that reminded me of that boy back at the cabin.

The one who chased me.

The Thatcher Reed who'd abrasively reintroduced himself into my life today was quite different from the one who'd made my life hell years ago. They were both evil, terrible, but they were different. Thatcher today was generally demonic in the sense where he liked to play with his food before he ate it. He liked to *tease*, and though that was scary as shit, the twelve-year-old version of him was even worse. There'd been a blankness there whenever I looked at him, a lack of empathy and soul, and I noticed that harshly each and every time he bothered to talk to me.

"You gotta eat, snowflake," he'd say or, *"Don't run. Don't be stupid."*

I did run eventually. He'd been gone a long time one day, and I'd seen an opportunity. I didn't know how my captivity would end, and my captor wasn't providing me information. I didn't know his endgame, and no matter how much I screamed… cried, he gave me nothing. He'd been like a shell back then with no emotion. I honest to God thought he'd kill me, so I ran.

And he caught me.

I tried not to think about that time. I'd spent many years and therapy sessions trying to get my shit right and just move on. It was a wonder I ever did anything else with my life creatively. It'd been sheer will and grit that got me through. That and my mom.

I loved my mother, and I thanked her every day for pushing me. She did what she felt she had to do to heal us both. It'd been a tumultuous time, and she'd gotten us both through it. She did despite going through her own tragedies. That was later, but she'd done that.

No fucking way was I getting into a car with Thatcher. He'd already warned me never to be alone with him after what I pulled today, and even outside of that, I wasn't fucking stupid.

"That's a great idea, son," Mr. Reed said, which swiftly jolted my already racing heart. He squeezed Thatcher's shoulder. "That's very kind of you to offer."

Mr. Reed clearly didn't see that darkness in his son. Thatcher was no doubt the apple of his eye, so Mr. Reed had no problem being enthusiastic about his son's offer. I, on the other hand, was not enthused, and before I could say hell the fuck no, the valet pulled up a sleek Audi. Thatcher immediately got the door for me, using his large frame to create a barrier between myself and his father.

"After you, snowflake." A sharp bite deepened his voice. It made it gravelly and even more cruel than his eyes. He was giving more emotion than he had before, but the demented gleam didn't put me at ease.

I wasn't going anywhere with this guy, and clearly seeing that, he guided a hand behind me. I shoved but there were already so many people on this fucking street, his dad included.

At the end of the day, people still couldn't know I was here, and my mom couldn't know about the Thatcher complication. Again, I'd have to explain too many other things.

Even still, I couldn't make myself get in this psychopath's car, and Thatcher quickly noticed.

"Get. In. Snowflake." He all but put me in his car, the seat warm, and the sweat gathered between my breasts. My boob-to-body ratio wasn't equal, and I always sweated there when I was nervous.

Or scared.

Terror took on a new face inside Thatcher's ride. The black interior felt like a cage, and the only ally I had was on the other side of the glass. Mr. Reed was on his phone after saying goodbye to his kid, and when his own ride pulled up, a dark Escalade, I had no more of his attention.

"Better buckle up, baby. You're going for a ride." Thatcher snapped his door shut after he got inside, and the cabin immediately filled with his sharp scent. I'd actually been turned on by that sea breeze aftershave he wore when we'd been at the rave.

Now, I just felt ill. *Now*, I wanted to scream, and before I could, Thatcher forced the gas pedal down. The car shot off like a rocket, and I grabbed the dash. "Thatcher!"

He wasn't listening to me, and I screamed when he zipped through a stoplight. He literally stopped traffic, his Audi gliding through cars like he was some racecar driver. At least, he thought he was. I grabbed the door. "Thatcher, stop!"

I got nothing but a dark chuckle. He sped up, then shifted into manual. Apparently, the car could do both.

"Seat belt, baby," he said, and I was nauseous. The term wasn't endearing. Not any more than his *darlings, sweethearts,* or *snowflakes* from before. He swung his blue eyes my way. "I warned you."

He did, but I didn't think he'd come to collect so quickly. I figured I'd at least have his dad's security and the ability to make a phone call for help.

My phone.

I wrestled inside my purse for it. I was obviously panicking and not thinking straight. Thatcher spotted what I was attempting in seconds and grabbed it first. Alarmed, my first instinct was thinking he'd throw it out the window.

That would have been better.

I watched in horror as he took the device and spread his legs. He shoved it directly between the seat and his cock, a sizable bulge there.

Like he was hard.

This crazy, fucking psycho was getting off on all this. He chuckled again. He only had one sharpened cross in his ear today. The other earring was a dark stud. He put his arm behind my seat. "Go for it."

He spread his behemothly large thighs wider, and I was disgusted. I did what he said regarding the seat belt, though, and I had no choice as he slammed on the brakes. He happened to actually stop at a stoplight this time, and I didn't want to go through the windshield.

"Thatcher, you made your fucking point," I said, gripping down on the seat. I was trying so hard not to cry, to not show this guy my fear, but his car shot off like a bullet again, and the blood pumped violently in my ears. I closed my eyes. *"Please."*

I didn't know why I was pleading with him. The guy was clearly a sociopath, and he didn't bother to laugh this time. He just drove. We ended up on the back roads (way outside of campus), and on an empty stretch of road, Thatcher decided to test the limits of his car.

He went so fast, so terribly, frighteningly *fast*, and I thought I would die. I thought this was it, and I'd be left with *him*. The scream I bellowed out was something out of a horror film, and I didn't even hear it over the sound of the car. Thatcher went at top speed, and the acceleration only increased upon coming toward a moving train.

It was like he was charging right for it, and I lost my voice at that point. There was nothing left. There was *nothing*. I thought he'd literally hit the train and kill us both.

He stopped just short.

The wheels labored, spinning out a bit. Burning rubber hit the air as the car stopped at an angle just before the start of the tracks. The train zoomed its final cars past us, and I was shaking by the time I swung in Thatcher's direction.

"You're fucking *crazy*. You're fucking…" I held it back. I refused to shed tears but I was so goddamn close. "What is wrong with you? Have you lost your mind? Did you ever have it—"

I stopped my rant. Mostly because he wasn't listening. He still had his hands on the wheel, facing the street in silence, and I didn't see the point.

Point or not, I was going to start in on him again, but I

noticed something else. Thatcher's hands were not only ghost white on the wheel…

But they were shaking.

His entire body was, his forearms, his biceps. His body was in a constant state of shake. Like he himself was scared, but he'd been driving. He'd been in control, so why was he scared?

"Thatcher?" My adrenaline was going down, my swallow hard. "Thatcher?"

He didn't hear me. Like he was a shell once more. That hollow vacancy had returned to his stark blue eyes, and my heart restarted its quick beats. Something looked wrong with him, and I didn't know why I reached out to touch him. I was scared as fucking shit and wanted nothing to do with him.

"Touch me, snowflake," he gritted just before I could. My fingers stopped mid-touch, his trembling bicep within inches of my outstretched fingers, centimeters… He faced me. "And I touch you back."

His words held promise and equal parts darkness.

Fuck this shit.

Fuck *him* and all this shit. I unstrapped my seat belt, shaking.

"Snowflake—"

I grabbed my purse, literally getting out of the car on the side of the road. I almost tripped in my heels and face-planted in the dirt.

"Snow—Aspen, get back in the car. Aspen, I'll take you fucking home!"

There was no way I was getting back in the car and certainly not with him. My heels caught in the dirt, and I was so desperate to get away, I took them off. I lost my sunglasses too with my initial stumble, but I was so frantic I left them.

"Aspen!"

I started running then. I had no plan. I had no phone, but I didn't care. I just had to get away from him, and my heart started swiftly once more at the memories that suddenly invaded my head.

This felt so familiar.

Me running… Thatcher chasing. He got me when I ran so many years ago, but not before someone saw me. I'd made it nearly to a local diner outside of the campgrounds the cabin was on, and it was that short escape that saved me. Someone had spotted me and called the cops.

They had because they'd seen Thatcher catch me.

I still remembered his weight on my back. He'd been younger then but still big, and there'd been emotion on his face when he swiveled me around. He had emotion for the first time. That dark and twisted boy had shown me something.

Desperation.

He hadn't wanted me to leave, and he made sure I hadn't.

"Aspen!"

I was pulled out of the image of him in my head when the image of him today stood in front of me. He was still quick and cut me off shortly after I made it through a valley of trees. We were in some kind of woods off the highway.

He'd cornered me.

Thatcher wasn't even out of breath. Not like I was. Part of that, I think, was adrenaline, but he wasn't even fazed. He lifted his big hands. "No more games. I promise I'll take you back to your dorm."

But how many pieces would I be in by the time he did? I snarled, "Fuck you."

This was madness, and he had to think me mad if he thought I'd get back in a vehicle with him. I took a step, my feet bare and cut up from the sprint without my heels, but Thatcher matched my step.

He got closer. "This is pointless, snowflake—"

"It's Aspen!" I hated that fucking nickname he'd given me, and where the fuck did it even come from? Was he calling me fragile? Weak? I didn't know, but I was sure it was some kind of jab and a way for him to hold dominance over me. I cringed. "Why are you doing this to me?"

I'd asked him that too back then. I just wanted to know *why*. I'd done nothing to this guy, but he kept coming after me.

Thatcher's expression was stoic, and I hated him in that moment. I hated him because he was so beautiful, strong, and I knew how powerful that large body of his was. I also knew how free it made me feel if even for a night. I still felt trapped in front of him, and it was almost a decade later.

But that had nothing to do with him.

It didn't this time, and I felt *ill*. I didn't listen to him, taking quick steps away. I started to pick up my pace, but once more, he got ahead of me. He was so quick, too quick.

"As I was saying, this is pointless," he said, his dark hair curling over his eyes. He'd made it more posh today. I assumed to go with his country-club look since he had it moussed back, but he had kept his earrings in. The one dangled in the soft light streaming through the trees, and I noticed he didn't answer my question from before. Like when we were kids, he still didn't explain why he was doing this to me. His eyes narrowed. "Despite the fact that you are barefoot, I play college football. You run, and I will catch you. I assure you."

My heart squeezed. My stomach clenched, and though I thought it would be from dread… it should be from dread, it wasn't. Something wild danced inside me when he said that. I started thinking about him chasing me, and for some reason, I wasn't scared.

You are fucked up.

I knew that. I knew that just as well as I was here going to college and not still on tour. I had the life of my dreams, doing what I loved musically, but I was here in the woods with a guy who'd tortured me in my youth.

Thatcher wet his full lips. They were charged red and flushed from his own run. "Now, turn around and head back to my car, and for fuck's sake, don't run." He appeared terse for some reason, frustrated when his lips pinched together. He wove his fingers through his inky locks, tousling it a bit before dropping his hand. "I will take you back to your dorm. I will get you there safe."

Safe?

He pocketed his hands. "Just don't run. You run and…" He huffed out a breath. "You just shouldn't run. *Please* don't run."

His voice had deepened an octave, and he already had a deep voice. Those glacial eyes of his scanned the length of me, and when he dampened his lips again, my thighs clenched.

Holy fuck… the way he was looking at me. He studied me as if I was something to devour, and I was well aware of how I looked. I was windswept from the sprint, my toes and calves dirty. My peach dress had even torn a little when I fell earlier. Not to mention my hair was a complete mess. My locs had fallen from the high bun I'd looped and put time in. Now, all my hair rested down my back and across my shoulders, and there were definitely leaves in it from my earlier fall. Basically, I appeared as if I'd been through something.

And he had too.

His shirt was open a little, displaying his massive chest. His cross chain flashed down the center, his large pecs rising and falling with breath. I hadn't gotten to see his bare chest that night at the rave. He'd been wearing a cutoff tee, but even if he hadn't, it would have been too dark to see him there, touch him…

It wasn't dark now, and Thatcher and I were in a standoff. I'd made things easy for him that night. I'd been an easy lay, and that was me out of my comfort zone. I just wanted to be different. I… my life was so goddamn tight, and he'd made me feel free for a night.

Thatcher stepped forward, just a step, and he had his hand out. It was like he was trying to calm a wild animal. Like I was the wild animal and he was trying to coax me into a sense of security. "No more running, snowflake. You run and I." He paused, my blood heating again when he appraised me, my nipples *tight*. His irises flared. "I won't stop."

I didn't know what he meant by that. I didn't know if he wouldn't stop chasing me... or what. My lips parted, my mouth incredibly dry. "Okay."

His eyes flashed, maybe wondering why I was making this so easy. He started to move, but then, I did. Just a step. His chest rose. "You said you wouldn't run."

Did I? I took another step, and those irises flared once more.

He shook his head. "Snowflake—"

I darted off and was completely unaware of why I had. He was faster than me, but something had my knees hiking up and adrenaline pumped through my veins every step I made away.

He got me in seconds.

His thick fingers encased my arm, that chunky ring he wore pressing into my skin, and he brought me down beneath him so fast. I dropped my shoes. I dropped my purse. I was pinned, and Thatcher Reed was on top of me.

"Snowflake..." He was breathing heavy. His big chest labored with heavy breath even though there was no way that short sprint and our struggle took anything out of him. This guy no doubt played on the football field for hours before getting tired.

Something had him breathing harshly now, and he wasn't getting off me. He stared down at me, his large hands cuffing my small wrists. "Aspen."

My breathing kicked up, my breasts literally in his face. I trembled, and his blue eyes darted in their direction. My boobs were basically spilling out of the top of my dress, my nude bra below pushing them up.

He could see that nude bra, my breasts pushed together like two half-moons above my dress. Thatcher's eyes blazed in their direction. Like he couldn't keep his eyes off them. I'd allowed him to put his hands on me that night, squeeze them…

You should push him off you.

Even if he didn't weigh as much as he looked, I'd probably be hard-pressed. The fact of the matter was, I should do a lot of things right now being in this position. I should scream even though no one was around. I should fight, again, even though no one was around. I should because that was a fight-or-flight response.

Thatcher also wasn't doing what he said he'd do. He said he'd take me back to my dorm with no more games, but this wasn't that. This was him staring at me like he wanted to fuck me again, and I didn't move when he let go of one of my wrists. His large knuckles curled above one of my trembling breasts, but he didn't touch me. He swallowed, wetting his full lips like he wanted to but didn't dare.

Instead, his eyes stayed on me, studying my moves and reactions as his digits hovered down the length of my body. Again, he didn't touch, but he watched me. It was like he wanted to see if I'd stop him, and when I didn't, his fingers eased toward the hem of my dress. My thigh twitched, but I didn't stop him.

A low hum sounded within the confines of his mighty chest when his fingers glided beneath the hem. He followed the material to my pussy, and when he hooked two fingers in my panties and tugged the material away…

I was wet, *drenched*, and he picked up on that real fucking quick. The rough pad of his thumb swiped one quick stroke between my pussy lips, and that was all he needed. I was wet, and *he made me* wet.

"God *fucking* dammit," gritted from his mouth the same time he locked ours together. His tongue invaded the space between my lips, and something wild unleashed inside me. It was something that had me struggling. I lodged a tight fist into his chest, and when I bit Thatcher's lip, he growled. He immediately stopped kissing me and got my wrist when I looked like I was going to sock him again.

He blinked. "What? You don't want to do this?"

I didn't know what I wanted. I didn't know what I was *doing.* I just knew I used my other hand to grip his shirt, and once I did, I had that mouth back on mine. I wanted it. I craved it like an animal, and Thatcher, being a dude, didn't stop me. He kissed me equally hard. If not harder, and when I punched at him again, his arms this time, he didn't stop kissing me.

"Fuck, snowflake," he ground out, and I was struggling so bad he had to lock my wrists above my head. His eyes flared, but not once did he stop kissing me. He used his weighted hips to pin mine. "If you're going to do that, you gotta give me a fucking code word or something."

His kissing got more intense, more aggressive. He moved to my neck, dragging his long tongue down my flesh, and I shuddered so bad I stopped fighting for a second.

He bit my skin. "A safe word or I'm not going to fucking stop. *I won't stop,* so you gotta give me something in case this gets too intense."

He was saying something I didn't even realize I wanted, him taking me out here and me fighting him. Him *losing control* with me having little to no means of fighting him off. It was something primal and untamed like it'd been at the rave. For a few wonderful moments, I hadn't known who he was.

And that got me off so fucking much.

"Music." I didn't know who this person was beneath him, talking to him. I wasn't this girl who liked getting fucked in the woods. I wasn't this girl who enjoyed being pinned down and dominated by powerful men. Every aspect of my life was timed and scheduled. I didn't get to the level I was at in my field without doing so. I had to be serious, controlled.

Perhaps that was what made the prospect of this so exciting. It was dark, sinful.

"Music," I repeated. That was my safe word.

"Music. Okay," he said, smiling a little. His tongue flicked my lips. He didn't seem to care about my matte lipstick, and I wriggled. He grinned. "Perfect."

He lowered to kiss me again, but I didn't make that easy. In fact, I did something so out of fucking pocket, but I was turned on, and I hated that I was turned on. I hated that I wanted this attention from him because I *loathed* this fucker, but that didn't stop my excitement from whatever this was. I kneed Thatcher Reed in his dick, and that threw him so fucking off. He grunted, cursing when he grabbed his junk.

"The fuck!" he roared, the sound radiating in the trees, but all I did was smile. Thatcher rolled off me, the whole point, and once I was free, I ran again. I left all my stuff in the woods and ran, sticks cracking and breaking under my feet.

If my mom saw me…

Eugena Davis would have a fucking coronary if she saw what I was doing. She'd never understand this, and hell, I didn't understand this. I just knew something about all this made me feel powerful, and when I glanced back to look for Thatcher, he was gone.

Because he was in front of me.

I swear to God this boy was a goddamn vampire he was so quick, and he'd obviously recovered from the kneeing of his balls. He stood in front of me, his burly arms crossed.

That was when the shirt went off.

He unbuttoned it quickly, aggressively. He ripped it down his thick arms, displaying an array of muscles and toned definition. Before I knew it, there was nothing on but his cross and pleated pants. He'd even taken off his shoes like a wild man.

Fuck.

Six-pack abs pressed into his chiseled abdomen like a chocolate bar. A dark smattering of hair disappeared into his pants, his cock hard and tenting the gray material. He looked like a centerfold made just for women, and he threw his shirt down like a promise. Like he was preparing for a chase, and the devious grin on his face matched.

"What now, snowflake?" he asked, and I took a step only for him to match it. So much blood charged behind my ears, but that only excited me more.

I doubled back, heading off deeper into the woods, and I had to say, he let me go for a hot minute. I got so far into the woods before he brought me down again and underneath him.

And this time, he didn't let me get away.

He used his entire powerful body to pin me tight, but that didn't stop me from fighting. I lodged a punch toward his pretty face, and he got my knuckles in one hand.

"Ah, ah, ah. You fuck that up, you pay for that shit, sweetheart," Thatcher crooned. Pinning my wrists to the ground, he drove his hard dick into my thigh. Instinct and adrenaline had me attempt to knee him again, but he was quick just like he'd been in the woods. He got the back of my knee. "Uh-uh, snow. You fuck that up? You really pay for that shit."

He slipped his hand beneath my dress after he said that, cupping my sex, and I wriggled, burned.

He chuckled hoarsely in my ear. "Want me to make this pussy sing, snow?"

The prospect gathered sweat between my breasts, my thighs. Even still, I couldn't let him win at this game we were playing. I rolled, or I at least tried to. All that got me was Thatcher using his body to lock mine tighter against the ground. Twigs stabbed my back as he forced the front of my dress down, and he exposed me when he eased one of my nipples out of my bra.

"Fuck." He massaged my breast with his warm hand, then used two fingers to tweak my brown nipple. "Goddamn does this need a taste."

I didn't fight him because I *couldn't*. His mouth felt too damn good when he latched on to my peaked nipple.

"Christ." My wriggling wasn't from fight this time, my head digging into the leaves, and what the fuck? I was not a nature girl, and my mother could tell anyone that.

Thatcher's chuckle was gravelly over my tit, and he knew what to do with that too. We'd both been fully clothed the last time we fucked, and he hadn't gotten to suck me.

Well, he was now, and I got my mind back when he made me cup his dick. He made me squeeze him, trying to force me to submit to him, and I bucked.

"Get off me, asshole," I bit out, getting back into our game, and Thatcher's response to this was to suck my tit harder. He laved that one before exposing my other breast and biting that too.

"Nah, these want me too much," he said between tastes, bites. His voice was like molten lava against my skin, and when he forced my dress up, I gasped. He groaned. "This sweet little pussy wants me too."

His hand dove into my underwear, and the sound I let out was feral. I was completely wet, soaked for him, and the moment he felt that, he allowed a finger to slide inside me.

"That's right," he said, my nipple popping out of his mouth. His previous work had his full lips bruised and beet red. He licked one before biting my neck, and I fought him again. His hands were all over me at this point, inside me and squeezing my tits, but not once did I use my safe word. This was something he obviously knew, so no matter how many times I called him an asshole or the dirty motherfucker he was (which was a lot), he didn't stop.

He laughed, feeling me and fucking me with his fingers. They were so *thick*. Especially when he added more than one.

"You're going to let me fuck this sweet pussy, snow. My dick needs a taste," he hummed over my throat. He kissed my warm skin. "And like a good little whore, you're going to let him use you, have his way…"

God, he was such an asshole and *so* filthy. I wasn't into guys calling me a whore, but when Thatcher did it…

Even still, I didn't make this easy for him. I actually struggled so much he had to use his bare chest to keep me from moving. I tried to touch it at one point, grab his cross and feel him, but he didn't let me. He just used his weight to pin me down, and our positioning allowed him to still fuck me with his fingers.

His ministrations were so *stimulating*. He had that chunky ring on, and I kept feeling it deep inside me. Eventually, he curled his fingers and gathered some of my wetness out.

"Taste yourself, snow," he said, forcing his thick digits past my lips. He invaded deep into my mouth, and at the sound of my moan, he groaned. "That's it, snow. Taste yourself like a good girl."

I bit his fingers instead, and he grabbed my throat. I lost air for a second, seeing stars. My eyes rolled back, and he kicked my knees apart.

"You're not seeing my face," he said, making me go on all fours. I heard a foil package rip, and I saw it when he tossed the empty condom wrapper in front of me. "You don't get to see it. Maybe next time."

Like there'd be a next time. Whatever this was between us… was crazy. It was toxic as fuck, and I had no intention of letting this guy fuck me again.

The thoughts were all well and good for the future, but at the present, I easily let him lock his big hands on my hips. He gave no warning before driving himself to the hilt inside me, and the invasion forced a sound to rip from my lungs. I gripped the ground, drawing blood against the leaves.

God.

Thatcher thrust, over and over until the labor had us both against the ground. My exposed breasts scrapped at the brush beneath me, and I knew I'd have cuts. I'd probably even have bruises.

I didn't care.

This felt too good, and I couldn't stop it, couldn't use my safe word.

"Yeah, take that shit," Thatcher gritted, still holding my throat. He used that and my hip for purchase while he drilled relentlessly inside me. "Good, snow. My good little whore who loves to please me."

"Fuck. *You*," I ground out, but it all felt so damn *good*. I was close, and Thatcher was too. One final thrust released a roar from him so loud birds literally flapped out of the trees. He woke the whole area up, but disturbed wildlife wasn't what scared me.

It was me who was scared. He awoke something carnal inside me, and I wasn't just turned on by it.

I was invigorated by it.

"Yes, yes, yes," I called out, my pussy vibrating around his cock. It was like he was literally making it sing, and I felt him so deep when we both collapsed and he milked me from behind. Thatcher said nothing while he did this, but I saw what all this was doing to him too. He may not have let me see him while he fucked me, but I saw his hands in the dirt. They were ghost white, and he probably had more cuts than I would.

"Fuck, snowflake. Fuck," he said, easing out of me. He fell to his naked back, and I fell to mine too. He stared at the sky. "Fucking hell."

Fucking hell was right, and once it was over, it was like a wash of something hit me. What we did right here, hit me, and my heart raced harder than it already was. It was like a literal fucking ice bath hit me, and I might have been able to think more about it if Thatcher didn't grab my hips a few moments later. He put me on all fours again.

And I forgot to fight him when he took me for a second time.

CHAPTER
EIGHT

Thatcher

Fuck, this girl was into some freaky fucking shit.

But so was I.

This was new even for me, but I embraced that shit. I fucked Aspen not once but two more times out in the woods and was shameless about it.

I didn't care.

I should.

This girl had the potential to trigger some deep shit in me, but I didn't care. She'd also been the reason I lied to my dad today, and though I wasn't Saint fucking Peter, I tried not to be dishonest with my dad if I could help it.

This was dishonest. This was *savage*, and I was making that pussy pay for not only making me lie to my dad but also Aspen's efforts to use my dad against me.

At least, that was what I told myself.

It was easy once I had myself buried in that sweet little snatch of hers, and I think the only reason we stopped was because we were both tired. We were also dirty, and though I didn't give a shit about it, I noticed we were both bleeding in various places.

She was bleeding.

I didn't know much about this romping-in-the-woods shit, but aftercare was a thing, and something about seeing her bleeding in the woods triggered me. It shouldn't. Again, I shouldn't give a shit.

Why do you?

I wasn't a complete barbarian, and I was fucking tired. She'd given my dick a workout, and I must have done the same for her because she didn't fight me when I offered to get us both clean and patched up. There was a convenience store nearby. Not a big box store, but it did the trick. They surprisingly had a change of clothes for us both, and we used them after I found us a motel.

More fucking happened then, and let's not even talk about the shower we ultimately took together. I licked every inch of her in there, and even ate her out, her long gorgeous leg over my shoulder. This chick had me on my goddamn knees, and I didn't even worship pussy like that. I took a good dick sucking like the best of them, but eating pussy took effort, and I typically didn't bother with it. I didn't see the point as the next good lay was around the corner.

Aspen smacked me after I patched her up. I hadn't been gentle about the antiseptic I put on one of the cuts on her shoulder, and that pissed her off. She called me an asshole, and I immediately parted her legs. I fucked her to the point of creating new wounds.

But those were only inside me.

This wasn't good, what we were doing. I was fucking this girl to ignore shit, and I knew that but...

It just felt so good, her pussy warm, inviting. Each time she called me a dick or a disgusting motherfucker, it just made me want to take her harder, faster.

Yeah, I'm fucked up.

I just knew I wasn't thinking when I was inside her. I forgot about bullshit, and even my friends blowing up my phone. The guys started to do that after I told them my dad had canceled lunch. They knew I was looking forward to seeing my dad.

"Fuck, Thatcher… Fuck!"

That's right, snow. Sing that sweet music for me.

I had both of Aspen's legs above her, her warm brown skin in my face. I kissed her bare foot. "That's right, baby. Bow down to your God."

She called me an asshole again, but didn't have the stamina to wriggle away from me at this point.

And what that shit did to me.

She wanted me to force her in the woods, and chicks I was typically with didn't do that. They wanted to be fucked by a Legacy guy, my friends and I legends. Only Bru, Wells, and I were single now, so we were hot commodities. Our partners didn't fight us. They *submitted.*

Aspen Davis didn't easily submit. Aspen Davis hated me, but that didn't stop her from parting her legs. She took my cock wonderfully, and she made me fight for it. That did something for me, *unleashed* something, and I think that was why I had us so bloody in the woods. I was getting off on it. Like a part of me needed it.

Something dark and equally savage had me closing my eyes, and Aspen's screams picked up. I slammed into her *hard,* and though I knew the back of those beautiful thighs of hers would bruise…

I didn't stop. If I did, I thought about shit, and I wasn't thinking about *fucking shit.* There was too much, and I refused.

"Thatcher, yes, yes, yes."

My kinky snowflake loved it, and I let go of her legs to fuck her deeper. I flattened against her on the motel's white sheets, wanting to taste those pert dark nipples. They tempted me each and every time I slammed into her, bouncing and shit, supple.

I brought one into my mouth on top of her, eliciting the most carnal noise from her full lips. She'd lost her lipstick a long time ago. Either in the shower or before. It was all over my mouth until I cleaned it off after the shower. She'd tried to kiss me other places, but I fought her.

She'd only get my mouth, and I fisted her tits as I drove inside her. Eventually, I let her tit pop out of my mouth so I could watch myself disappear inside her. She was unshaven, dark curls coiled on the most perfect pussy.

Fuck, get out of my head.

I kept seeing her as more than a lay. I saw her as more than a *temporarily* good time, and the potential of that shit terrified me so fucking bad. This couldn't be anything, and I picked up the vigor of my hips. I drowned myself inside her, forced the thoughts of anything else and this moment out of my head.

Snowflake…

Her kiss was potent, a drug, and any fight I had to create distance between us evaporated when she rose up on her elbows and pressed her mouth to mine. It was one of the rare moments where she wasn't calling me shit or cursing me out.

God.

This girl was doing some terrible shit to me, and she didn't even know. She went for my hair, but I braced her wrists and pinned them to the bed. I took her deeper there, covered her with my whole body. Well, as much as I could without suffocating her.

Aspen was so tiny below me, fragile, delicate. A soft hum moved from her lips into mine, and I found myself kissing her sweetly. I wanted her to like this.

I wanted her to like me.

Fuck…

I came so hard over her mouth, and she did too. Her

back bowed, and her pussy tightened around my cock, but I was the only one shaking. My body physically shook like I had behind the wheel of my Audi. I let myself get in my head a bit this afternoon. I was thinking about my dad, my gram…

I wasn't thinking about that now, the tension completely releasing from my body. It all escaped in a *whoosh* as Aspen's mouth took over my entire fucking being. I ended up having her face in my hands, my attempt to dive deeper into the feeling, make this last.

Snow…

I was losing myself, and though I could feel that, I didn't stop. It felt so good. Something about this girl was drugging me out.

"Thatcher?"

Her effects were apparent when I was hugging her after, *long after.* I had Aspen in my arms after we fucked, a place I put her. "Yeah?"

"You falling asleep?"

I had been, which was crazy. I didn't fall asleep easily lately. Things in my household were pretty fucking stressed. It didn't matter that I was away at school. I faced Snowflake, following the silhouette of her body in the dark. How long had we been fucking lying here? It hadn't been dark when we got here. I closed my eyes. "Maybe."

It was kind of nice being here with her, warm. I grabbed her hip with my eyes closed, massaging her ass, and she shoved at me.

"Well, we can't. I…" My eyes popped open when she shifted away. I didn't like it. She huffed. "I should probably get back to campus."

I didn't know if she was concerned about classes in the morning or what because today's were shot. She started to move across the bed, but she was little, and I wasn't. I got her back easily, which made her balk, but she didn't fight. I closed my eyes again. "Snowflake, you missed whatever classes you had today, so you might as well sleep."

The same went for me, and school was about the only thing I still had a lock on. It was the only thing I could control in my life lately, so I didn't miss shit.

I had today. I had for her, and if I thought about that shit too much, I'd probably try to escape this bed too. I grasped Aspen by the hip, keeping her close, but she made more of an effort against me.

She wriggled. "Dude, I can't sleep here."

"Why not?"

"Because I can't." She sat up. Mostly because I let her. She turned on the light, and even though the fixture was shoddy, it set a glow to her that distracted. I kissed the lipstick off her lips, and though I think the shower had done the rest of her makeup, that didn't matter.

She was fucking flawless.

Honestly, *flawless* wasn't a good enough word for how good this girl looked completely fucking natural in front of me. Girls usually overdid that makeup shit when it came to me, but nothing did it for me more than a girl fresh out of the gym or just out of fucking bed. Aspen Davis had that shit in spades, her face flushed, her braid over her naked shoulder. She'd done that with her hair after we got out of the shower, and it rested near one of her brown bandages. This one was on her arm, and I traced it with my finger.

She let me for some reason, following it with her big eyes. I didn't know why I was touching her, or why she was letting me. She bit her lip. "I can't stay."

"And you've yet to tell me why."

"Why do you want to?"

Her mouth parted, as if to say something else, but she paused. She'd been self-assured before and a fucking badass in the woods, but seemed hesitant to be that way now.

Was Aspen Davis being fucking shy? I'd seen it before at the rave, but she'd put it away.

She studied my finger again. I circled a mole on that space where shoulder met chest. She was so soft.

A shift moved in her throat. It was slight, but I noticed. Her teeth lodged into her lip again. "Anyway, I can't. I don't mind sleeping naked, but I need something for my hair. I'm not putting my head on these pillowcases."

She eyed them warily, and I noticed she'd completely glossed over the first question she'd asked me.

I was kind of glad for that. I didn't have the answer, but if she was worried about her hair, I got her on that. I got out of bed.

"Where are you going?"

I shrugged my boxers on. "To get you something for your hair." It took a second to get dressed, and by the time I turned around, Aspen's full lips had parted again. "What? I'll be back. I might have to drive around for a bit, but I'll find you something."

She blinked. "Find me what exactly?"

"A silk pillowcase, right? Or a bonnet." Her eyes expanded to the width of her face, and I chuckled. "Aspen, you're not the first black girl I've dated. I got you. I'll be back."

Grabbing my keys, I went in quick time. Mostly because I didn't want to see her reaction to what I just said. I mentioned dating, and I didn't know why I said that.

I left before I thought too much about it. It was dangerous for me when thoughts caught up. It was best to outrun them.

Otherwise, I'd have to deal with them.

CHAPTER
NINE

Thatcher - age 10

"What are you doing over there?"

I closed my eyes tight, trying not to flinch, trying not to *cry*. I said nothing, and a deep sigh came from behind me.

"You came here, didn't you? You did, so get from over there and come here."

I flinched, a sound behind me, movement. It wasn't close but far away.

A ripping noise filled the room, like a scratch. It reminded me of my neighbor's cat when I accidentally stepped on her tail. I didn't always see Piper. She was so fast sometimes and liked to hide.

I wished I could hide now, but I didn't. I never did. I couldn't.

Music sounded after the scratch, a record player. I'd never seen one before, but now, I saw them all the time. They played in my head on autopilot, old music like what my gram listened to sometimes through her radio. She liked to listen to old music, but never this.

This wasn't *music.* It was noise that made my stomach tight and made me want to throw up. It always played when I came here. It was so loud, and even if I cried, no one would hear. I guess that was why it played.

"Kid..." Another loud sigh, and I flinched again. I couldn't help it.

Be brave. Be brave like Dad.

My dad wasn't scared of anything. He was so strong. I had to be strong too. I had to be for my friends, my brothers. I couldn't let anything bad happen to them too.

"No one's making you be here," a deep voice said. "Remember, this is your choice. It always is."

I opened my eyes, then played made-up movies in my head. I liked to pretend.

If I did, it didn't hurt so much.

CHAPTER
TEN

The music had woken me up, but then... Thatcher.

"Thatcher?" I sat up, his body quaking beside mine. We'd both fallen asleep. *What time was it?*

I didn't care about the time when Thatcher hit the pillow. On his side, he forced his fist right into it. It'd been my pillow, but I obviously wasn't there anymore since I was sitting up. My heart raced. "Thatcher, wake up."

He wasn't, and the noises falling from his lips sounded tortured, pained. He let out a cry that quite frankly clenched my fucking stomach, and the music was coming so loud from somewhere. Thatcher and I were still in this motel room, so it must have been next door.

My hand hovered over him, hesitant to touch him since he was shaking so much. He was such a big guy, and this was honestly scaring the shit out of me. "Thatcher, you have to wake up."

The noise he made next was something between a strained

bellow and a bloodcurdling whimper. He sounded like a small child being beaten, and I didn't fucking play around anymore. I rocked him, terrified myself since he was so large, and I had a right to be when he snapped awake. He swung his big arms just barely missing me, and his blue eyes were so wild.

"Thatcher…" I was shaking, but he was too. He paled, his dark hair curling over his rapidly blinking eyes, and his hands gripped the bedding so hard his fists were ghost white. "Thatcher?"

His attention zoomed in my direction, his earring dangling when he turned his head. He blinked again. Like he was just now aware of himself and me sitting here.

His mouth parted as if to say something, but then he faced the wall.

His eyes went wild once more, wide and crazed. He scanned the wall, all that noise… all that music behind it, and the next thing I knew, he was out of bed. He had on nothing but his boxers since that was what he'd come to bed in. He did after he'd driven around for over an hour finding me a bonnet.

I wore that now, thinking it was so sweet he'd done that but I was really freaking confused. I was confused about a lot of things, and the latest was watching Thatcher rip the door open of our motel room in nothing but a pair of boxers and the cross chain he wore. His dark hair was strewn about, something normally really sexy on him, but now, it made him appear wild and untamed.

He disappeared into the night air. I saw nothing but his naked back and broad shoulders when he moved swiftly into the night. He was barefoot, and I was too when I ran after him.

Normally, I'd care about being braless. I literally had on nothing but the T-shirt and shorts we'd bought earlier at the store. Well, that and my bonnet.

My mother would really keel over seeing me out like this in public, but my appearance was the last thought on my fucking mind right now.

Thatcher was slamming his fists into a door.

His mighty knuckles punched, already bandaged from our time in the woods, but now, they were bruising, bleeding. I screamed. "Thatcher!"

He was leaving blood on the door, streaks every time he hit the thing again and again, and that music was *so loud*. I covered my ears, I think overly stimulated between the music, the ringing in my head, and Thatcher hitting this door. It was old music, a male soloist with a sound that came out of the 1960s or something.

The guy's voice was drowned out every time Thatcher slammed his meaty fists against the door, and eventually, his punches turned into kicks. Using his bare feet, Thatcher shot his foot into the door, and alarmed, I started to grab for him but thought better. I knuckled my hands. "Thatcher…"

In the end, it only took two kicks. That was how strong this guy was, how big, powerful. The door in front of us fell off its hinges, and Thatcher thought nothing about going inside this person's room.

"What the fuck do you think you're doing, man?" A man ran from the bathroom in nothing but a towel. Steam came from the room he'd been in like he'd been in the shower, and Thatcher ignored him as he headed toward the back of the room and the source of the music. It was a vintage-looking radio. Our room had one of those too, but we hadn't used it.

This guy would no longer get to use his, because as soon as Thatcher got to it, he ripped it out of the wall. He then threw it at the wall, then charged his bare foot into it for good measure.

I wished it would have stopped there.

Thatcher took his bleeding and bruised fists and punched at the radio, over and over again despite the fact the music stopped long ago. I watched him, horrified, and I must have been screaming, and he must have finally fucking heard me.

Because he faced me.

He'd done so on autopilot, sweat on his brow, his chest. He also had blood going down his fingers. It dripped to the floor by his feet, which were also cut, bleeding.

Awareness blinked into his eyes again. Like it had before when he woke up and realized I was there beside him.

I swallowed. "Thatcher..."

Instinctually, I reached out. He just... I couldn't help it. He appeared like an animal, confused.

Lost.

He very much looked like a werewolf after it transformed and destroyed everything, and I hesitated my reach when he glanced around. He was able to see now what he'd done. The broken radio at his feet. The man in the towel staring stunned at us both.

Then there was the fact that he was bleeding.

We both had small cuts from the woods, but this was different. The bandages he still had on his hands were gone or bled through. I stepped forward. "Thatch—"

My voice made him cringe, and he stepped back. He became animal-like again, cowering like he'd hurt me. I didn't understand and even more so when he rushed past me.

"I'm calling the fucking cops," the guy in the towel said behind me, and once he said that, I got out of there too. I went after Thatcher, but I wasn't quick enough.

He was already in his car.

I stood on the sidewalk with bare feet and shaking limbs, nothing more I could do. My ride and the only person I knew backed out of his parking spot with smoke literally on his wheels. Thatcher shifted, then peeled off into the night, leaving me, and my back hit the wall. I could hear inside my head now that the music wasn't playing. I could hear my own voice.

It was screaming.

CHAPTER
ELEVEN

Thatcher

"Bro, what the fuck?" Wells shot, pausing. "Where are your clothes?"

My buddy Wells was getting his dick sucked, a girl on her knees in front of him in the middle of our living room.

I blew past them both, heading to the bathroom. They technically did have on more clothes than me. I had no shoes on or even any pants outside of my boxers, shirtless…

"You're also… bleeding. Thatcher, what—"

I blew chunks into the bowl on the first floor, effectively drowning out Wells's voice. He'd followed me.

I didn't stop.

Once it started, *I couldn't*. No matter how hard I gripped the bowl and willed for that shit to stop. No matter how hard *I tried*.

"Thatch." Wells was beside me in seconds, a fury of fake blond hair. He dyed his hair. He was normally a brunet, and there wasn't a bunch of room in the bathroom, but he got in beside me. We were both large motherfuckers. He was more so tall where I was wide. He was working his Pembroke Football hoodie over his bare chest, but stopped when he spotted me in here. He fell down beside me. "Thatcher…"

"Is everything okay—"

"Get the fuck out of here!" Wells roared, and the girl who'd sucked his dick twitched before fleeing from the bathroom. Apparently, she followed me into the fucking bathroom too.

Christ.

I had no time to think about that shit. I had no time to *think*. All I could do was fight the images in my head, the music.

Make it stop. Make it stop. Make it stop.

Just like throwing up, I couldn't. This shit was a chain reaction.

Wells's hand hovered over me. "Bro, did you eat something weird?"

I'd laugh at my friend if I could. He knew I had an iron stomach. I ate fucking everything and had to.

I wished what he said had been the case. I wished to fucking shit it was. Fucked-up food didn't have me like this. It didn't have me gripping the fucking toilet bowl like a little bitch.

It didn't have me shaking.

Wells saw that too, and his green eyes flashed. He wrestled his fingers through his white hair. "Buddy, let me go get Wolf."

Wolf was one of our other best friends, and though I should have let Wells go get him… Wolf would know what to do, I didn't. Wells started to leave, and the first thing I did was let go of the bowl.

"No, please don't leave." I felt so cold, so fucking dark. I grabbed Wells, not caring that I got blood all over him. My hands were bleeding, my fists. I shook my head. "Don't leave. Don't leave. Don't leave."

The words I spoke just played in my head. Honest to shit, I didn't even know what I said. I just knew I couldn't be alone. I knew he couldn't leave.

The voices…

His voice. His fucking smell…

The bile threatened to come again, and thank fuck for my buddy's strength. I was bigger than him. I was bigger than everyone, but Wells managed to handle me bracing him within an inch of his life.

"Okay. Okay." Wells braced me right back and let me hold on to him. He was lanky as shit, but he didn't let go. I was even ripping this dude's fucking hoodie. He placed a hand on my back. "I'm not going anywhere. Okay?"

He couldn't if he wanted to, and I closed my eyes. I did because I knew that *he knew* to do this.

Because he'd done it before.

I let a sound escape then, and I knew that shit sounded familiar. I knew *she'd* heard me do it before, seen me…

Aspen had seen me like this.

The shakes hit my limbs again. I was on the verge of throwing up once more, but from the far-off spaces in my mind, I heard voices. There were two voices suddenly in the bathroom with Wells and me.

"What's going on? Noa and I heard yelling."

My eyes shut tighter, my best friend Dorian's voice in the room. The other voice had been his girlfriend, Noa Sloane-Mallick, and as soon as I opened my eyes, I cringed. Sloane had her hand to her mouth, and Dorian had his hand on her.

"Go get Wolf," Dorian urged her. Wolf was her twin, and the two looked similar. They were both tall and looked like Latin models with tanned skin and flowing dark hair. I supposed they both were Latin and Middle Eastern and white.

I couldn't even look at Dorian when he came over. He was blond too, but it was natural.

I should be stronger than this shit.

I should have been, and I didn't want Sloane to see me like this. I didn't want anyone to see me like this, but especially my buddies' girlfriends. Wolf had one too, and I saw Fawn when she entered the bathroom with Wolf.

She was his fiancée now, a redhead with tattoos. Wolf had some too, but not as many as her. The two had recently gotten engaged, and she had moved into our house. I shared one with my friends, and Dorian had been pissed about the engagement. He was happy as shit for Wolf. We all were, but Dorian was in his feelings that Wolf had gotten the jump on him. It was common knowledge Dorian wanted to propose to Sloane, and he had his back up about not being able to propose first.

I had a feeling neither of my friends were thinking about that now, that beef. They weren't with me on the fucking floor like a little bitch.

Fuck. Fuck. *Fuck.*

I couldn't stop fucking shaking, and I couldn't let go of Wells. I kept hearing that goddamn music. I kept hearing it…

"Hey." Wolf had his hands on my shoulders. His real name was Ares, but we called him Wolf because he played like a beast on the football field.

I didn't know how all of us were in this tiny-ass bathroom. I barely fit in here, but Wells, Dorian, and Wolf managed to get in. Dorian was wide like me, and Wolf was goddamn tall. He was closer to seven feet than six.

Wolf braced my shoulders. "Look at me, buddy. Okay?"

Dorian knew to get Wolf. Hell, Wells had too, but I hadn't let him.

"Ares…" I cringed again, rocking, and I heard whispers. Sloane said something to Fawn by the door, and shortly after, they both left. They both thought it best, leaving us guys, and they said that.

I cringed once more, buckling over like a little fucking bitch. I should be able to deal with this, handle this.

She saw me like this.

I shouldn't fucking care. Who the fuck was Aspen Davis to me anyway? But I didn't like anyone seeing me like this. Weak…

"Thatcher?" Wolf urged, physically making me look at him. I ended up releasing my hold on Wells only to grip Wolf instead.

The music. That fucking music.

"Make it stop, man," I called out, that shit drumming in my head. I was tearing Wolf's clothes now, his sweatshirt. "Make the music stop, *please*."

"You're hearing the music again?" Wolf questioned, his voice calm, steady. It always was when I had these panic attacks, which was why the others had wanted to call him. He knew how to deal with these because he had them sometimes. "It's in your head again?"

I nodded, shutting my eyes.

Wolf gripped my arm. "You listen to me, okay? You're here in this room. You're here with us. *You're safe.* You are because you're here with us guys. Your boys."

My eyes shut tighter.

"You're safe, man. I swear," Wolf continued. "You're with us guys. You're okay."

I knew that, and though I wanted to be here in the present, it was hard. This shit didn't easily stop when I was trapped in the sea of the moment. I got lost in it. So fucking lost.

Even still, my friends attempted to help me. Dorian put a hand on my shoulder, and I felt another on my back. Wells ended up hugging me from behind, and they all put me in a cocoon.

"Safe, man. You're safe." Wolf kept repeating, and eventually, I heard whispers again, Dorian.

"Where's Bow?" I heard him ask the others, and it was Wells who responded.

"She's at the library with the kid," Wells stated. *The kid* was Sloane and Wolf's brother Bru. "They'll probably be gone for a while. You know how they study."

They were whiz kids, the both of them. I didn't do bad myself, but I was more into the tech stuff, coding and hacking.

It made sense Dorian would wonder about the location of my sister. Rainbow (we called her "Bow") may live at the dorms, but she was always over at our house.

"Good," I heard Dorian say, and he wasn't bothering to keep his voice down. I mean, we were all here in this tiny fucking bathroom, so what was the point? Dorian squeezed my arm. "Good. He wouldn't want her to see him like this."

My friends knew me so well, and out of everyone, my sister couldn't see me like this. I was her big brother, and I had to be strong. Especially right now and what we were both dealing with back at home.

The music…

I let myself be weak in the bathroom. I didn't have a choice. I let myself be broken.

I did until I didn't.

CHAPTER
TWELVE

Aspen

Me: Hey, it's me. Are you okay?

    Me: Me again. Thatcher, what happened was really scary. You also left me at that motel and… yeah. Just get back to me, okay?

    Me: I'm not angry. I should be, but I'm more so freaked out. You didn't look good that night. Are you okay?

    Me: So, I've left a few texts. I obviously haven't called, but it wasn't cool how things were the other night. Like I said, I'm not angry. Just get back to me. I'll give you space.

———

I stared at my phone on a Monday morning, days after what had happened with Thatcher the previous week. I stared at unanswered texts, and I should be fucking pissed about what happened.

I should be…

Like I'd told Thatcher, I wasn't angry. I was just

concerned. He didn't look well when we'd been together, and I'd gotten the hell out of there after the shock had worn off. That guy had been threatening to call the cops, and I didn't need the bad press. The guy gratefully hadn't recognized me, but considering that motel had been in the middle of bumfuck nowhere, I was sure I wouldn't be seeing any classical music fans who enjoyed fusion with hip-hop. I mean, it was possible but yeah. Far-fetched. My music was pretty niche.

My thumb hovered over my message thread with Thatcher. I hadn't heard from him since he left, and again, he hadn't looked good. It was like he'd been entranced. Like someone else had infiltrated his body, and he raged all over that guy's room. He obviously hadn't liked the music, and it had been loud.

Just text me back.

It was like a silent plea, and crazy considering I really wasn't *Thatcher Reed's* biggest fan. I mean, I fucked the guy. Well, he fucked me. He fucked me damn good, and I couldn't get him out of my head.

I wished that was the reason why I'd been in a constantly flustered state. That I wished my booty call would text me back so I could yell at him, and not that I was pretty frickin' concerned about him. He'd turned into someone else when he'd woken up.

Fuck this.

I wasn't paying attention to my history class, so there was no point in me being here. I got up in my lecture hall, very aware when someone got up with me on the other side of the room. The ex-Navy SEAL had been hired for me by Thatcher's dad's company. I'd gotten security like Thatcher said.

Wetting my lips, I kept my head down and tried not to feel some kind of way that a grown-ass man was following me out of class. Mr. Reed's guy was discreet. He made himself look like a college student with baggy jeans and an oversize hoodie, but he looked more like a dude casing the place than he did a college student.

These people around me were none the wiser, though, and I didn't let my thoughts linger on my security. I just let him follow me out of class.

"Everything all right, Miss Davis?" he asked me once he noticed I lingered outside the lecture's double doors. Unlike Franklin, this guy wasn't an actor and was nearly as big as Thatcher freakin' Reed.

Thatcher…

I didn't want to text him again. Honestly, I didn't want anything to do with the guy, our history notwithstanding. He hadn't looked right the other day, and I was human.

I told my security guy I was cool. His name was Phil.

This is stupid.

A few things in my life were, and though I needed space, I allowed Phil to do his job. He followed me across the quad, people playing Frisbee and hanging out. Again, I kept my head down, but no one noticed me since I'd come to Pembroke. I always wore my shades and my hat.

Me: I know that I said I wouldn't text again, but just give me something so I'll stop. I need a status on you, and I'll leave you alone. Are you good? Just let me know.

Thatcher couldn't possibly be good. At least, that night. I pocketed my phone, then decided to head back to my dorm. It was a long walk and Phil offered to drive me (or ride the bus with me), but I opted out. I just needed the time to think.

"Give me a text if you decide to go out again today, Miss Davis," Phil said when we arrived at the dorm. "If you need me, I'm on standby for you."

Mr. Reed had worked it out where Phil would be staying in a nearby dorm on my floor. Ironically enough, that was a similar situation I'd had my own fake security do.

I nodded at him, and the brawny dude left me as I approached my door. I'd almost gotten the key in the lock when heavy steps suddenly sounded down the hall, startling me.

"Eh. You Aspen Davis?"

Okay, so no one should know who I was here. I made sure of that. I mean, my disguise could be better, but no one should know I was here besides Thatcher.

This guy did as he stalked down the hall toward me and despite my disguise. I had my hoodie's hood up and sunglasses and hat on. He still clearly knew who I was, though, and I was well aware of how good-looking this guy was. He was also tall and blond. Though, his hair looked bleached considering the dark roots. My mouth parted. "Uh…"

He was on me in seconds. Well, not on me per se, but he came at me so fast that I backed up, dropped all my stuff, and then he kind of was on me. He towered over me, his nostrils flaring, and that good-looking face of his appeared straight-up pissed.

My back hitting the door, I raised my hands. "Whoa—"

"You're Aspen Davis, right? Looks like you." The blond eyed me up and down, and his face was as red as a fucking cherry. His green eyes were also wild. Like he had crazy in them. They narrowed into slits. "It's been a long time, but I recognize you. Anyway, stay the fuck away from my buddy Thatch."

Uh, double whoa, and where the fuck was Phil?

Right.

I'd let him go for the night, thinking I didn't need him, and I'd be naive if I said I didn't have threats. Of course, I had threats. I was a public figure, but…

My fists curled, fight or fucking flight. I probably couldn't take this guy, but the body couldn't help but try to defend itself. He'd mention Thatcher, though, and it took my brain a second to catch up that he had. My mouth parted. "You know Thatcher—"

"Yeah, I know Thatcher, and you're going to stay the fuck away from him. I saw the fucking texts you sent him, and you're going to stop that shit if you know what's good for you."

So, this guy knew Thatcher, and he also had access to his phone because he saw my texts to him. What I didn't understand was why he was so pissed at me, or why he said it'd been a long time since he'd seen me. Like he knew me or some shit, but I didn't know this guy.

The guy managed to get closer, smelling fresh like the sea. It reminded me of Thatcher in a way, but there was nothing surfer or laid-back about this guy. He was big, and he had beef with me. I certainly didn't feel safe. Especially with him hovering over me. I put a finger in his face. "I'm warning your ass. I've got security and—"

"Wells, back off. It's not her fucking fault."

Another dude made his appearance—well, two. The one who'd spoken was an even larger blond if one could imagine. He wore combat boots and faded jeans and a sweatshirt that said Pembroke Football on the front. The guy behind him was even taller than him and incredibly tan. It was a natural tan like he may be mixed race or Latinx. He also had these pretty kickass curls I wished I had before I loc'd my hair. They breezed behind him like he was a walking shampoo ad, and both guys picked up their pace once they spotted this Wells guy getting closer.

It was like Wells hadn't even heard the blond, and the guy with the hair pulled him off me so fast. Wells hadn't gotten to me *yet*, but he'd been about to.

Wells shoved the guy with the curls. "Back off. You saw the shit she did to him the other night. How he was all sick and shit and fuck that."

My eyes widened. Thatcher was sick. In what way?

I mean, he hadn't looked good. Not at fucking all, and he left me so fast. He had after being, well, kind of sweet. He hadn't been sweet in the woods at all, but that had been the point. I hadn't wanted him to be sweet, and he hadn't been.

And then after…

After had been different and nothing I'd expected. I never would have thought the guy who threatened me and over-powered me so many years ago would take care of me. He patched us both up, then got me a bonnet for my hair. He'd even brought food back with him.

It'd been sweet.

The shower, though brief, had also been nice. Thatcher had *washed* me like an actual nice guy, and I'd let him. I'd wanted him to. It'd felt good, and before he'd woken up and freaked me out, the cuddling part had been nice as well. Being in his big embrace had been nice.

This wasn't nice as I watched these guys shove each other back and forth. It was like observing clashing titans, and the blond dude (the one in the combat boots) pulled them apart. I had to give it to the guy with the curly hair. He hadn't been wanting to fight and had been more so trying to deescalate the situation. The guy who yelled at me, Wells, had made it hard, though. Wells shoved back his hair.

"She's still doing shit," Wells said, shooting his finger in my direction. Red crept up his chiseled jawline, and he clenched it before snarling at me. "She broke him, and that shit doesn't sit well with me."

I broke Thatcher? How so?

I was so fucking confused and just stood there. "What's going—"

"You don't fucking talk." Wells stalked up on me again, but with his friends there, he wasn't getting an inch. The guy with the curls pushed Wells back once more and pointed two fingers at him.

"And again. It's not her fault," the curly-haired guy said, and the guy in the combat boots was sighing, his hands on his hips. All these guys were fucking huge.

Combat Boots shook his head. "Don't do this, Wells. You know Wolf is right. We both are, so take a fucking walk before you do something stupid."

Wells didn't want to take a walk, but his friends gave him no choice. He stalked away in a huff, and I could finally breathe again with him up off me.

I didn't get anything from the other two guys. Absolutely nothing before they followed after him. They didn't apologize for their friend or anything.

And wouldn't even look at me before they left.

Aspen

It wasn't hard to find Thatcher that night. In fact, I wished it would have been harder. I wished it would have taken effort to figure out where the next rave was being held. I wished it would have been laborious to assume that was where he'd go after he went AWOL and his friend came after me on some confusing-as-shit warpath.

But it wasn't.

As it turned out, it was hella freaking easy to find the guy who'd been dodging me. He had been at another rave once I got the location, and he was chilling just like the rest of the strung-out college students there. The rave was at another warehouse, and though Thatcher wasn't in the center of the room, he was one of the star attractions. He was in some dodgy corner with a bunch of chicks and dudes around him.

And one of the girls was naked.

Well, mostly. A cute little thing, she pressed her pert little breasts in Thatcher's face. This was easy to do since he sat in a chair smoking a blunt. The girl was actually *on his lap* and was completely topless.

My face heated, the girl doing a slow grind on Thatcher's lap while he virtually ignored her. He had his head back, smoke billowing in the air from his lips. The girl hovered over his cock, doing everything she could to get his attention. He wasn't really giving it to her. Actually, he wasn't looking at her at all and seemed more consumed by his smoke. He just sat there, hazy eyed as he stared up at the ceiling, but that didn't stop the pang in my chest.

I swallowed, watching that cloud of smoke gather above Thatcher's tousled locks. His hair appeared inky black tonight in the room filled with strobe lights and ass, and eventually, he closed his eyes. Like he was completely unaware of the activity around him and the fact a basically naked girl was on his lap.

I felt unsteady, just standing there with a tight throat and rapidly beating heart.

I mean, what else could I do?

I stood there for a time, staring, wavering. I felt tossed right in the center of some stupid fucking 1980s movie. One where the girl went after the boy only to find him doing dumb shit that had absolutely nothing to do with her. He never cared about her, not really.

I stood in my own version of a 1980s film in an oversize coat and my blonde wig, trying to blend in.

Trying to disappear.

Thatcher turned his head in my general direction, but there were too many people around me. He didn't even see me when I snapped a picture of the spectacle, that girl on his lap.

Why do you care?

I didn't. Not really. I mean, what was I to him, but I had been concerned and confused as fuck since his friend came at me earlier tonight.

I felt stupid for that concern now, and though I intended to text him the picture I took and show him what an ass he fucking was, I didn't. I just left, flustered more than I wanted to be.

Idiot.

I wished I'd been mentally calling him that, but I wasn't. I went to that rave like some dipshit checking on a guy who was, well, not all completely there. He fucked like a god, but he was insane, and I didn't know what I was thinking.

My chest hurt.

I rubbed it upon heading back to my dorm, chugging stomach relaxer along the way. I had my rideshare driver stop at a pharmacy before taking me home. It was actually my second stop. The first had been a pizza place where I proceeded to devour half a deep dish like an idiot.

Hence the hurting chest.

I didn't typically have acid reflux, and I blamed the sharp burning in my chest completely on that.

I rubbed beneath my nose, sniffling. I hadn't told my security I was going out and, honestly, hadn't thought to. The only reason I really got security was Thatcher, and he clearly wasn't coming after me.

I rubbed my chest again, tucking my Pepto Bismol in my purse before tugging off my wig. There was no way I was going to fucking classes in the morning after staying up half the night, and I had no idea what time it was by the time I got back to my dorm.

I stopped in the center of the hallway. In fact, I stopped dead fucking center, and the person sitting in front of my door was well aware.

Thatcher Reed looked like shit. Hell, he looked like shit mixed with hell and a side of fucked up. His dark hair was strewn about like it always was, but it was the bags under his eyes and fatigued expression that made him look like hell. He appeared exhausted on my doorstep in the ribbed tank and jeans he'd worn at the rave, and in the hallway's clear light, I could see the body glitter on his dark tank and jeans.

Her glitter.

I fought the bile in my throat, and upon seeing me, Thatcher got right up. He filled the whole fucking hallway with his bulky frame, and I hated myself for the intrusive thoughts I had. How I noticed just how well those jeans sat on his chiseled hips and the way that tank hugged his huge pecs. His tank top fully exposed how ridiculously large he was, how broad…

"Snowflake…" Thatcher stepped forward. Well, stumbled. He appeared drunk on top of everything else, and the light in the hall appeared to bother him. He squeezed his eyes before focusing on me. He pocketed his hands. "You didn't come home last night."

He hadn't either. Though, I was sure he didn't know I knew that. He was clearly high as hell at that rave. I bunched my arms. "You obviously didn't either."

I mean, he was sitting at my door.

I can't do this.

The drug from the pharmacy was just starting to work. Even if it was only kind of working for my issues. I still had that harsh beat in my chest, that searing pain…

Not letting Thatcher see that shit, I maneuvered around him, and I heard him sigh like he had any right to do that. He'd ghosted me for days after leaving my ass at that motel. And let's not forget the fact that he probably fucked that bitch at the rave.

It didn't matter. None of it mattered, and for some reason, I couldn't get into my dorm. The key wouldn't maneuver into the lock, my hand shaking too bad.

"I wanted," Thatcher started, but then stopped upon seeing I was struggling. He eased between the space of the lock and my hands, and I was so goddamn flustered I let him take the key.

I nearly barked at him, wondering what the hell he thought he was doing, but then he opened my door for me. He did that even though he was clearly inebriated and I wasn't.

He opened the door slightly but didn't give me back the key. Nor did he move away, and I loathed how much he filled the hallway with his smell. He still smelled so good, fresh and airy. He wrestled in his dark locks, his earrings dangling. "I wanted to apologize."

Okay, so I wasn't expecting that. An apology. I folded my arms, waiting for the laundry list. "Well, that's—"

"My friends texted and told me Wells came over. He did, and that was completely out of line, and I'm sorry about that. He shouldn't have done that, and that was shit."

I had to say. I stopped talking. Mostly out of clear shock.

Out of all the things he'd done, *that* was what he was apologizing for? I mean, he should apologize for that, but that was only the tip of the frickin' iceberg.

I was shocked, enraged, and my face heated so fucking bad I thought I'd physically spit lava. Well, if that was possible, I would have. I eyed him. "You're fucking joking, right?"

"What?" He really was not all there. He kept shaking his head, and every once in a while, he'd stare daggers at the lights in the hall like they were wreaking havoc on his blue eyes.

Good. The jerk deserved some fucking pain, discomfort.

He pushed back his hair. "Why would I be joking about that? I'm sorry he came over. I didn't ask him to do that, and it made shit worse."

He was right about that. It had made shit worse, and done with this shit, *his shit,* I grabbed my fucking keys from him. I attempted to maneuver around him after that, but he stopped me with his big body.

"Aspen—"

"Don't fucking touch me." I was keeping my voice down,

but one scream and my security would be out here. I didn't know why I was keeping my voice down, but I was for some reason. I pointed at him. "You left me. You left me *by myself* after breaking down someone's door basically naked."

He'd been mostly naked like that girl at the club, and those images I didn't fucking want. I wanted to burn my fucking *eyes out* before I saw them again.

Thatcher twitched. Like he was thrown that I'd actually call his shit out there. He raised a hand. "I know."

"You know." I nearly laughed. "You fucking asshole."

"I know that too. Just—"

He tried to touch me again, but I gave myself a wide berth. This fucker was not touching me again. It'd been a mistake the first time. All the times. I swallowed. "You scared the shit out of me, then left me in some seedy fucking motel. I didn't even know where I fucking was!"

I'd gotten a rideshare out of there. I had after I'd gotten myself together. I'd been crying…

I was just so scared, and I wished that'd been just for myself. Thatcher had *lost* it. He had, and he was covered in blood and had just left like that. It'd been like someone had taken over his body when he had been so kind earlier. He'd been so nice after all the freaky shit we did, but I wanted him to do all that freaky shit. We both had. It'd been fun, then he'd gone insane.

I was shaking in the middle of that hallway, and I knew my security wouldn't come. I'd shouted at Thatcher, but I'd whisper shouted. Like I was protecting this guy from repercussions when he clearly didn't give two shits about me. He left me, then tonight I found him at a party with some girl all over him.

Thatcher threaded his hands above his head. "I knew you were okay."

How could he know? How could he possibly? I shook my head. "You're a dick."

"Maybe, but I knew you were okay. You were okay." He nodded to himself. Like he knew or something. He wet his lips. "Anyway, I'm sorry about that too."

He was sorry about that too… now, after being prompted, he was sorry. My jaw moved. "And I suppose you're also sorry that you ghosted me. Oh, and really sorry that you fucked some chick at a rave tonight, which I saw because I went to that rave looking for you because I was worried like a goddamn idiot."

His blue eyes zoomed in my direction. His hands dropped. "You were at the rave?"

That was all he said. He didn't deny the accused fucking or anything.

You really are an idiot.

I got some weird emotional attachment to my stalker, my kidnapper. It was textbook Stockholm syndrome and had to have happened just because this dude fucked me well.

I backed off, backed away, but his one step took three of mine. His throat flicked. "Aspen, I didn't fuck that girl."

And like I could believe him? Like I should care enough *to* believe him, but I did. I fucking did. Again, I was an idiot. I raised and dropped my hands. "I don't care what you do, Thatcher."

"Well, you should. Aspen—" He got my arms, but I worked them away. He lifted his hands. "I know what that probably looked like, but I swear nothing happened. I just… I just needed a night to get fucked up. *To get high*, and that's the only reason I went to the rave. That's the only thing I did at the rave."

And get drunk, but he failed to mention that. He'd clearly been stumbling earlier.

He released a large breath. "Things have been stressful lately. Things at home, and then all that the other night… The other night with you…" He cringed. "I swear nothing happened with that girl."

"You swear." I pressed my hands together, touching them to my mouth. It was the only thing I could do not to lose it, *cry*. I faced him. "It doesn't matter if you swear because I don't give a shit. I don't, so you can go get fucked up, Thatcher. You can go get stoned out of your mind for all I care, and you can fuck whoever you want because I. Don't. Care."

It was lies, point-blank.

But I made them sound like they weren't.

There was no waver in my voice, and I stood tall when I got in his face. I stood confident. My throat thickened, tightened. "You wanna know why I don't care, Thatcher? Because you're insane, but you also happen to fuck me really well. You do, so I overlooked that, but I don't want anything more to do with your psycho ass."

He didn't cringe. The guy didn't even wince in front of me. In fact, those blue eyes darkened and went so cold *I* nearly wavered. I nearly backed down because they reminded me of the last time I truly feared him. I feared his capabilities because I didn't know the extent of what those were. I didn't know what was inside this guy.

But he'd given me a snapshot. I got a great visual of the true terror he could unleash upon me. The monster.

Thatcher Reed got right in my face, and that was some scary shit. He was big, powerful and all-encompassing. He stood in front of me like a colossal giant, and I was the tiny life-form in his wake. His nostrils flared. "Fuck this shit. You're right. I did fuck that bitch, and she was a lot better lay than you."

I winced, feeling stupid that I did, weak. I'd said stuff to him too, but he hadn't been affected. Not like me.

I swallowed as he left his scent in the hall, leaving me standing there. He stopped at the end of the hall, and I thought he'd come back. For a second, I thought he would, but he didn't. He strode away and disappeared around the corner, and my back hit the wall.

It did before my butt hit the floor.

CHAPTER
FOURTEEN

Thatcher

Pembroke University was aware Aspen Davis and her celebrity had made it on campus.

I think that had something to do with the fact she wasn't hiding anymore.

Maybe her security gave her confidence, but not only was Aspen not hiding behind a ball cap and inconspicuous clothing anymore, but she was out in the open. She had her shades on, but she was actually using them to block the sun.

Because she was sunbathing.

Legit, this girl lay in the middle of the quad *completely exposed* in a pair of short-ass shorts and one of those lacy bra things girls wore. She wasn't exposed in the sense she was flashing her tits, but she might as well have been. Her nude bra thing blended well into her brown skin, and those shorts barely covered the curve of her ass. Actually, her ass would be full out if she'd been on her front. She had an arm crooked over her head, acting as if she had not a care in the world.

And I wasn't the only one to notice.

Again, Pembroke University noticed they had a celebrity in their midst, and Aspen got nearly as much attention as my friends and me did whenever we went, well, fucking anywhere. Every once in a while, someone would be brave enough to approach her, and my back went up every time. That was until I realized she had security, and the guy had changed too. When he'd first been assigned to her, he dressed like another student, but now, he was in a whole-ass suit. That was typical for the guys who worked for my dad.

I was well aware of what kind of security Aspen had and even the guy's name. I knew more than I wanted to know about Aspen and her situation.

And I couldn't stop fucking looking at her. I wanted to carve my fucking eyes out, but I couldn't help it. People were being decent whenever they approached her. They were just asking for her autograph or even a selfie from where I sat, but my heart raced every freaking time.

Especially when she *looked* at me.

Snowflake attempted to be discreet, but then again, she fucking wasn't. Actually, she was making a whole-ass display knowing I was watching her. Especially when someone asked her for something. She obliged, giggling and being all bubbly when that was the opposite of who she fucking was. That girl was a pill. A completely hard-to-swallow bitchy-ass pill, and that shit made me so fucking hard. It was kind of sick how much it did, but that was me. Fucking sick.

Aspen definitely knew I was watching. Hell, she knew where my friends and I sat, and that was on the other side of the quad. Everyone knew where my friends and I chilled out. We were here nearly every fucking day, and today was one of the rare days it was just myself, Wells, Dorian, and Wolf. Normally, Wolf and Dorian had their girls, but this afternoon one of them had a class while the other hung out with my sister. All three of the girls were good friends, but Sloane and Bow hung out the most. I didn't know what Sloane and my sister were doing today, but I knew they'd left the quad early to hang out.

The only other person missing from our crew was Bru. It was impossible to keep that dude out of the fucking library though, so that was probably where he was, and our area was even more sparse since Wells or I didn't have a groupie out here. It wasn't unusual for one of us to be fucking with someone in our space. We never fucked *per se*, but my friend and I were indecent enough to have our tongue down someone's throat on occasion. The fuck did we care about that shit?

I hadn't brought a conquest out here in a while, and ironically enough, not since Snowflake had come around. There was no irony. In fact, those two events were hella fucking correlated.

I growled, pretending to code on my laptop, and Aspen faced me after finishing another autograph. I couldn't see those dark-brown eyes behind her shades, but I saw her flip her long hair in my direction. She did that before flinging her arms up and lying back down.

That little cunt.

That little beautiful, sexy-ass cunt whose pussy tasted like candy and whose ass I wanted to bury my cock in. I hadn't gotten to do that, but I would have if I'd had more than a goddamn night with her. I would have pillowed myself all up in that shit, and Wells hit me right in the middle of my depraved vision.

"Bro, she's goading you, and you're letting her do that shit," he said and wasn't even bothering to act like he was studying or doing anything productive. He had his back to a tree, his cell phone in his hand. His dark eyebrows narrowed. "You know she's doing that shit to you on purpose."

Oh, she totally fucking was. I'd pissed her off with what I said, and this was her trying to give that shit back to me. Her hurt must have blinded her because no way in hell did I give any indication that anyone at all could have ever been a better lay than she was when we'd been together. She fucked as good and hard as me, and that was saying something. I fucked a lot and pretty fucking hard.

And then there was the fact that I'd lied to her about that girl at the rave. I hadn't fucked that bitch. I had been stoned out of my mind (and drunk), but I hadn't fucked anyone. That girl hadn't smelled like Christmas candy and chocolate. Nor did she have dark eyes I could fucking drown in.

My fingers curled on my keys. I was no doubt fucking up all my coding. I'd lied because Aspen had pissed me off too. She'd called me crazy, and I wasn't fucking crazy.

I grunted in response to my friend, and my other two were pretending not to watch us. Dorian was on his cell phone too, and though Wolf had a novel in his hands, they both had their eyes on the situation. They had good reason to considering what had happened the other night after I'd found out Wells had gone after Aspen. The dude had found my text messages from her, then dove deeper into my shit when he realized who Aspen was. I'd gathered a lot of information recently on the girl from my past, and it wasn't hard to find considering I had a folder for her on my desktop.

My friend thought he knew me, and I guess he did know me. We'd been boys since the womb, and I'd also had a file on Aspen back then. I had even though I'd only been twelve, and Dorian, Wells, Wolf, and I had all been at football camp that summer. There wasn't anywhere I went where my laptop didn't go with me.

Wells knew that. He did because he knew me, so once he found out who Aspen was, he knew exactly what I'd do. Stalk her.

Personally, I got why he had his back up about the situation. Aspen and I were complicated, *our history* was complicated, but no way did that give him license to do what he had. Dorian and Wolf had said he threatened her, which was completely bullshit.

Especially since shit wasn't her fault.

Things had gotten pretty violent after I found out what my friend had done, and the only reason I hadn't fully laid his ass out was because I had been stoned and wasted. I had at least fifty pounds on the guy, but my inebriation gave him the advantage. We'd both been equal that night as far as strength had been concerned, and if Dorian and Wolf hadn't stopped our brawl, the two of us probably would have killed each other.

I loved my buddy, but he was definitely out of line that night. What was worse was he knew that. Wells folded his arms. "I think you know your attention needs to be somewhere else, and actually, we should probably be hanging somewhere else if she's going to be around."

I growled at his complete disregard to the fact that he was overstepping. "I'm cool, and I told you, that night wasn't her fault."

They all knew as I'd ended up telling them everything. There hadn't been a point to lying. I told them everything regarding Aspen's reappearance in my life and that what had happened the night we fucked again wasn't her fault.

Things had never been her fault, even back then, and once more, Wells knew that. He did, but he was overprotective just like we all were when it came to each other. That shit blinded us sometimes, so that was the only reason I wasn't holding any beef about him coming at Aspen.

But that didn't mean that shit sat well with me. It didn't, and I would kick my friend's ass if he continued to push. Again, I loved the shit out of the dude, but I would hand his shit to him for being an idiot.

Wells's green eyes shifted dark, and they were a sharp contrast to his hair. He'd dyed it as blond as Aspen's white wig that night at the rave. "I know it's not her fault, but you need to stay away from her for obvious reasons." He tossed his phone in the grass. "She's clearly triggering for you, which makes her dangerous."

My laptop touched the grass, and that was when Dorian intervened. He was a combination of Wells's height and my build, so he was easily able to put space between us. He was also quarterback for Pembroke's football team, so he was quick. He pointed at Wells. "You? Shut the hell up before you get your ass kicked. I don't think I need to explain that this guy isn't baked today, so he actually can kick your ass if Wolf or I let him."

I smirked, and Wells lifted his eyes.

Wells shoved Dorian's hand off his chest. "Whatever."

"And you." Dorian directed his dark eyes at me. "Open your ears and actually fucking listen to what this idiot has to say. Wells's delivery may be shit, but he's not far off that you probably need to keep your distance from Aspen Davis."

So that, I wasn't expecting, and when Wells started to smirk, I went for him.

Dorian stopped that too. He could hold his own against me. At least, for a little bit. Dorian frowned. "I'm just saying there is something to what he has to say about Aspen being potentially triggering for you."

"I told y'all what happened," I said, shoving him off me, and Wolf put down his book. Things would get crazy if he got involved. The dude had a wingspan like the missing link and probably a good amount of the strength. I rearranged my shirt. Wells got a hold of it before Dorian forced us apart. My eyes narrowed. "Aspen had nothing to do with what happened that night."

She hadn't. Point-blank, and Dorian scrubbed into his blond hair.

"You know, we all know that, but you can't deny you wouldn't even have been in that situation if you hadn't been with her."

There were no lies there, but I didn't want him to be right.

Because I didn't, I fully intended to start a completely baseless argument, but hesitated when I spotted a familiar woman on the quad.

Oh no.

My mom's petite stature set off alarm bells in me, and not thinking much of it, I put my laptop away and got up. The guys did too, but by the time they had, she was nearly over to our group.

"Hey, babe," Mom stated, going to hug me first, but my wingspan nearly swallowed her up. I'd say my mom didn't fit in our family with how small she was, but my sister was really tiny too. Mom was a blonde, though, whereas my sister was a brunette like my dad and me.

"Hey," I returned, and the guys greeted her too behind me. When it came to all our parents, we were all pretty close. In fact, each set of my friends' parents were like my own and vice versa. Our parents had all been friends since long before we were born, so that made sense. I pulled away. "Everything okay?"

It was unusual her being here. Home was like hours away, and normally when things went wrong back home, she called.

Which was why my stomach was all clenched to shit right now.

Those emergency calls had been pretty frequent this entire goddamn year, but before I could take off on the ground running with my panic, my mom lifted her little hands.

"Everything's fine, baby. Sorry to freak you out," she said, putting her hand on my face, and the guys behind me ran their hands through their hair like me, fidgeting. Dorian, Wells, and Wolf definitely all knew my trauma shit, and like stated, they were family. Mine was theirs, and though things at home hit me closer, they felt it.

They all felt what was going on back home with me, and after they greeted my mom with hugs, Mom asked if she could steal me away for a bit. Apparently, my sister texted her where the guys and I were this hour.

Mom asked if I was busy, and of course, I told her I wasn't. I never would be when it came to my family.

"I'll see y'all around," I told the guys, getting my things. My mom walked away after saying goodbye to my friends, and I let her for a second before facing them. I nodded in a certain direction, and they didn't even need to look that way to know what I meant. Aspen Davis was still over there flashing her little tummy.

And she was looking at me too. She was, but she was trying not to. She had her arm still draped over her face, but I one hundred percent noticed when she faced my way as my mom approached. Snowflake was aware of me.

Just like I was aware of her.

Wells had something to what he said about her purposely goading me, and she could play her little fucking game if she wanted to. I didn't care, but what she wasn't going to do was get herself hurt because she was fucking mad at me.

That was what my nod in her direction told my friends. We all had been keeping an eye on her even though she had my dad's security. My friends had been doing that casually while going to their classes, and I had too between my own and football practice. There was a reason I knew Aspen had been okay the night I had a fucking panic attack. I parked outside her dorm after washing the vomit and shit out of my mouth.

"*Please*," my eyes told my friends, and Dorian and Wolf instantly nodded. They were more mature, older by a year, and though they weren't particularly happy about the situation with Aspen and me, they were aware her life had literally been threatened. They were, so they'd watch out for her for me. I'd asked them, so they would.

Wells, on the other hand…

He wasn't as mature. Fuck, neither one of us was. We were

both juvenile little assholes sometimes, but I needed him to do me this solid.

And I knew he would. He would because it was me, and we were boys. Wells grunted at first, but eventually, he nodded too.

Good.

My friend could be in his feelings as long as he did what I said. That shit that had happened the other night wasn't Aspen's fault.

It never was.

Aspen probably recognized my mom. Mom was there through all that drama shit all those summers ago.

Aspen's arm lifted from her eyes a bit when my mom and I passed her, but my mom was none the wiser to Aspen's presence. Mom probably knew about Aspen being around anyway due to Dad telling her, so there'd be no problem there anyway. My parents thought Aspen Davis wasn't a problem for me anymore.

And that was how I wanted it.

"You said everything is fine—"

"Yeah, hon. And." Mom paused after we distanced from the quad a bit, laughing a little. She was a spritely little thing like my sister, Rainbow. Really, the only difference between the two was that my mom was blonde and more outspoken than my sister. Don't get me wrong. Rainbow Reed could hold her own. I mean, she was my sister, and I taught her well. Mom adjusted her purse on her shoulder. "Everything is good. I swear. That's actually why I'm here."

Not knowing what she meant, I couldn't be completely at ease, and I had to miss more than one football practice this week due to emergencies. I'd had to trek the two-plus hours back to my hometown, Maywood Heights.

Gram needed me.

Mom walked by my side. "I was actually wondering if you could consider coming around when things are good."

"What do you mean?"

Mom stopped walking, then smiled a little. It was a forced smile, but not necessarily a sad one. It was one of a woman who'd had to give up a lot like all of us. She got to be at home in all of this with my grandma, in the thick of it. She rubbed my back. "It'd be good to be there when things are good. It would help, I think. Couldn't hurt?"

It couldn't. Probably wouldn't. I nodded. "Okay. You and Dad talked about this?"

"It was discussed," she said, and when I said nothing, she touched my hair. "Thatch, I know how hard this is for both of you. Maybe coming around when things are good will help. She'll see you. You know, when she's good."

"Yeah."

And Mom put on another one of those forced smiles. She did even though she was hurting. This was all hard for her too. She let go. "If you're free sometime today, it would be good to swing by. Bow's going to make her way down today too. It'll help Grandma to see her too when things are good."

It wasn't too bad for my sister. I mean, in my grandma's eyes. Probably because Bow was a sweet little nonthreatening thing. My gram could be friendly with her, my sister's face a nameless nonthreatening one in a crowd to her.

I'd come to find out in all this with my grandma that threats weren't always those of intimidation. Sometimes threats were memories. Ghosts.

My hands in my pockets, I continued my strides beside my mom. I had a half day of classes still, but I didn't care. I'd wrap things up, then come home. I always went home when I needed to, and if my mom felt that would help, I would. I'd do anything for her and my gram. I'd do anything for my dad.

Fucking anything.

Aspen

I fully expected my mom would call me. I'd outed myself, my location, and expected to hear from her. I also expected to feel sick because I knew what she'd do. She'd freak out, and then this detour to Pembroke University would be short-lived.

I expected this.

What I hadn't expected was the news she was giving me now while I sat on my bed, and I was sick.

I was damn near nauseous.

"You might as well," she stated, continuing on after breaking the news to me. "Everyone in this world knows where you are, so you might as well do some good."

Some good. I nodded. "A charity concert?"

It was the first thing she mentioned when she called me. She didn't ask how I was doing or even rant about how I'd outed my location. Of course, she'd heard about it. The minute people saw me here at Pembroke, the selfies went up on the internet and the news reports followed. A few reporters tried to come down to break the story, but Pembroke's chancellor took care of that real fucking quick.

Fuck, you're an idiot.

I normally didn't give in to my temper. With a momanager like Eugena Davis, not giving in to daily frustrations was damn near impossible. I had to be in control, cool in all aspects of my life, but Thatcher fucking Reed took me to my breaking point. He'd read me the riot act outside my own damn dorm room.

He hurt you too.

I'd like to say I didn't fucking care about what he said to me. I'd like to believe my heart was steel and I didn't care, but I was a goddamn human, okay? I had a heart. I had a soul, and he'd trampled all over that shit. I was a stupid girl who literally got attached to someone who abused me in the past. Basically, I was a goddamn idiot.

I knew that too.

I brought my legs up. "Are you sure that's a good idea?" I normally didn't question my mother. I mean, what was the point as she nearly always got her way. My jaw moved. "Mom, the threat…"

"Oh, don't talk to me about that right now. You've let the whole world know where you are, and the only reason I'm not pulling you out of that place is because Chancellor Richards and *your security* have guaranteed to me that they have the situation handled." She paused, rustling around. I figured she was in downtown LA today. She enjoyed shopping. "I still don't know why you fired Franklin, but this new firm seems good."

And God fuck did she *not* know that firm was the Reeds'. She would pull me out of Pembroke.

You should let her.

I'd self-sabotaged deciding to work with Thatcher's dad's company. Mom would definitely have an issue if she knew I was close to the Reeds, but I hadn't cared when I'd done it. Thatcher just made me so fucking crazy.

Physically making myself calm down, I closed my eyes. "But a charity concert? I know I'm here, but I probably should continue to lie low."

It wasn't that I didn't want to do something for charity. In fact, if my mom told me to go down to the local Red Cross, I'd work myself to the point of blisters and exhaustion to help them out. I really enjoyed helping others, loved it. It was just…

My mom's sigh was evident, but best believe it was impatience, frustration. The sound caused my stomach to flip, and I remained silent. "You're going to do it, Aspen, and I've already set up your appointments with Mare and Jillian."

My stylist and nail tech. Of course.

"Speaking of appointments, I was surprised to hear from your personal trainer that you've been dodging her emails," she said, and my stomach flopped again. "She's been trying to contact you to set up a time to check in and see how you're doing with your solo workouts."

I really had nothing to say to that. Just that I hadn't been doing anything but lying around and binge-eating since Thatcher Reed had called me a bad lay. I tended to emotionally eat when I was stressed…

That guy had way too much power over me, and I got to hear another one of my mother's sighs in my ear.

"I don't think I need to inform you that you're a public figure and have an image to maintain, Aspen," Mom said, and I glanced at the ceiling. It wasn't just enough the music had to be perfect, but I had to be as well. Perfect body. Perfect playing… "Maintaining yourself physically also helps with your stamina. It keeps you playing at your best for long periods of—"

"I know." I heard the growl in my voice, but I couldn't help it. My mom was always too fucking much.

"Well, if you know, show it. I better not hear again you're dodging your trainer. And dear God, if I hear you haven't been keeping up with your meds..."

Like I needed another thing to worry about. Especially because I tended to flare when I was stressed out. I gripped the bed. "I have, okay?"

"Okay." Mom sounded busy, moving around. "I get it. You're in a stressful situation, but you will make that situation worse by not taking care of yourself. That means eating well, doing your workouts, *taking your meds*, and keeping up with your self-care. All these things affect your playing ability, honey, and you know that."

I knew my mom meant well. She did. She wanted the best for me. *She cared* even if that care made me feel like I was drowning...

Which it did more often than not.

I said nothing about that, of course. Never did. I just let my mom continue on, and my ears perked up when she started talking about my cello.

"Speaking of your playing, I know you've been keeping up with your practice, so I'm not even going to address that," she said, and I nearly laughed. I hadn't played in weeks let alone practiced. "And with this charity concert, I expect you'll be doubling if not tripling your practice time. I'll contact Deborah—"

"No, I'll do it," I said, the both of us referring to my teacher. Deborah Hays also hadn't heard from me in a while, but fortunately, she didn't have to. She sent my practice music and expected me to just do it.

They both did.

"Fine," Mom said, and my heart settled a bit.

That was until she mentioned...

"I have been working with the police, and we haven't found anything regarding those letters. That sicko who threatened you is still unfortunately out there, but best *believe*, honey, we will get him. We will, and when we do, we'll make him pay for detouring your life."

I blinked, my eyes closing slowly after. I lowered my head. "Mom..."

"And then we'll get you back on tour," Mom said, her voice changing, different. It swelled with something, and I only heard it when she was talking about the future. My future. "We'll get you back on track and things will be just like they were."

I was sure they would be, and I thought about that long and hard after my mom finally got off the line. She let me go so I could practice. So I could be perfect for that charity concert, and eventually, things could go back to normal.

I stared at my cello for a long time that afternoon, the case still on it. I stared until I couldn't anymore.

In the end, I got up, taking a hoodie with me, and when I left my dorm that afternoon, I failed to tell my security.

I guess it slipped my mind.

CHAPTER
SIXTEEN

Aspen

I had to give it to my security. It took about two-point-five seconds for Phil to realize I was gone, and apparently, he did his job too well.

I didn't care. I felt overwhelmed as fuck and needed to get out. I ignored Phil's texts and just drove.

I could do that now that I had a car.

Something else I corrected after everything with Thatcher was getting a vehicle. I wouldn't be stranded anymore at the mercy of someone like him.

I feel like I'm going to throw up.

Honestly, being behind the wheel was a stupid decision. I felt dizzy pretty much the entire time, but that certainly hadn't stopped me from keeping my foot on the gas pedal of the Range Rover. I kept the car moving and ended up on the highway. I drove through miles upon miles of cornfields and had no idea where I was going.

Again, I didn't care.

I was frustrated that my mom got me like this. She got me in my head sometimes and thinking about my cello, playing it after what happened…

I kept the Range Rover cruising, and eventually, I came across a sign ahead. It came up really freaking fast.

Welcome to Maywood Heights.

I missed the population size, but the town appeared to be fairly large. It had rolling hills and the city itself had a skyline. It kind of looked like a mini Chicago or LA.

I guess Maywood Heights was about to have one more resident.

Obviously, I was just passing through, but now that I was here, I couldn't be numb to the distractions of my head or my body. My stomach grumbled, something I'd purposely ignored on the road due to my mom still being in my head. Her constant hounding made me be aware of my body and caused me to feel insecure sometimes. I knew this wasn't her intention, but it didn't stop the fact from being true.

A sign for Jax's Burgers came up while I drove, and I instantly took the exit to the fast-food joint. I loved Jax's. I'd been to a handful while on the road, and there were a ton on Pembroke's campus.

I thought about going through the drive-thru to get a salad (yeah, my mom was still dictating my fucking actions), but I decided to go inside instead. I mean, why not? It was in the middle of the day on a Wednesday, and I highly doubted anyone would be looking out for the cellist who played hip-hop and toured with Beyoncé.

Oh, yeah, and she'd been threatened.

I had been threatened, but I didn't think in the way most people thought.

Just calm down. You'll feel better.

My mom had been right that I needed to be conscious of my self-care, and lately, I hadn't really been thinking about all that. I mean, I kept up on my meds. I had an autoimmune disease and that was necessary, but there was certainly no self-care in my life lately. Self-care for me wasn't getting on that fucking Peloton, though. It was paying attention to my mind.

It was caring about myself.

"How can I help—oh, my fuck. It's *you.* What are you doing here? You're the girl who plays with Beyoncé, right? The cellist?"

So that came from the person who came to my table at Jax's. Jax's was a fast-food restaurant, but their tables had a call button for the servers to come by and take your order. I smiled up at the girl in a 1950s-style apron. "Yeah, that's me."

I was recognized all the time, so it didn't surprise me to be spotted. The girl was cool about it, though, and of course, I didn't mind taking a selfie. She got that, then took my salad order.

I picked at it when it came around, staring off into the open space of the restaurant. I started to fork some in my mouth when I noticed a woman looking at me, an older woman with graying dark hair and, honestly, gorgeous-as-fuck eyes. They were a haunting blue. Like stunning marble.

Her eyes were warm in my direction, and I made sure mine were the same. She probably just knew who I was like that girl.

I thought the woman would peer away eventually, but she didn't, and she was dressed peculiarly. Her silk gown was nearly as dark as her hair and glittered, sparkled even. This woman was dressed for a night out at the ballet but was here at Jax's with me.

Of course, that wasn't my business, and after smiling at her, I glanced away.

"I'm sorry for staring, honey, but I know you, right?" she said, her table directly across from mine. Her head tilted. "You play classical music."

I did, and there wasn't a point to eating this salad. I

wanted fucking fries not a salad. I wanted anything but a goddamn salad. I placed my fork down. "Uh, yeah."

"I knew it. It is you." Her head shook. "I love your music. I have some of it on vinyl actually."

Okay, so I didn't hear that one a lot. My smile widened. "Really?"

"Oh, yes. It sounds best that way." She completely shifted in my direction, sparkling gown and all. It was really unusual, but again, that wasn't my business. "What brings you here to Maywood Heights? Do you have a concert? I feel like I would have gotten tickets."

I didn't have a concert, and the thought of a concert kind of made me sick. I shook my head. "I'm not playing right now. Not anything really."

I have no idea why I admitted that. Maybe it was because of the woman's calming nature, but the words just tumbled out of my mouth.

Even still, I thought she'd understand why. It was very public what happened to me, but there was a possibility she didn't follow social media since she was older.

The woman frowned. "Oh, I'm sorry to hear that."

I chewed my lip. "Maybe I will again soon."

I said this, but I wasn't sure. Millions of people saw what happened to me on the night in question between the live audience and the telecast. I was playing Carnegie Hall, the biggest concert of my dreams, *my life*. I literally had been working toward the venue since I started playing. It should have been the best night of my life.

And it turned out to be the worst.

Those millions of people saw that, the world saw that, and I was left in the aftermath of the ashes. A cello player who couldn't play cello.

My hands shook for some reason like they had that day, and I put them together. Closing my eyes, I physically tried to keep my heart from racing, but of course, I couldn't. I kept remembering that night and…

"Well, you're wonderfully talented, and I hope the world gets to hear that again soon. You too. I hope you get to hear that."

I opened my eyes after what the woman said. She was up on her feet now. Her sparkling gown touched the dingy Jax's Burgers floor, and she really was beautifully stunning. Her face also reminded me of someone's. Like I knew her too in some way, but I didn't of course.

Her bright eyes managed to warm even more when I didn't say anything. "I really hope you get to hear it. You're the most important ear, after all."

No one had ever said that to me before. That I was the most important ear, but she was right. I suppose I forgot.

My smile was completely genuine in front of this woman. "Thank you."

I was thankful she said that, grateful. I did forget sometimes. That what I thought, what I felt mattered.

The woman nodded, and I noticed she didn't have any food on the table, not empty wrappings or anything like that. Even still, she turned back as if she was going to grab something from the table, but when she spotted it empty, her expression changed. She blinked.

"Well, that's unusual," she said, then placed a hand on her head. "Very unusual."

"What is?"

"I…" She stopped, then backed up into the table a bit. "I don't know. I guess I don't remember why I'm here. I came for my son. I…" She touched her dark hair, shaking her head.

I got up. "Are you okay, ma'am?" She didn't look okay. She looked kind of panicked. "Can I help you?"

"Oh, no, I…" she started, but then her expression shifted again. Her face screwed up. Like she was confused, and when she sat down, I came over.

"Let me help you, ma'am," I said, then noticed her purse on her arm. I pointed at it. "Do you have a cell phone? We can call someone for you."

CHAPTER
SEVENTEEN

My sister was crying, panicking.

I didn't blame her.

"Thatcher, what are we going to do? If we can't find her, I..."

Bow hiccupped with her tears, damn near hyperventilating, and I got her shoulder. My sister and I looked a lot alike in some ways. We had similar features since my father's were so strong, as well as his dark hair, but other than that, we were yin and yang. She was sweet whereas I was an asshole, but I had my moments when my sister was fucking crying. I had her look at me. "Breathe, okay? We're going to find her. Everything is going to be okay."

I could be lying to my sister, but there were no other options as far as I was concerned. I entertained no others because shit would be okay.

I'd make it okay.

I'd been hesitant to call my parents when my sister told

me what had happened this afternoon. My mom had finally gotten a day off, a spa day, and my dad was working. They were finally getting to not think about stuff at home because my sister and I were in town to take over. Bow had gotten to our parents' home first since she left before me, and I'd arrived only mere moments from Pembroke University before I came across my sister, panicked and ripping through the house. She told me she'd only gone to the kitchen for a few moments, seconds.

But sometimes that was all it took.

My chest locking, I resisted my own panic. I resisted the fear that came with the not knowing that something truly could be the worst fucking thing *ever*, but you couldn't freak because you had to be there for someone else. Bow had looked on the cusp of vomiting when I'd come home. If fact, she wasn't able to talk she was crying so much.

"Thatcher..." Bow gasped, pointing behind me. It'd been the most focused she'd been since she told me the news that had made me nearly throw up. I thought there couldn't be anything worse than losing one of the most important people in your life in every way but the physical. I thought there could be nothing more terrible than the actual death of someone, actual loss. But my gram going missing...

That cut just as harsh, and even though Bow and I scoured the neighborhood, we couldn't find her. We'd searched for almost an hour, and I was about to call my parents.

But it turned out we didn't have to.

My sister left my side, and I wavered, in shock really. Nothing else could define the feeling I had seeing my grandmother approach the gates of my parents' home in her Sunday best. There was a girl at her side...

A girl I couldn't get out of my head.

Aspen Davis was like a permanent fixture in my already fucked-up mind. I couldn't get her out with a damn crowbar and here she was not just a vision. Here she was *at my house* with my grandmother.

And they were laughing.

God, were they laughing, the two like old friends. My grandmother had said something to Aspen, and Aspen put her head back in the sun, her laughter light and jovial. She didn't laugh much with me. In fact, she spent more time insulting me and me her. That was just our dynamic and how that shit had me *gone.* Our banter was fucked, but I loved it. It got me hot. Got me hard.

But seeing her smile.

Something was different about her laughter, and that shit got all up in my chest. It nearly distracted me from the fact that she was with my grandmother, the two walking toward the gates of Reed Manor together.

What the hell?

My sister and I had been on the cusp of another search, but while we looked, I'd been about to break down and call my folks. I hadn't wanted to, but I had no choice. My gram was missing.

At least, she had been.

Aspen spotted my sister first. Bow had been faster. My shock of Aspen being here (with my gram) legit slowed me down, but after seeing Bow, her gaze passed over to me.

Hey there, snow.

The sight of me rattled her, and well, consider her not the only fucking one. Her expression went from shocked to stony, but that didn't stop her from being one of the most beautiful fucking things on this block to me. She wore not a stitch of makeup today just like that night at the motel. Her hair was bundled atop her head and her shorts were nearly hidden under a gray pullover hoodie. She looked the most basic she could look in her low-top Nikes and was a far cry from the red-carpet goddess I'd seen torturing the Grammys and MTV Video Music Awards. She had pictures from all those events on her social media, the girl high in demand since she performed with celebrities. She looked different today.

But different wasn't bad. In fact, different let me see her, and despite the scowl she reserved for me, I was slowing for a different reason. I was just in fucking awe of her.

Wake up.

The guys were probably right that Aspen Davis was bad for me, and even though I was still pissed from that shit she said to me the last time we'd been together, I wasn't caring about that shit right now. I ignored Aspen's shocked expression and went toward my gram. I followed after my sister outside of our gates.

"Gram!" Bow started, getting to Gram first, but as soon as she did, she bit her lip. "I mean, Evangeline. You know you can't just leave the house. It's not safe."

My sister realized her error, and even though I'd seen her do similar recoveries in the past, it didn't stop the cringe I made that she had to do it.

Nor the tightness in my stomach.

That shit locked me all up, but I didn't allow that to play across my features. My gram's attention went from Bow to me after my sister's correction, and her expression immediately brightened. Gram waved. "Nighty!"

Nighty.

Knowing that was me, I made my grin strong. I came forward, and when my gram brought me into her arms, I held her right back. She smelled like cinnamon and days by the fireplace or the piano. I didn't play anymore, but my gram had taught me everything I knew. My hand covered her back. "Hey, Mom."

I wouldn't allow myself to cringe saying it. Actually, I said it so much lately that word just flew out of my mouth. My gram had fewer and fewer days where she was lucid. In fact, damn near none lately.

I peered over my gram's shoulder, well aware Aspen was

still standing there. She'd hung back, and her glare had shifted to something else. A heavy confusion narrowed her dark eyes, and I didn't blame her for that. This shit was confusing.

But only from the outside.

Unfortunately, my entire family had been having to deal with this lately, so Aspen was the only one confused on this residential street. I pulled away from Gram. "Nurse is right. You can't just leave—"

"Oh, stop it. You both worry too much," she said, swatting my arm. Nurse was my sister some days. Most days. Gram touched her sparkling gown. "And I should be mad at you. I waited for you at our place, and you weren't there."

Christ, that was where she was? This whole time…

I closed my eyes. "I'm sorry."

"Yes, well, I'm only not upset because of Aspen here," Gram stated, and my sister's and my attention flew over to the girl who was trying to blend into my parents' well-trimmed hedges. Actually, if Bow and I hadn't done that, I was quite sure Aspen would have backed up and run. One of her Nikes had definitely been out to ease away. Gram waved at her. "Come here, dear. Meet my son and my worrywart nurse. Her name's Rainbow. We call her Bow."

Gram still knew my sister's name in all this confusion, and that gave my sister something I didn't have. Bow wasn't always my grandma's nurse in her eyes. Sometimes Bow was her granddaughter, but I was never her grandkid. Not anymore. It was too confusing for her.

I never considered it a curse to look like my father. In actuality, I used that shit to my advantage each and every day of my fucking life. Looking like my dad got me laid, but that shit had become a curse when my gram got sick. It was just too confusing for my grandma.

An understatement.

"She plays cello," Gram continued, the pride beaming on

her face. Her eyes sparkled. "I've been following her career. She's so very talented."

She was talented, and I'd heard Aspen play. Not in person, of course, but I'd brought up YouTube videos in the past.

I wished that had just been because she appeared on my campus.

Aspen Davis hadn't been a constant thought over the years since all that drama when we were twelve, but she'd been a thought. I was secure in myself enough to admit that I checked up on her every once in a while. I supposed I couldn't help it. I wanted to know if she was okay or whatever.

"I…" Aspen started, and Bow beamed at her too. My sister knew about the Aspen drama, but she'd been young when it'd all gone down. We were all young, but my sister was *young*. I wouldn't be surprised if she didn't even remember all of it. Let alone Aspen herself being at the center.

And bless her for that. I wasn't a really religious guy, but God was looking out for me for that. Sparing my sister. Yeah, he or she was looking out for me.

Aspen was basically shoved in front of me right when my grandma said…

"And this is my son, Knight."

Aspen's eyes flashed, more of that confusion on me. Her full lips parted, and before she could say anything, I nodded.

Just go with it, snowflake. Please.

And she did so quickly, so quickly understanding when she put out her hand. "Hello. My name's Aspen Davis."

"Hi." It was weird taking her hand, touching her. I'd touched her in so many ways, but a handhold got me all up in my head. "Nice to meet you."

"Likewise."

Our handhold lingered, more damage to my already fucked-up head, but Aspen was smart. She eased out of my grasp with the finesse of one who was pristinely talented in dexterity. I supposed she played music for a living.

I ignored the heat in my digits. "How did you two—"

"She was at our spot, Nighty," Gram said, shocking me further. It was the fact Aspen was there. "Our spot" was so far from campus. She touched Aspen's hand. "And she was so nice to walk me home."

"It was no big deal, Evangeline," Aspen stated, and it didn't look like one considering how she beamed back at my gram. Warmth touched her brown eyes. "I'm just glad we could get you home safely."

I was still confused about all this, but I was grateful.

Gram stared off a bit, not uncommon with her, and once she had, Aspen made eye contact with Bow and me.

"She looked confused when I ran into her, and I was able to see her ID. I found her address," Aspen whispered, and my chest soared. She got my gram home. Safe.

I had no words, but gratefully, my sister had some. Bow's face flashed cherry red. "Thank you so much," Bow said, and I mouthed something over my sister's head.

"*My sister,*" I stated, explaining our real relation to Aspen, and both girls nodded at each other, understanding. The small exchange was enough time for us all to understand how we got here.

She brought my gram home.

I was feeling some kind of way about that, but couldn't really react to it. Not with Gram here. Bow took Gram's hand. "That's probably enough excitement for today, yeah?" my sister said, her laugh an emotional one. That was another way we were different. Bow definitely wore her heart on her sleeve while I kept that shit on lock. Bow smiled. "Why don't we get you inside now?"

"I suppose." Gram allowed Bow to guide her by the arm, though she looked like she'd rather stay on the street. She turned to Aspen. "Can you come too, honey? Rest your feet a spell. I want to thank you for walking me home."

"Oh, I don't know about that—"

"You should," I said for some reason, and Aspen directed her gaze up at me. Her eyes met mine in a wide width, and her sugar scent hit the breeze. She always smelled like holiday gatherings and sweet candy. I wet my lips. "I was going to make Mom cocoa. I'm pretty good at it."

I was mediocre at best, but I wanted her to come.

Because you're stupid.

I was, and the guys wouldn't love this, but who the fuck cared?

I think it'd been my gram to convince Aspen to come up to the house in the end. It certainly hadn't been me because her denial of the request had been adamant. Yeah, even to my cocoa invite she turned me down, but one was hard-pressed to say no to my grandma. Once she got a thought in her head, she saw it through, and that was how Aspen Davis ended up in my house. Well, my parents' home. She toured the marble halls and polished floors, and her gray pullover was immediately taken by our main housekeeper, Janet.

I wished she'd kept it on. She wasn't wearing one of those lace bra thingies like on the quad, but she might as well have been in her sports bra and Juicy Couture shorts. They reminded me of those shorts cheerleaders wore at practice except they were fuzzy and sat drastically low on her trim hips. Her belly button out...

How had I not noticed she was *pierced*?

She had a jewel in her pert navel, one I would have certainly noticed and tasted around. She caught me looking at it and, well, her, but I directed my focus to getting her in the kitchen.

"Nice house," she said, peering around. My sister and Gram had gone ahead. "Really nice house."

I almost recorded her statement, the only compliment I'd

probably ever get from her after what happened between us. I nodded. "Thanks. It's been in the family a while."

My dad and his dad lived here. I didn't know how far back it went from there, but the Reeds prided themselves on tradition.

It was weird having Aspen Davis in my kitchen.

She perched her bubbled, Juicy Couture ass on one of my parents' barstools at the kitchen island, and I was happy my sister and Gram chose to sit in the breakfast nook. If Aspen and I were in the kitchen by ourselves, I didn't know what would happen.

She'd probably knee you in your shit, then you'd make her ride your face.

And I would. Fuck would I, and that was some fucked-up shit. Aspen and I were really toxic, but that didn't seem to matter.

I saw her notice me too as I maneuvered around the kitchen. I had to reach above her to get the cocoa out of one of the high cabinets, and she was definitely staring at my abs when my shirt rode up. That was after I caught sight of her staring at *my ass* when I got cups from another set of cabins. Her dusky eyes lingered on my dark jeans for the briefest of moments before I turned, and something told me this girl still liked what she saw despite our history.

Like I said, toxic.

"So Evangeline," she said. I think my parents' bar was a safer place for those dark eyes. Her gaze remained there after staring at my ass. Her black-polished nail picked at the marble. "She's, um…"

"Not well," I informed, and I could say that since my parents' kitchen was so fucking huge. The breakfast nook was on the other side of the room, and my sister had Gram occupied. She had one of my gram's favorite games out, one Gram used to play with my sister and me. Gram's doctors said it was good for us to do familiar things with her whenever we could. It might help her condition.

It never helped, but who was I to question doctors?

I glanced up from the milk I had bubbling in a pot. "Dementia."

The word was poison, vile, and one that twisted my insides again. Not from the word itself, but the way Aspen looked at me when I said it. A ring of sympathy rounded those brown eyes when, the last time this girl and I had been together, there'd been nothing but hate in her eyes.

I guess that'd been before she found out certain things.

Aspen's nod was subtle. Her dark hair touched the counter, thick strands that framed her face that were loose from her high bun. I googled and found out she wore locs. Her lips turned down. "I'm sorry."

I was sorry too. I shrugged. "She gets confused, as you can see. Thinks I'm my dad more often than not. We look alike."

I suppose she knew that. She'd seen my father.

I'd added cocoa to the milk, and Aspen was silent for so long I gazed up. She was staring at my sister and grandma playing Monopoly.

"That makes sense," Aspen said, chewing her lip. She shook her head. "She was so confused. She wasn't at first, but then…"

Gram had moments where she was lucid, or at least seemed to be. From the outside looking in, one could talk to her and not know something was wrong at all.

But her family knew. How could we not?

"I ran into her at Jax's Burgers," Aspen said, confirming something I already speculated. Gram had mentioned "our place." Aspen played with her hands. "She said she was meeting her son."

I stopped stirring, then gripped the counter. "Jax's didn't use to always be Jax's. When my dad was in college, he and

Gram used to go to the place it was before. They'd do that after they went to the ballet. They used to do that a lot."

That was kind of how the tradition started with my friends' dads and us guys. We'd do the ballet, then dinner all the time. Though, our dads typically used ballet outings to punish us.

"Oh." The remorse on Aspen's face was there again, sadness. It was weird seeing her direct that toward me. Our argument had been a volcanic eruption.

"That's on me for not thinking about that place," I said, chewing my lip. "I should have. That was their place. Hers and my dad's."

I wanted to fucking kick myself but resisted in the moment. That didn't stop the guilt, though.

"Thank God she let you walk her home," I said, and Aspen nodded. I faced my sister. "My sister said she turned her back for only a moment."

Again, sometimes that was all it took.

The two continued to play their board game, my gram in so much bliss. Bow was too. She always was seeing Gram happy. Even if she wasn't always there.

Aspen hugged herself, studying the two with a sad smile. "Me too. I asked if she had a phone after I noticed she was confused. I was going to attempt to call one of her contacts for her, but she didn't have one. At least not on her, and eventually, she let me look at her ID. Again, I found her address."

And she took her home. She'd done that for a complete stranger.

Aspen's throat shifted. "I'm sorry."

I didn't know what her apology was for. I guess the situation in general, which was fucked up.

She didn't know the half.

After taking the cocoa off the burner, I didn't serve it right away. I stared at the brown liquid. "My gram was in a coma for a lot of my dad's life. An accident..." My fingers tapped the bar. "Anyway, she came out of it when my dad was in college. She missed his entire childhood for the most part."

"Oh my God."

"Yeah." I pushed off the bar. "She woke up, and she had a college student now instead of a little boy." I gestured toward my face. "My gram's memories recognize this face. This is the one she saw when she woke up."

"Which is why she thinks you're…"

"My dad, yeah." It really was messed up. It was fucking tragic, but not just for me. Nah, it was nothing for me. Not compared to what my dad got on the other side of all this. "My gram doesn't know me as her grandson. It's too confusing for her memories, but it's worse for my dad. Her mind doesn't know what to do with him at all, and he can't ever mention who he is to her. She panics. She has these episodes and… it gets bad."

I'd downplayed that shit. The struggles… the tears. My gram would have these breakdowns, and that was when I was placed on speed dial. The early days of her disease I had to be at the ready. I had to drop everything because if she saw my face, my dad's face, things were okay. I made things okay for her. I calmed her.

"Thatcher…" Aspen's hand reached out, and she had a look in her eyes I'd seen before. It was that day I'd had a panic attack. I'd barely been lucid myself, but I recalled that same look in her eyes. The one of concern, remorse. It'd been there all of two seconds before it shifted to her own panic, fear. I'd scared the shit out of her that night.

But it hadn't even come close to matching my shit.

Aspen stopped reaching for me in the end. Maybe she thought better. Maybe she got smart. I didn't know. She hugged her arms. "Is this what you were dealing with at home? You said that. That you were dealing with something."

My head lifted. I'd dropped my head at some point. My jaw shifted. "Yeah, but there were things I shouldn't have said to you that night." There was a lot of shit I had said. Shit I regretted. I swallowed. "I didn't sleep with that girl."

I could tell that hadn't been what she expected to come out of my mouth, and when this conversation started, I would have thought the same. I didn't hate this girl, but I strongly disliked her sometimes. I disliked my potential to spiral around her.

To be vulnerable around her.

I didn't like being vulnerable, and my friends could tell anyone that. Vulnerability made you feel shit. It made you emotional and unstable, and that was one thing I couldn't be. I had too many people looking to me for stability. People like my sister who was going through this shit at home too. I had no excuse for instability because when it came to all this tragic shit at home, I got the good end of the stick. I still had my grandmother in some way, and if my dad could lock down his feelings and take care of everyone around him, I could too. I could be strong too like him.

Aspen... she rattled my shit, though. She made me feel vulnerable. She made me *feel*, and I didn't like that shit. It wasn't her fault, but I'd be naive in saying the guys weren't right about the shit she could bring up. She was there during some of the most turbulent times in my life.

She just didn't know it.

And she never would as far as I was concerned. Some things were just better left forgotten, easier that way and not just for me.

It took me a minute to realize those brown eyes hadn't left me, but there was no longer sympathy there. There was something else, and whatever that was had my stomach clenching and shit. Flipping. Aspen reached out, and when she took my hand, I let her. She stared at our fingers together, hers so slender and warm brown, mine thick and pale.

"I feel like I knew that," she said, smiling a little to

herself. It was rare I saw her smile and definitely not because of me. It was so much different than her scowl, softer.

My stomach flipped again. I really hated this vulnerable shit. "I guess you pissed me off calling me crazy." Honestly, it was completely valid for her to think that from the outside looking in. I probably had looked crazy, but it still hadn't felt good.

She sat back in her chair, her grin wiry. I liked that too. She smirked. "*I* pissed *you* off? You pissed me off."

I knew that as well, which was why I'd said what I had. We were tit for tat, the two of us.

"And I shouldn't have said what I had either. You had pissed me off, but I shouldn't have said it." She was still holding my hand, but it changed suddenly. Aspen unlaced them, and the next thing I knew, she had her hand out for a shake.

"Friends?" she asked, her hand resting on the counter. "We could try being that instead of... well, being whatever we are."

She laughed after that. I didn't know what for, but I took it as nerves. I honest-to-fuck had no desire to be this girl's friend, but whatever it was I think I wanted to be had me reaching for her hand. The handshake was easier, smarter.

Way smarter.

"Friends," I said, and it was easier than being her enemy. We could at least be on the same campus together without wanting to come for the other's throat. I let go. "And thanks again for bringing my gram home. You don't know what that means..."

I was getting up in my head again, but Aspen saved me from it by breaking eye contact. She had her gaze over on my sister and Gram, the two still playing their game. "It was no problem. I'm glad she got here safe."

I had no idea why Aspen was in town. She was a long

way from Pembroke-U, and when I asked her, she shifted uncomfortably in her seat.

"Just needed a drive to clear my head," she said, and I finally started pouring the cocoa into mugs. I handed her one, and she gripped it.

"Without your security?" I decided to call attention to that. This girl was being awful cavalier about the whole threat thing and had been from the jump since I first saw her. Her lack of concern about it all was dangerous. "Dad said you're here hiding out on campus, but the world kind of knows about you being here now, don't you think?"

That was something I found out recently from my dad. Her real reason for being here. Her being in hiding and no one knowing about that was the only reason in my mind she'd ever travel without her security, but she didn't have the anonymity now that she'd had before.

Aspen's head shot up before she chewed her lip. "I guess I was leaving quick. I..."

Her phone buzzed, and she pulled it out, glancing down. She pushed her loose locs out of her face. "Well, I guess my mom knows I left now. She says they told her."

They I assumed meant her security. I started to come around the bar, but she backed away.

"Thanks for the cocoa," she said. "But I should probably head back to campus before my mom sends the military after me."

I recalled her mother back when we were kids, and she'd been scary but only in the ways a mom was when it came to protecting her kid. She had that mama bear energy, but that shit had been warranted. I mean, I had taken her daughter, and Aspen and her mom hadn't had any pull back then. We were the Reeds against the Davises, so yeah, there hadn't been any pull. "Can I take you back to campus?"

I didn't want to leave, but my sister and Gram seemed to be doing okay. Actually, more than okay. My sister didn't smile a lot lately when she was home. It was hard when Gram was either mentally not here or in the hospital. She got sick sometimes like older folks do, but her condition had her susceptible to pneumonia and stuff. She was basically sick all the time except for when she wasn't, but today, she was good.

She was perfect.

I loved my gram, and I cherished every moment I had with her while she was here. Aspen caught me looking at the breakfast nook, at my sister and Gram. Aspen smiled a little. "No, I have a car. I left it at Jax's."

"So, I can run you over there—"

She had her hand up right as I met her around the bar. She placed it on my stomach, and that shit *burned* through my shirt. Like hot fucking fire it scorched, and it took all I had not to brace my hand around hers and do something that definitely wasn't friendly.

What are you doing to me, snowflake?

I didn't care about girls unless they were my sister, and of course, my mom and Gram. My friends' mothers were under that umbrella too since they were like second moms, but any other female connections were rare in my life. Women tended to be messy, but I made their shit look legendary. I gravitated toward drama. Not to mention I loved to fuck. Picking one girl meant I was missing out on a cornucopia of the rest.

But I didn't think that with Aspen. Actually, other girls were the last thing I was thinking about when she was in my head.

"You should stay here," she said, testing the boundaries of our new friendship when she allowed her digits to linger on my abs for just a smidgen too long. The muscles formed beneath my dark shirt when her fingers made the material go taut, stretched. She let go. "Thanks, but I'll be fine. I'll see you on campus."

She let me make her cocoa to go, and she used that time to say goodbye to my gram and sister. I supposed she could have just left and denied me again, the cocoa, but she didn't. She sat with my family, and I watched her while I made her cup. I didn't know why I felt so protective over that girl. Even when we were kids, she'd messed my shit up, but that would have been worse if she'd done anything remotely close to what she had for my grandmother today back then. Aspen had helped my gram out, a perfect stranger. Before today, I thought Aspen Davis was dangerous for me.

But apparently danger was only the beginning.

CHAPTER
EIGHTEEN

Aspen

I heard it from my mom about leaving campus without telling anyone, but considering how far away she was, she couldn't really do anything. I got a stern warning, and I appeased her because I didn't want her uprooting me back home. Things would go back to the way they were, and I wasn't ready for that yet.

I just wasn't ready.

I needed time, and with it, I knew I would be okay. I would wake up every day and be who I used to be.

I would.

I held solid to the notion, but tried not to think about it too much. If I did, it'd rattle me, so I let go and moved on. I decided that was the best course of action, but blocking my mind from those thoughts meant others could drift in. Thoughts about Thatcher and his family and how he suddenly seemed human. A big, large human with problems just like me. I had problems, and he did too.

And his were heart-wrenching.

I couldn't imagine someone I cared about forgetting about me. I had a grandmother, grandparents on both sides. My dad may not have been in the picture, but his parents were. My dad was absent in the sense that he had another family, but his family actually gave a shit. I saw his mom and dad on holidays and my mom's parents too.

I just couldn't imagine.

And then all that with the coma and his dad… It was just tragic, and yes, it humanized Thatcher in ways I wished I didn't know frankly. It was easier to hate him when he was just insane for no reason.

But people always had reasons, didn't they?

Maybe I was giving him more credit than he deserved. I still held that trauma he inflicted on me when we were kids, but today's Thatcher may not be so easily written off. I wanted to write him off. Fuck had I wanted to just toss any sympathetic thoughts for him aside, but that was hard.

Especially when he showed up at my door.

He startled me actually. I was leaving and heading to a class, but there he was, his fist mid-knock. He wore a cutoff tee that showcased his big muscles and broad shoulders. He'd never been one of those guys who was cut in the ways you saw every muscle, but he was huge like he didn't go to the gym but lifted boulders for sport instead.

Or trains…

Okay, trains was a bit over the top, but this guy could easily bench-press a dude or two. Then there were his thighs that hugged his dark jeans like sin. Thatcher Reed gave emo energy depending on what day it was. He looked like a country-club pretty boy with his dad, but today, he opted for the bad boy. He had a couple nails painted black again, and he used those large hands of his to juggle coffee and fast food. The Jax's Burgers logo was stamped onto the bag, and the two coffees in his hands were in a carrier.

"Morning, snowflake," he said, then completely threw me

off by handing me one of the coffees. He smiled at it, his cross earring dangling. "Didn't know what you liked but decided to play it safe. It's just coffee with artificial sweetener and almond milk."

I blinked. That was exactly how I took my coffee. I brought the coffee to my chest. "Thanks?"

He bumped a laugh at the clear question mark that was on the end there.

"No problem." He sipped his remaining coffee, looking like a complete god in the hallway, and I wasn't the only one to notice. Since people did know I lived here now, I'd get the occasional lurker. They usually wanted autographs, and I always did because I loved that part of the job. I truly enjoyed meeting fans, but I wasn't getting their attention today with Thatcher Reed in my hallway. A couple of girls giggled at his jean-clad ass, and I bristled in a way that surprised me.

"Ladies," he said to them, oozing the same charisma that got me to fuck him in a dark club… in a mask. I'd had no idea who he was, but he'd done that. Not to mention, he hadn't even spoken.

The giggles erupted from those girls like a volcano upon being acknowledged, and when Thatcher tipped his chin at the guys a few paces behind them, they tripped. Like full-on tripped in the hallway over themselves.

"Hey, Thatcher!" One of the guys waved like he was trying to take off in flight, and after he cleared Thatcher and me, he held his head and cursed. I literally heard him mumble to himself that he was a fucking idiot, seemingly chastising himself for his greeting.

Holy fuck, the power Thatcher Reed had. I mean, I knew it. He had gotten me to fuck him in that club.

But had he…

I guess I needed to acknowledge the fact that I'd kind of thrown myself at him. But that had been before I knew who he was and our history.

It scared me that my brain didn't automatically think about that anymore. Whenever I saw him, fear used to be the first instinct, not anger that he said hello to other girls or sexual frustration because he probably had the best ass I'd ever seen on a guy outside of a porn star. I'd stared at it a little too much in his kitchen when he'd been making cocoa.

"Up here, snowflake."

And his cock, which bulged even though he probably wasn't even fucking *hard*. The guy was just big everywhere and those tight-as-fuck jeans outlined what he had.

My face heated at being caught looking, and Thatcher smiled behind his cup. That little smirk he did pouted his full lips and never ceased to tickle me in places I definitely didn't want to be tickled. My draw to him was confusing because I wasn't sure it just surrounded how he looked. I mean, he was fucking hot, but I hadn't even seen his face in the club.

Yeah, it was confusing.

"Breakfast sandwiches," he said, surprisingly not putting me on blast for staring at, well, his cock. He lifted the bag. "I got a plant-based one and a meat one. Again, I was playing it safe."

I didn't take the food like the coffee. Instead, I closed my door and locked it. "Okay…"

"Good morning, Miss Davis." My security dude, Phil, approached from his own room across the hall. He walked me to class every day, and since I'd blown my cover, there wasn't a point to him blending in anymore. He wore his dark suit like he did every day now, and upon seeing Thatcher, he nodded. "Good morning, Mr. Reed. Didn't expect to see you today."

I didn't either, and of course, he knew Thatcher. Phil was employed by Thatcher's dad's company.

"Clearly, Miss Davis didn't know either," Thatcher teased, then flashed me a wink over his big shoulder. It made my knees go weak, and I cursed at myself just like that guy had who tripped. Thatcher angled around. "I've come to walk you to class. That is, if you'll have me."

Well, color me fucking shocked. "Um…"

"We are friends, right?" He angled close, again his voice teasing. "Well, I walk my friends to class sometimes. Our first classes also happen to be close by, so I figured why not. We walk, and we have breakfast."

He lifted his grub, and the proposal was sweet. Like really freaking sweet.

You did tell him you wanted to be friends.

I didn't know why I said that in his kitchen. Thatcher and I were the last thing that could be considered friends, but looking back, I think the proposal had been a defense mechanism. I'd felt for him and his situation with his grandma, and I'd reacted.

I'd friend-zoned him.

I didn't want to feel anything for Thatcher, and though I may sympathize with him, I didn't want to want him. Friends felt like something easier, but that friendship was just supposed to be a formality. Something on paper and not real. It was a way for him (and me) to stay away from each other.

We needed to stay away from each other.

Thatcher and I had something weird going on, and though all this today seemed sweet, I couldn't help but question his angle. He had to know I hadn't really meant what I said, right? At least, not in the way that we'd be hanging out.

"Snowflake?"

I blinked out of my thoughts.

Thatcher grinned. "Come on. You're going to make us both late for class."

I think I decided to go in the end because I had security as a buffer. I didn't think Thatcher would try something, but with Phil being there, nothing weird could happen anyway. Weird being Thatcher and I losing our minds and playing predator/prey in the woods again.

Yeah, I looked that up after we fooled around. It'd been hot what we'd done, and I'd been curious about it.

God, he got me crazy.

He had, and that made him dangerous for me. I'd turned into someone else, and though that someone else was exciting, I wasn't sure it was healthy to give in to it. Healthy for me anyway.

The walk to class was surprisingly quick, and Thatcher had good taste in breakfast sandwiches. I chose the plant-based one since I heard my mom's voice about diet in my head, and I ate while Thatcher did all the talking. He definitely liked to talk, and his charisma didn't just ooze in the bedroom.

He was actually funny. Genuinely so, and I was surprised that I was sad when we arrived at my class. I was sad our walk was so short-lived, and I thought he'd linger for a second after it was over, that he'd try something but he didn't.

"Good breakfast, snowflake," he said, balling up our trash. He tossed a wrapper at my head, and I was in such shock that I laughed. I mean, he tossed a wrapper at me like we were friends and he was being funny. He eyed it on the ground. "I'd pick that up, snow. Don't want anyone thinking you're a litter bug."

So he totally tossed that *at me.* I picked it up, throwing it at him, and he dodged in the way a football player did on the field. I guessed he did play football. He told me that, and from what I heard, he and his friends were pretty fucking good. People around here called them Legacy because of their families' influence on the school.

Thatcher backed up in his boots. "See you around. Have fun."

And then, he was gone, leaving Phil and me in the hallway.

I shook my head. That was the last way I thought I'd

spend my morning, and another thing about that surprised me, as I entered my class with Phil behind me. I didn't so much mind being walked to class by Thatcher Reed, but what surprised me the most (and alarmed me a little) was that I really was sad it was over…

And that I hoped we got to do it again.

CHAPTER
NINETEEN

Thatcher and I did get to walk to class together again. In fact, he was at my door every morning with coffee and breakfast sandwiches. Each morning, I opted out of the sandwiches. They were a bit heavier than what I was used to in regards to calories, but that didn't bother Thatcher. He still brought them even if he ended up eating both of them.

And my God was he *funny*.

I'd gathered that from our very first walk, but the fact had become more and more evident as I spent more time with him. And spend more time with him I did. That first week had only been early morning walks, but then our meetings turned into mid-morning walks, and eventually, lunches. Yes, I started eating lunch with Thatcher Reed on *occasion*. It wasn't every day. Sometimes he had football practice at odd hours, but he always seemed to find time to meet with me at least once a day.

And I didn't hate it.

Actually, I looked forward to it, which was fucking crazy.

We really were acting like friends, and he was like not insane. He just walked me to class or he made me laugh over a meal. Hell, the dude didn't even make a move on me, which kind of disappointed me at first. I was very much attracted to Thatcher, and even though a casual hook-up situation would be a terrible idea with our history, I couldn't honestly tell myself I'd resist him if he tried anything.

But he didn't. Not once. We both traveled into friendship territory very quickly, and I think that was why our walks eventually evolved into lunches and things. I felt comfortable with him, and there was no pressure. It was just us chatting and him making me laugh.

It was normal.

I often asked him about Evangeline during our meetups. I couldn't help my thoughts traveling her way, but each time I asked, news was only good about her. Thatcher visited her often during the week, which was awesome because his hometown was over two hours away. There weren't many guys I knew or had dated in the past who'd ever make that kind of accommodation.

Thatcher Reed was just different.

It was kind of crazy how comfortable I was starting to get around him and him around me. He had no problem giving me a hard time, but not in a cruel way. Like today when he dropped an entire trough of food in front of me that certainly did not include my regular order of a chopped salad and a side of fruit. I frowned at the cheese fries, tacos, and burgers. "Where's my food?"

He eyed the grub, looking like literal sin in his scarlet-toned jeans and a dark Henley that hugged every bit of his bulky exterior. He was what the British would call *fit*, and just because we were friends didn't mean I ignored the fact that he was literally gorgeous. I had eyes, and I used them.

He did too. I caught those glacial eyes lingering in the direction of my top before he sat down. My shirt happened to be flesh-toned and cropped and also pushed my breasts up in a way where the swell nearly spilled over. He hadn't been obvious about it, but he did it, and that let me know he was still aware that I was a woman. He was also very much a man, and that was something I was aware of when he pressed his big body up against me at our usual table in the student union. He always sat on my side, and with as large as he was, he couldn't help getting close. The heat of his thick leg pretty much smoldered through my jeans, and even though my face played that off, I couldn't deny the rosy tint suddenly flushing across my chest.

Thatcher noticed that too, but didn't call attention to it. Sometimes I wondered if we actually had fucked with the way he didn't engage with that part of our previous relationship. I just kept reminding myself I told him I wanted to be friends. Even if I hadn't actually meant it. Actually meaning it or not, that was what we were now, and it did take the pressure off. That was good, of course. Great.

Thatcher displayed the food. "Pick your poison."

That would certainly be easier if my food was there. My head cocked, my locs touching the table. "I don't see my salad."

"And you won't. Not today," he said, then made a display of opening a napkin and placing it on my lap. I let him just because of the sheer audacity, and it made me laugh. His blue eyes danced. "You order things that no one in their actual right mind would eat every day unless they were held at gunpoint. I mean, what the fuck are kale chips?"

"Delicious?"

He made a face. "That's fine, and I respect you wanting to eat healthy. I got to do that too for football." He opened a Gatorade. "But I don't eat like that every day. You're in college, snowflake. Have a fucking treat day on occasion."

I liked how he called them treat days instead of cheat days. I folded my arms. "Why do you call me snowflake?"

It was something I never asked, and it was kind of a sore spot for us. I mean, he'd called me that *back then.*

We never talked about that time, he and I. It was obvious why we didn't, and as I spent more and more time with him, *back then* and *that time* really hadn't made sense. I get that we were kids. He'd been *a kid,* but today's Thatcher and that Thatcher seemed so different. Today's Thatcher was cool and funny. He was charismatic, and the old one was so with-drawn. Dark. Truly, they were like two different people, but I found it hard to believe this version of Thatcher wasn't in there back then. And if that was the case, I didn't get why he just didn't talk to me. If he'd truly liked me, he could have just talked to me. I probably would have liked him, and maybe even had a crush on him.

Thatcher smiled a little. It was a wobbly smile while he ate a cheese fry. Like he was shy or nervous, and maybe he was a bit talking about this. He shrugged. "You don't remember that necklace you used to wear?"

"Necklace?"

He nodded, then finally faced me, and whoa. His face was red. Like a full crimson charge had chased up his neck and filled his cheeks. He passed a hand over his dark hair, his spiked earring bouncing when his arm clipped it. "Yeah, that necklace. You used to wear one. It had, uh... had a snowflake on it."

He busied himself by drinking his Gatorade after that, and my eyes flashed. Not because of how weirdly nervous he was acting, but that I did recall I had a necklace like that. I'd worn the thing all the time. I think I'd gotten it at a carnival the summer before we met, and I'd worn it everywhere.

I sat back. "You remember that necklace?"

"Yup." He rubbed his hands down his pant legs. "Surprised you don't. You never took it off."

I hadn't, and he remembered that.

Our history was so weird, and though it should have put

me off the nickname's origin, I was more in awe that he remembered any of that.

He studied my food. "You going to eat or…"

"Yeah." I took a fry. He was right. I should treat myself on occasion, and my thoughts mulled over a different scenario. One where he had just talked to me back then, and our whole history had been different. Where he'd been this Thatcher, sweet and charismatic, and gotten me to loosen up and just eat some fucking fries. How different things could have been.

But it wasn't, though. That wasn't what had happened, and that fact became very apparent as suddenly we weren't alone at our semi-private lunch. Thatcher tended to pick a table that was out of the fray of the student union. Between who I was outside of here and his Legacy status, we often got people approaching us. It never bothered me, but Thatcher always sighed before it happened. Like he just wanted to spend time with me, but that was probably in my head.

"Brilliant," Thatcher gritted, his arm going behind my chair. It brushed my neck and distracted me a bit. He never did that or touched me, but suddenly, that was what he was doing as several people approached our table. They were people I definitely recognized.

I mean, one had chewed me out.

I was suddenly very uncomfortable upon seeing his friend Wells. The bottle-dyed blond was stalking his way over, a determined look in his eyes, and I found myself tucking under Thatcher's arm. I played it off, of course. At least, I tried to when I flipped my hair, but Thatcher instantly drew a look down when I scooted. Suddenly, that arm hugging my chair was hugging me. It was discreet, but he hooked it around me more. It made me wonder if that was why his arm had hit the chair at all. Like a territorial measure.

A protective one.

That was probably in my head too, considering Thatcher appeared like he was forgetting more and more that I had a vagina and was, well, a woman, but at the present, I didn't care why he was so close. I was just glad he was as Wells came over with his and Thatcher's other friends. I recognized the one they'd called Wolf too. He had his arm around a curvy redhead with a lot of tattoos and a nose ring. She was gorgeous, just like the other girls in their group. One girl was standing close to the guy who wore combat boots the night I'd gotten yelled at. Combat Boots was hand in hand with that girl, so they must have been together too.

The last girl in their group was the only one I recognized, and as soon as their large party saw me, she waved. Thatcher's sister, Rainbow, was super adorable and hella friendly. She didn't intimidate me like her brother, but she was with a group of guys who certainly took up a lot of space. Outside of Wells, Wolf, and Combat Boots was another guy, and though he didn't look nearly as serious as the other guys, he was fucking huge. He was big and broad like Thatcher. Not as big and broad, but still built like a linebacker.

He might have been. Thatcher played football, so he might too. I heard about how good Thatcher and his friends were on the field.

"Hey, Aspen!" Bow skipped ahead. She had a lunch tray, and the others had other forms of grub with them—drinks, wraps, fries, etc. The only one empty-handed was Wells, who had to navigate to his side when Bow pushed around him. He borderline sneered at her when she did it.

What the fuck was this dude's problem? He obviously had one and hated my ass. That sneer definitely directed toward me after it left Bow who got to Thatcher and me first.

"Hey, Bow," I said, and she beamed.

"You guys eating lunch?" she asked, her hair up in a tight bun.

"Uh, yeah." Thatcher sat up, and though his arm navigated back to the chair a bit, it didn't leave. Wells arrived behind Bow shortly after she did, and Thatcher tapped his fist. "Not much room at the table, though…"

"Don't worry, bro. We can fix that." Wells took the initiative and physically brought a table, connecting it to ours with a screech. It made half the student union look over and several of their friends cringe. Most likely from the sound. Wells sat backward on a chair. "There. All fixed."

The two passed a glance between them, Thatcher's terribly icy before looking at me. "You know Wells. And I swear he's only an asshole ninety percent of the time."

"Only ninety percent?" Wells whistled. "Must not be on my game lately."

Thatcher visibly growled at him. Especially when Wells casually snatched one of our fries. I tipped a chin at him in greeting. "Hello."

"Hi," he returned, chewing. I was dismissed after that and certainly hadn't gotten an apology for being yelled at.

I supposed I'd take the cold rather than more yelling, and by then, Thatcher's other friends had come over. I assumed they were the rest of who was considered Legacy here on this campus. Thatcher and his friends were pretty influential around here, and I'd heard about that.

"You also know Wolf and Dorian," Thatcher stated, introducing the guy with the long curly hair, then the one wearing the combat boots respectively. I had to say, Thatcher was pretty fucking gorgeous, but all his friends managed to hold up to his looks. The guys were Greek gods, even Wells who was grimacing sourly into the open air during the introductions. He obviously still didn't want me around Thatcher, but I didn't really understand why. I should be upset by what had happened that night. Not the other way around.

There was still confusion surrounding that night for me, but I didn't touch it with a ten-foot pole. This was for my mental health because Thatcher and I were cool now. I actually liked spending time with him and didn't want to self-sabotage over some confusion.

Dorian and Wolf were a lot more polite than Wells. I had to say, they'd kind of dismissed me that night things got crazy too, but today, Dorian shook my hand, and Wolf introduced me to his fiancée, Fawn. The girl had a rock on her finger the size of Texas, and after he introduced her, he looped his long arms around her waist.

"Hey, Aspen. I'm Sloane," the girl standing next to Dorian said. She was tall and gorgeous and looked kind of like the girl version of Wolf. This made sense because in the next breath she said they were twins, and the last guy in their group (the really freaking big one), she introduced as their brother Bru.

Bru got his own greeting in, waving, and after he did, Dorian got his arms around Sloane's hips in the same way Wolf had claimed Fawn. Dorian tipped his chin over her shoulder. "We don't want to bug you guys. We were just passing through and looking for somewhere to sit."

"Well, there's plenty of room," I said. There was since Wells had brought that table over. I gestured toward the extra seating. "I don't mind."

Thatcher looked like he minded. He kept trying to make eye contact with Wells, who wasn't making eye contact. Apparently, after his initial venom, Wells was all tapped out. He continued to stare into open air as he ate our fries, and with the invitation, the rest of Thatcher's friends made themselves at home. The others brought chairs over, and it was kind of nice being in a group. I'd spent a lot of time alone lately, which was the opposite of my normal life. I was usually always surrounded by people.

It'd been nice to have a break, but I liked it today. Especially getting to see Bow again. I asked about her and Thatcher's grandma. He told me things were fine with her whenever I asked, but of course, I wanted to check in.

"She's really good, and I can't thank you enough for what you did that day," she said sweetly. "We got a bunch of your albums after that happened, and Gram loves to play them."

"Really?" I studied Thatcher, who nodded. He'd never mentioned that. I braced my arms. "That's wonderful. Makes me so happy."

It did. I was glad my music brought people joy. That was what music was supposed to do. It was supposed to make you feel warm and free. Yes, it was.

My gaze hit the table after the thought, but I lifted my head when the group started to give me questions. I got questions about the music business and what it was like to go on tour with celebrities. That was one of the really kickass things about the job, and I loved that.

"Oh my God, how was playing at the Grammys?" Sloane asked me, but I hadn't mentioned the Grammys. She laughed. "Bow and I looked you all up after she told me what you did for her grandmother. You played with Alicia Keys?"

"Not to mention Beyoncé at the Oscars. Ah! So freaking cool." Bow grinned, and I laughed.

"Yeah, it was pretty cool. A dream." I'd played with some of the biggest artists and on the biggest stages. My life truly was a dream.

"Then there's Carnegie Hall, which was probably pretty cool."

I froze, the high I'd been on from the conversation completely gone.

Shattered.

It was like a bucket of ice water hit me. It locked up my vocal cords and stopped any engagement I had in the conversation. I couldn't speak, and suddenly, Wells (the one who'd spoken) was no longer looking into open air.

His sight was very much on me.

Everyone else's attention was on me too. Even those who hadn't been entirely engaged in my conversation with the girls. It wasn't that the others were being rude or anything, but they had their own conversations going. Those conversations stopped, though, and the way they all looked at me, borderline sympathy in their eyes, let me know *they knew* why I reacted this way to what Wells said. Carnegie Hall was the one venue I hadn't really gotten to play. My dream venue. I'd been working literally my whole life to get there, and when I finally had, I'd frozen in front of millions of people.

I'd frozen.

I'd ended up walking off stage, my bow and instrument in hand, and later that night, there'd been the infamous press release. *Concert Cellist Aspen Davis Freezes At Carnegie Hall…*

Following Threats Made Upon Her Life.

The news had been *everywhere*, and even if one didn't follow me, they probably would have heard about it. I was trending on Reddit and shit and…

It was like the energy had been sucked out of the room, and Thatcher grew like a size and a half next to Wells. He towered over his friend despite being seated, but before Thatcher could say something and put things out there more than they already were, I got out my phone. Thatcher looked at me then as I started to type.

I got up. "I actually need to go, but it was good meeting everyone."

Everyone knew I was lying, and *I knew* by the way they all averted their eyes. Most of them landed on Wells, who clearly knew what he'd said. He did, but he hadn't cared, and odds were, he'd said what he had on purpose. He'd acknowledged one of the most embarrassing moments of my life—in front of everyone—on purpose. He clearly didn't like me when my past with Thatcher was not my fault—at all.

Thatcher's mouth parted. "Snow—"

He didn't get the full word out.

I walked away.

Thatcher

I went after Snowflake, but she was fucking quick.

Fucking Wells.

Normally, my friend wasn't this much of an asshole. Actually, he was very much that much of an asshole, and normally, I was right there with him.

But this was different.

This was Snowflake and him continuing to come at her like this wasn't fucking cool. I lost Aspen somewhere between the Chick-fil-A and Chipotle store fronts in the student union. The place was fucking crowded, and she'd obviously been determined to get away.

I growled, fucking livid. I doubled back to our table. I'd left my things there, and even my fucking cell phone. I noticed her security's table was empty on my way back, though. Phil usually sat nearby, but never with us. He wanted access to Snowflake, but also gave her the space she needed.

I wished that calmed me down a little more. That she at least wasn't alone, but I had just as much fire as when I left.

Especially when I saw my friend still sitting there.

Wells started to stand up when I got back, but he went right back down the minute I swung.

I didn't fucking miss.

My sister—hell, all the girls at our tables—shrieked when the punch landed, and I'd given them a good reason. I was wearing my gorilla ring below my knuckle, and an ocean spray of blood flew from Wells's big-ass mouth.

"What the fuck!" he bit out from the floor. He touched his bloody lip. Like stated, that shit landed. My ring was also big and chunky, so that shit did some good fucking damage.

I never thought I'd lay my friend out like this, but he'd taken shit too far.

Wells snapped up on his feet, quick. A small crowd had gathered in the student union, but the moment Dorian yelled at everyone to go back to what they were doing, they headed back toward their tables. My friends and I had a lot of power on this campus, but even with Dorian's yelling, everyone was still looking this way.

Wolf got up then, eyeing the room, and *that look* got everyone looking back at their salads and shit. Wells started to come at me, but Bru (Wolf and Sloane's brother) got between us. He was a big ol' boy, but he still didn't have shit on me. Bru studied us both. "Hey, you guys. Don't do this fucking here."

"Nah, let them handle their shit," Dorian directed, I think surprising both Wells and me. The girls all had their hands up. They all covered their mouths, and my sister appeared horrified. She started to approach us, but Sloane touched her shoulder.

"They should deal with this on their own," she urged, both Dorian and Sloane the two leaders in our group. It made sense they were together on this. Especially because they were together. She glared at Wells. "And that was low. Even for you."

It was low what he'd said to Snowflake, and that wasn't in my head. Everyone knew about that concert and how Aspen had been threatened. It'd been news, and it was everywhere whether someone followed her music or not.

Wells had taken things too fucking far, and rather than talk to his ass, I gathered my things. I made my point with his bloody fucking lip, and even after our friends left, I didn't talk to him.

"Thatch—"

"Fuck you." I swung around. Okay, maybe I did have some things to fucking say to him. I shot a finger at him. "Don't talk to me. I ain't ready for it."

His mouth would see my ring again if he said the wrong thing. He gripped the back of a chair. His mouth still bled in the corner. I guess I hadn't busted his lip after all.

What a shame.

I started to go, but he cut me off. A noise rumbled in my chest. "Move."

"No."

The alternative was his ass on the floor again, but when I approached, he lifted his hands. He shook his head. "I wasn't trying to be a dick."

Well, he had a shit fucking way of showing that.

He wet his lips. "I wasn't, and I probably shouldn't have said that to her."

"Really?" The sarcasm dripped from my voice, venomous, lethal. My eyes narrowed. "You have no reason to have a vendetta against her."

"I don't."

"Then what the fuck was that shit?" We were getting a crowd again, and I sneered at the room. "The fuck's everyone looking at? The show's over."

I was sure on the outside it looked like it was just beginning, and it might if Wells continued to say stupid fucking things to me.

He posted his hands on his hips, the two of us more than at fucking odds lately. He didn't like having to look out for Aspen. He didn't like that I asked, and he certainly didn't like the fact that I was looking out myself by spending more time with her. Dorian, Wolf, and Bru were indifferent. I'd gotten Bru caught up on everything and gotten him in on the Aspen shifts. He was cool and had been more than ready to help. He was the nice one out of all of us.

There was blood on Wells's Pembroke Football shirt. He spat blood. "You know what the issue is. It's one thing to look out for her, but the amount of time you're spending with her is not fucking good for you."

Yeah, Snowflake wasn't good for me. She was terrible, and he was an idiot on top of being an asshole if he actually fucking believed that. I shook my head. "Yeah, she's really fucking terrible."

"Isn't she, though?"

I refused to believe my friend was this much of a dumbass, and I hated this shit. I hated that *this shit* was putting me at odds with him so much. This guy wasn't just my friend. He was *my brother* in every sense of the word.

And I felt like I was losing him because of all this.

This Aspen thing was putting a wedge between Wells and me that I didn't like, but I was standing my ground on this. I put my finger in his chest. "Yeah, she's really fucking dangerous. So dangerous in fact that I'm not getting fucking drunk off my ass these days and higher than shit." Or had he failed to notice I hadn't been at the raves lately? I hadn't. I hadn't had the urge in days, weeks. My jaw clenched. "I'm not even fucking partying anymore. Yeah, Aspen Davis is so fucking terrible for me."

Wells's mouth parted, his dark eyebrows narrowed, and I wasn't surprised. I think I too was realizing in that moment that I hadn't been doing those things. I really hadn't had the urge. Zero urge in fact.

Blinking, I shifted away. Wells called after me, but I ignored him. I needed to find Snowflake.

I needed to apologize for my dumb-as-shit friend.

Thatcher

I attempted to get in touch with Aspen over the next few days, but she really wasn't having it. She avoided all contact, including me showing up to her door to take her to class. I stayed outside knocking until just about making me late for my own classes.

Fucking Wells.

My buddy had fucked up whatever this was I had with Aspen. I didn't know what it was, but I didn't hate it. I liked walking her to class. I liked just hanging out, which was fucking crazy. I didn't hang out with girls. Especially when I was attracted to them.

I texted Aspen too when I realized she was going to class without me. She responded to those, but they were one- or two-word answers. They were clearly a brush-off, and she was ghosting me.

I was the one who usually did the ghosting, so I definitely wasn't used to that shit. Being ignored didn't sit well, and since I wasn't used to it, I nearly got desperate and dropped in on one of her classes. I knew where she was at pretty much every moment of the day, but that felt like I'd be laying things on too strong.

Especially considering our history.

I hadn't respected Aspen's boundaries back when we first came into each other's lives, and though that situation was completely fucking different, I knew I had to play this another angle. Friends didn't stalk friends.

Even if I wanted to.

I saw her sometimes even though she avoided the quad and the student union. I mean, Pembroke was a decent-size campus, but I would see her from time to time walking to her next class with Phil behind her. I'd always want to approach her, but she tended to have a fan club constantly following her.

I wanted her alone.

An opportunity came to do that when one of my frat's annual charity events rolled around. I didn't live at my frat but was an active participant. Many of the guys who were in it came from my hometown and the club we were all a part of there. It was called the Court, which was where the gorilla ring I had came from. Dorian, Wolf, Wells, Bru, and even Sloane and my sister were a part of the Court, but hardly anyone had been active since high school ended. My sister and I had been more involved, but only I had gotten into the Greek-life thing. That was more to connect me with my father since my frat was the one he'd been in when he was in school.

My dad wasn't terribly involved in fraternity events these days. Not like he had been in the past. He was working a lot and stuff, and though my gram wasn't actively sick, he didn't like being tied up too much away from home.

I got that, understood that, but I had looked forward to the days where we could both be involved in the fraternity. Obviously, sometimes things changed.

I held the invitation to my frat's charity event in my room one day, my phone in hand. We sold tickets to this thing, and all my friends were going. Frat brothers got comped for their tickets, though, and it included a date.

I wanted to invite Aspen.

I wasn't dating this girl, but we were friends, and it'd be nice to have a date that wouldn't be all over my jock all night. I tended to work the charity event since I was involved and wanted my hands and attention free.

Yeah, that was why you wanted to invite her.

It was, and I'd tell myself that to the fucking grave. I couldn't get out of my head what I'd told Wells that day he'd been an asshole to her. I was pretty much clean these days outside of the occasional joint and hadn't had the urge to party or use until recently. Being with Aspen kept me busy, focused. My head wasn't fucking clouded anymore with trauma and shit, drama.

I actually wanted to be in my head.

I ended up tossing the extra invitation away and going to the charity event alone. My friends would be there, and that was a big reason why I decided to opt for that option. All this shit started because of opinions that had to do with Aspen and me, and I wouldn't subject her to any more shit.

It wasn't fair.

The whistle noise came when I left my bedroom that night of the event, and I flipped all my friends the bird when I came into our living room. All of them were in various dress from the Regency era. That was the theme of the event, but apparently, I was the only one who'd gone all out and worn fucking tights.

The comments immediately started about how nice my legs were, and I hadn't gotten the memo that tights were optional. I refused to wear a fucking powdered wig, though, and wouldn't take my earrings out. I flipped my friends off again. "Fuck you guys. You ready?"

They all looked to be and the girls (my sister, Sloane, and Fawn) had really gone out with their ballgowns. They had fans too and had kind of coordinated together.

"We're just giving you a hard time," Dorian said, his hand in Sloane's. They both wore gloves. Dorian grinned. "But still, nice legs, buddy."

I growled. Especially when he slapped my chest. I appreciated them supporting the charity. Tickets for this thing were 5K a head and included dinner.

Wolf ruffled my hair, and I really almost lost my shit since I'd spent so much time on it. I nudged him and would have landed a footprint on his ass but he was too fast. He'd skipped out in his Regency garb, his long hair tied back. He was the only one outside of me who wore his natural hair. Probably because it was fucking awesome. The guy could do shampoo ads. Sloane and D looked pretty badass, though, in their powdered wigs. They did the whole king-and-queen thing in their intricate outfits, and everyone wore masks since it was a masked event.

Ironically enough, the only one who hadn't given me a jab was Wells, but that was probably because we weren't really talking these days. He nodded at me from behind a black mask on his way out. I got his arm. "Thanks for coming."

I appreciated it, and all this was for a good cause. It helped literacy in local schools.

"You know I'd always be there," he said, tapping my fist. I still wasn't happy with him, but all us guys always burned hot fast but cooled just as quickly. For the moment, Wells and I had put our beef on the back burner, and we all went to the event together. Bru planned to show up a little later since he had a night class, and my sister stayed close to the girls since she didn't have a date.

My sister wasn't dating yet, which was completely fine with me. I didn't feel like beating any dudes down who weren't good enough for her, and her single status also made it easy to keep an eye on her after we all arrived to the chateau that night.

My frat had gone all out.

The rented castle was in Winchester, a town over, and there were even fireworks upon arrival. It was kind of a trip but was on par with my frat's previous charity events. One year, we'd done *The Great Gatsby*, which was pretty badass.

"Everything looking good?" I asked one of my frat brothers. I'd lost my friends sometime between the fireworks and the circus performers at the door. There were actual fire breathers and shit here, and the alcohol was pouring. People were dancing in both Regency style and modern depending on what room they were in. The main ballroom was reserved for Regency, but anywhere else people could do whatever. We had a DJ outside of the ballroom, but live performers were under the main ballroom's chandelier. A string quartet with piano accompaniment played modern classical tunes, and people looked like they were having a good time.

I think my frat brother told me everything was okay, and normally, I would have listened. I cared that things looked good at our event. Especially since I had an active role in the planning, but a girl over by the punch bowl took my attention.

I wished it was just because of the dress.

A lot of people stood out in this fucking place. People were trying to go all out with the wigs, masks, dresses, and shit. There was glitter everywhere, and there was color, but I'd never seen someone encompass the Regency era more than literally the girl who just had a small fan and a white dress on. Perhaps, it was because her outfit was subtle compared to everyone else that she stood out.

She just couldn't help herself.

I strode over to Aspen, her gaze scanning the crowd of

people dancing in ballgowns to an old Motown song played in a classical style. Her hair was up and pinned intricately, her brown skin flushed and heated under the bright glow of the chandelier. She had a mask in her hand too, but it was on a stick, and her lips parted as I arrived at her side. She wore neutral tones with her makeup tonight, and her lips had never appeared more kissable.

"Fancy seeing you here tonight." I could do better with my line, but honest to fuck, I was just trying not to look at her in a way that was the opposite of friendly. The white dress made her look virginal, innocent, even as it pushed up her flushed tits and made them a gorgeous swell above her dress.

And what that shit did to me.

I'd been *dying* since we'd started hanging out and did everything I could to ignore the fact she was a woman (who I'd fucked). I actively had to ignore our history on the regular every day, and that wasn't easy. Sometimes she wore these jeans that would just…

Again, it wasn't easy, and though there were none of her jeans in sight, my second-favorite things… her beautiful full tits were on full display. The fact that I wanted to hug my cock between them because she appeared virginal was fucked, but it was what it was. Aspen Davis was a hell of a drug.

But once more, I had to pretend we were just buds and was hard-pressed when her gaze circulated over me. She tried to be passive about it. That she didn't notice the tight fit of my long jacket across my shoulders, or the fact I wore my cross below the ruffle of my white shirt.

Yeah, that's our cross, snow.

It was the one she'd played with while I fucked her, and that rosy tint bloomed in her brown cheeks before her lashes flittered away. She smiled a little. "Nice tights."

A jab. A condescending, bold-as-fuck jab, but for some reason, I wouldn't have that shit any other way.

I think her smile had something to do with that.

It was small, but it was there, and I think I realized in that moment that was why it was so easy for me to deep-dive into this friend-zone shit she'd put us in. Old Thatcher didn't make Aspen Davis laugh. Smile. Old Thatcher scared her and made her fear him. I shouldn't care about that.

I shouldn't care.

I scanned the crowd next to her. Some of my frat brothers and their dates were doing a coordinated waltz for the alumni, and I could say some equally condescending shit. She deserved that after she ghosted me.

"You look beautiful." Instead, I chose to say that, bold myself when I peered down to see her reaction. Aspen made a look like my compliment didn't affect her, but I didn't miss how her hand delicately maneuvered over the skirt of her dress. Like she was trying to fluff it out and favor herself.

"Thanks," she said.

I smiled.

"And I guess you look nice too," she continued. Her lashes flicked up. "Punisher."

She noticed my dark mask, simple, and though it wasn't my neck gaiter, I think its presence might have done something to her too. Suddenly, those fingers were gathering up in her skirt, and her mask and fan hit the floor. She dropped them, and I immediately picked them up for her. The problem was she went for them too, and we nearly collided.

Yeah, it was dangerous being this close to her. She was a breath away, a kiss away, and that shit made me drunk in the head. Dizzy.

Back off.

I really should ream out this girl for what she'd done to me recently. She'd literally ghosted me, but here I was wanting to kiss her.

I wanted to more than kiss her.

I was sure she saw that in my eyes. The hunger there. That

depth. Neither one of us moved, but she took the mask and fan when I handed them to her.

"And now for our special entertainment. Concert cellist Aspen Davis is here amongst our ranks tonight, and we're honored to have her. Aspen?"

I recognized the voice as one of my frat's alumni. I'd talked to the guy dozens of times, but in that moment, you couldn't even ask me what the guy's name was. I'd get it wrong a hundred times over.

And I think that strongly had to do with Aspen.

Gone was the heat in her eyes, and though the flush in her cheeks was still there, it accompanied a look of dread. Her dark eyes flashed at me, and she didn't immediately move.

"Aspen? Aspen, are you out there? We're ready for you up here."

The alumnus summoned her again, and though she didn't move, I took her hand. She was wearing short gloves. "Snowflake?"

She blinked. Like she'd been in a trance, and since we were both hunkered, I held her up.

The alumnus ahead grinned. He put a hand out toward her. "Aspen Davis, everyone."

The ballroom immediately erupted in applause, and I lost Aspen to the crowd. Her fingers left mine to gather in her dress. She headed toward the front of the ballroom, but very much appeared to be on autopilot.

I clapped for her too, of course, and despite my hand in tonight's event, I'd had no idea she'd be playing her cello. I was happy she was, though. I'd never heard her play in person, and even in all our hanging out, she never mentioned her music really. I brought it up a time or two, but she always changed the subject. I had a buddy who was into the arts, and since he never really liked to talk about his art, I figured she was the same.

That made the fact that she was playing tonight all the

more special, and I got as close as I could to the front. This happened to be near the now vacant piano, and our hired string quartet was gone now too. Their instruments were still there, but the players were gone, and in front of their setup was a chair.

It was for Aspen.

Snowflake took her seat, removing her gloves and placing down her things, and as soon as she did, someone came over with a cello. It must have been hers, but she didn't immediately take it.

The crowd was silent now, and I watched on, curious when she finally took it. She had a music stand in front of her with sheet music.

There was silence.

No one was even breathing. I think we were all waiting for Aspen's music, but it didn't immediately come.

Whenever you're ready, snowflake.

I was excited to hear her, but when she didn't play, that anticipation shifted into something else. It made my heart race, and eventually, my hands clenched.

She wasn't playing.

Aspen just stared at her sheet music blankly, and everyone started looking around. Maybe they thought they were missing something, and that drum in my chest hit violently.

Come on, snowflake.

No matter what my silent chants were, she *wasn't* playing, and something made me grab the piano player next to me. He stood idle, waiting too. I angled down toward his height. "Hey, do we know what music she's playing?"

The guy was surprised I spoke to him. His eyes flashed, but he nodded. He took a book off the piano and thumbed to an arrangement, and thank fuck it didn't appear too difficult.

I hadn't played in a while.

Honestly, this was a rash decision, and I'd chalk it up to

my incessant need to continue to run into the flames for this girl. For some reason, I couldn't stop.

I was addicted.

The music that filled the ballroom wasn't confident at first. Again, I hadn't played for a long fucking time, but sheer adrenaline was pushing me on. I pumped that sound into the ballroom, but only the beginning notes. I looped them around, and in the second playthrough, Aspen shifted around. I saw her in my periphery but couldn't look up from the music.

Come on, snowflake.

I prayed she'd save my ass, and suddenly, it was me waiting for her to save me. This was awkward as fuck, and my notes weren't as strong as they could be. They could be stronger.

And they were when she finally started playing.

She came in during my third playthrough, joining me, and I slowed to match her speed. I was rushing and trying to get through it, but I wasn't anymore.

And the way she played…

I'd heard Aspen's music before. She was famous for a frickin' reason, and she showed this whole room her talent. She played out, killing it with a modern R&B song arranged in a classical style. I only wished I could watch her.

You got this, snow.

She did, and it was sheer adrenaline that got me through my own playing. That and wanting to hear her finish. We ended up doing that together, and when the room erupted in applause, I made sure that wasn't for me.

I got up, applauding with everyone else *for her*, and I think mine was the loudest because eventually, she gazed over her shoulder at me. She had a look on her face I'd never seen, an awe in her eyes like she couldn't believe what was happening.

Like she couldn't believe I'd helped her.

I clapped hard, and a smile lifted her eyes. It pinched in the corner of her mouth too before she faced the crowd again. Holding her cello, she bowed a little, and wanting her to have her time in the sun, I eased from behind the piano. I allowed myself to fade into the crowd, and I didn't stop hearing applause until I made it into another room. That was how loud it was.

I couldn't believe I'd fucking done that, and my gram would be proud. She was the one who'd taught me piano like a million years ago.

It was rare I smiled from a memory of her and me these days. Memories of us usually made me sad, but today, they didn't. I smiled wide, my hands in my pockets. I was kind of distracted in my thoughts, so it took me a moment to realize someone was in front of me.

I got nothing but the smell of cocoa and peppermint when small arms wove around me.

I huffed out a breath, as Aspen's hold formed and her face buried into my ruffled shirt. "Snowflake?"

She didn't answer, and I didn't know what to do. I had my hands up like someone was holding me at gunpoint. I wasn't hugging her back. I guess I'd been taken by surprise.

But with her continued warmth around me, I slowly gave in to her. My arms formed around her too eventually.

And once they did…

That shit felt too good. Especially when I lowered my head. I rested it on top of hers, drinking her in.

"Thank you," she said, and I recalled what I'd just done for her. I'd forgotten about it that quick.

I'd do it a hundred times over if I got a hug like this. "No problem."

She laughed a little. That raspy, light sound like its own kind of music. I hadn't made her laugh in a while, so much time had passed, distance. She settled into our hug. "No, you have *no* idea what you just did. You have no idea…"

I guess maybe I didn't. I'd just done it.

And the hug was over too soon.

She fell away from it first, and then I felt obligated. I noticed her wipe her eyes a little after, and I realized she had tears in them.

Their presence alarmed me, but as she seemed to be attempting to hide them, I didn't call attention to them. Instead, I gazed around in the room we were in, my sight falling over various states of Regency dress. Soft music chimed in from the main ballroom, and everyone in this room started dancing to it. I held out my hand. "Snow?"

It'd break up the tension a little, a dance, and maybe take her mind a bit off what just happened. I didn't know someone like her would ever get stage fright, but maybe that was a common misconception amongst artists. No matter how big they were, I supposed they could get it too.

Aspen studied my hand, but eventually, she took it. She pocketed her fan and mask in the deep pockets of her dress first, and the moment her hand touched mine, I realized me asking her to dance had another objective.

She felt right up against me the moment she was there, and I drank that shit in greedily. It was rare the two of us weren't arguing or hurting each other. The closest we'd been to that was our short friendship, but she'd taken that away.

I slow-danced with her, and eventually, she gazed up at me.

I smiled. "What?"

She didn't say, a subtle smile so warm on her full lips. She just proceeded to press her face against me, and that silenced me.

I tried to draw our dance out as long as I could, but all good things always come to an end. It did end, but when I asked her if she wanted to get some punch, she took me up on my offer.

We ended up taking it upstairs, and only my frat brothers

had access to the high levels of the chateau via the elevator. The owner had given us access codes since we'd rented the whole place out, and lots of my frat brothers planned to stay here tonight since we did. I mean, when the fuck did we just have access to a fucking castle? Needless to say, the brothers were taking full advantage of it. Aspen and I passed a few of them stumbling along drunk, which looked hilarious in their old-timey outfits. Many of them had a girl or guy on their arm, and I had a feeling they'd be taking up use of some of these bedrooms.

I probably would have been too if not for Aspen. I was a fuckboy like the rest of them, but I actually hadn't had physical sex with another person since she'd come into my life. My hand got plenty of action, and there'd been invitations, but I hadn't taken up any offers.

It was something I didn't address with myself, just like the fact I didn't get high off my ass or party anymore.

"You tell Phil where we are?" I asked, Aspen and I settling against a banister. We were at the top of the chateau and could see people milling around at the bottom. They were a sea of colorful dresses and feathered masks, so it was kind of a trip. My lips turned down when Aspen didn't say anything. "I haven't seen him tonight."

That didn't mean he wasn't there, though, and he was paid to be discreet. I knew for a fact he hadn't come with us, though, because only myself and a select few had access to the top level of the castle. Perks came with being a Reed, and it was trippy how silent it was up here. It was like the walls were speaking history with the old statues and paintings.

Aspen opened her mouth, but then closed it. She'd taken off her gloves and placed them and her stuff on the floor. She studied the people below with a small smile. "He's around."

I was sure he was, and he was probably freaking out. I took out my phone. "Should we text him?"

I had his number and planned to give him the code for access up here so he could do his job.

Aspen waved her hand. "You don't need to."

"Are you sure?"

"Yeah."

I put my phone away even though I didn't agree. Aspen was talking to me again instead of ghosting, so I figured we'd be okay for a minute.

Her smile directed toward the punch in her hands. "So you play piano?"

"Uh, yeah." I rubbed the back of my neck. I shrugged. "If that's what you want to call it. My gram showed me a thing or two."

She'd taught my sister and me both, and my dad before that.

"I feel like she showed you more than a 'thing or two.'" She nudged me with her arm, her punch shifting in her glass a little. The area she touched was kind of warm after, but I ignored it. Her eyes warmed. "Seriously, thank you for that. You saved my ass."

"You would have gotten there," I said. She was an artist, and even if she did get some stage fright, she would have pulled it out. I nudged her. "You just needed a nudge."

"I needed more than that." Her stare lingered where I'd brushed her too, and that might have been because I didn't pull away like she had. I probably should have, but what could I say? I was a selfish fuck.

She let me stay in the end, then took down her drink like it was a strong shot. I didn't call attention to that either, but wanted to address something else that had happened. My fingers touched the banister. "Can I ask you something?"

"You don't seem like the type to ask for permission," she said, her dark eyes teasing. She chuckled. "More like an easier-to-ask-for-forgiveness kind of guy."

She was right about that, but I did ask when it mattered.

When it meant something. I braced my arms. "Why were you crying before? After the performance, I mean."

She blinked up, surprised by my question. Her lips lifted. "You noticed that, huh?"

Hard to miss as that shit rattled my insides. Something about seeing this girl in pain did something to me. That was ironic considering the conditions in which we spent lots of time together in the past, but I didn't like seeing her suffering.

I guess I was kind of like that with everyone in a way. My buddies joked that I was an empath, and I called them assholes until I looked up what that meant. It kind of made sense.

"It probably sounds silly, but I was just happy."

I shifted in her direction. "Happy?"

She nodded. "I was happy that I still like what I'm doing." She laughed a little. "Relieved, I guess. I love music, and I was relieved I love it."

Her smile turned sad, and I moved in closer. "Do you not always love it?"

This was probably an invasive question, but again, I had her *talking*. This girl legit was an enigma sometimes to me. She was guarded and worse than some of my friends. I didn't consider myself an open book either, but when I felt comfortable, I opened up with people.

Aspen didn't do that. Not really. Her throat flicked. "I guess sometimes you just forget, Thatcher."

She pushed off the banister, and I followed her with my eyes. I wanted to push her more, but worried doing so might achieve the opposite effect. Instead, I got out my phone.

"We should probably text Phil," I said, scrolling to his name. "I can give him the access code to up here so he can be nearby."

"You seriously don't need to do that."

"Why?"

"Because I lied, Thatcher."

My eyes drew up, my attention. What Aspen said came out in a fit of laughter, but nothing about her expression read funny.

If anything, it was sad.

She lifted and dropped her shoulders. "I lied, so I fired him. It felt silly wasting his time and mine. I don't need his services. Not really."

I didn't understand, but I put my phone away, and Aspen did the oddest thing.

I watched the most rod-straight posh girl I'd ever seen sit on the floor in a white gown. Like… *sat on the floor* and didn't mess with her dress after. She crossed her legs beneath her, and when she put her head in her hands, I sat beside her. I didn't give a shit about my outfit. It was rented and who gave a shit?

"I lied about the whole thing. The threats?" she stated, and my mouth parted. She lifted her head. "It was all bullshit and a way to save face. I froze at Carnegie Hall… a dream I'd literally been working toward my entire life." She shook her head, tears in her eyes again. "I cracked under pressure, so I made up a lie. If people thought I'd croaked because I was scared, that would make sense. If my mom thought *I'd failed* because of that, that would make sense."

My mind circulated over the information. Especially the last part. Her voice had changed when she mentioned her mother. "So none of it was real? The letters…"

"No, none of it."

"Why? I mean." I paused, staring away. "Were you just embarrassed? People get stage fright all the time, snowflake. It's not a big deal."

"No, it's not," she said, that haunted smile on her face again, and I didn't like that. It wasn't like the other one. The real one. She lifted her legs. "It wasn't stage fright, though."

"What was it, then?"

"Me hating my entire life." She laughed, dry. She dropped

her head. "Me feeling trapped and hating everything about what I do. What I worked so hard toward my entire life that meant so much to me…" She cringed. "Me learning to hate it because of schedules. Because of the glitz and glam. Because of the workouts. The diet."

"The diet?" I frowned, knowing she liked to eat healthy, but I figured that was a choice.

"Perfection." Aspen sat up, her back straight. "I have to be perfect. I have to play perfect. I have to make everything we worked for matter."

"*We?*"

"My mom." Her lip moved over the other, her jaw shifting. "She and I have worked so hard. She's given her entire life to me. From the moment I said I wanted to play, she was there and…" She glanced up. "She's dedicated everything. She's been there in the trenches. She's pushed me to be the best."

"Yeah, but if you're not happy, snowflake… If it's making you hate what you love, then that's not cool."

"No, it's not, but—" She bit her lip. "I'm all my mom has. We're all each other has, and that got even worse after Joe died."

I bristled, twitched.

Aspen didn't notice, her stare on the floor. "I'm assuming you know about that. He was your football coach."

It was my turn for my gaze to hit the floor. My eyes narrowed. "Your mom took it hard? His death?"

Of course, she had. The two had been engaged, and that was something I'd known back then. We all had. I mean, it was Coach, and we knew about the woman he'd brought around to football camp that summer. He'd brought a woman and her daughter. Their relationship was new, fresh.

The blood pumped into my brain, adrenaline pulsing, and I forced myself through the mental cloud.

Relax. Relax.

My breaths were slow in and out, focused. I wouldn't get lost in this shit. Especially with Aspen sitting next to me.

"Yeah, Thatcher." Aspen played with her hands. She brought her legs up again, holding them. "I mean, I barely knew him, but my mom was in love. And when he died and the way he had…"

It was a fire. His house in the country had gone up in flames around him. It'd been tragic. It'd been unfortunate.

I forced my jaw to loosen, to listen to Aspen instead of getting caught in my head. At the end of the day, history was fucking *history*, and the moments now were not. These moments now I had to be a part of.

And so I took Snowflake's hand. I made her focus on me, but the action turned out to be just as difficult for me. I braced her little hand, and mine went so white.

Stop shaking.

It was hard, but I made myself. Aspen's other hand touched mine, and when it did, she gazed up.

"I can't disappoint my mother. She's had so many disappointments and…" She had no idea what she was doing to me. That she was calming me down by restlessly rubbing my hand when I was supposed to be helping her. Her touch was like a healing agent, a soothing balm, and that shit calmed every ounce of my fucking soul. "She just wants the best for me. That's all she wants, so it's the least I can do. Be the best for her. Do my best—"

Her hands slipped from mine because I touched her face. I still didn't like seeing this girl so fucking sad and couldn't help it. I smiled. "I think your best, snowflake, isn't having a quarter-life crisis at twenty-one."

We were the same age, and I remembered that.

My thumb brushed the flush on her cheek. "That's exactly what happened at Carnegie Hall. You hate what you're doing, and it'll eventually make you hate everyone who's making you do it."

There might be irreversible damage between her and her mom once it got to that point, and she didn't want that. Life was too fucking short to hate the people who were responsible for the foundations of your life. You could lose them. You could lose them any fucking time, and it wasn't worth it.

I should know considering everything with my gram.

I was lost in my thoughts, my fingers lost when I played with some of Aspen's locs. I liked the way her eyes closed when I touched them and her cheek, and I couldn't stop. I was addicted.

Touching her slowed my heart.

She fixed my soul in the best way, and now, my thoughts were legitimately here. They were here with her and in this moment. They weren't on the past, and I didn't even have to try. Aspen Davis did that to me. She calmed me in every way.

"I don't get it." The words were a whisper from her lips, her eyes still closed. Her face moved into my touch, and I cradled her cheek more. She touched my hand. "Why didn't you just talk to me? Back then, why didn't you just talk to me?"

Her eyes opened, and I scanned them. They appeared so sad again.

"If you liked me…" Her voice cracked a little, and she touched my face now. She did, and that shit felt like fucking heaven. Her brow touched mine. "If you did, I would have listened. I would have seen this. I would have seen *you*. Who you are…"

Her words flared something in my insides. She licked her lips, then licked mine.

A sound rolled in my chest. "Snow—"

I moved to close the distance between our mouths, but she denied me. She guided my mask down over my eyes. I'd moved it up when we came upstairs.

My head literally spun when she did that, breaking the

trance I had on her mouth, and my cock was so hard. I thought that shit would break off in my pants it was so stiff.

Her cheeks tinted, her brown skin flush.

"Keep this on," she said, rising to her feet. She tucked her stuff away in her pockets, and those ended up being the last words she said to me because in the next moment...

She ran.

CHAPTER
TWENTY-TWO

Thatcher

I caught her in seconds. I was out of breath, hard, and very aware of what a bad idea all this was.

But that hadn't stopped me from chasing her.

Again, I'd done so in seconds. I had her delicate wrists in my hands as I husked out breath over her trembling lips.

I wasn't even tired.

It was pure adrenaline that had me this way, and the fact that we were wearing all this Regency shit only added to the game. We were doing such impure shit in what was considered a pure era.

"Snowflake…" I scanned her dark eyes, fully aware we hadn't done anything yet, but I had a feeling I knew where this was going. I'd chased her before, after all. My nose dragged along her neck. "Snow."

She quaked beneath me, her tight curves hugging me all through my costume. We were on the floor in the middle of the hallway.

I'd caught her between two suits of armor.

We were all alone up here beneath flickering candlelight, and I had a choice. I could honor our agreement. We could be cool. We could be friends, and I wouldn't create any more beef with my friends. I could walk away, give her space.

Instead, I gripped her wrists, bringing her body closer. I closed my eyes by her ear. I had something important to say, and she was going to fucking hear me.

"You don't leave this floor," I instructed, and I swear to God, I physically felt the blood pump beneath her skin, her neck warm under my open lips. "You can go anywhere you want, but you don't leave this floor."

We were alone up here, and no one was about to fucking see what I was about to do to her.

She blinked, and I wasn't sure she understood what I was telling her.

But then I said what I had next.

"You get five minutes to hide, run," I said, those dark lashes of hers flickering again. I bit at them. "I'll even close my eyes before I come find you."

And I would find her. I'd find her every time. I didn't care how big the fucking castle was or how many rooms were on this floor.

I'd find her.

Aspen didn't speak, but she needed to. I was all about consent when it came to her.

"You understand?" I asked, my finger curling. It touched her neck. "And if it gets too intense, you use your safe word."

It would be hard to stop, but I would.

Her mouth parted, and I'd never seen her so fucking gorgeous. The tint in her brown cheeks was so goddamn pretty. It made me wonder if her ass changed to the same color after a quick slap of the hand. I planned to test that theory.

"I understand." Her voice had gone raspy again, deepened. She wriggled. "But you're going to need to get your big ass off me."

Oh, she'd pay for that. I bit at her again, and she sucked in a breath.

Who's playing with who, snow?

That was her trying to take back the power, but she lost that the moment she insinuated I should chase her.

I let her go with a quick action, orchestra music playing all around us. Folks were dancing downstairs while we were up here, and there was something depraved about that shit. Naughty.

I closed my eyes, and Snowflake didn't miss a moment of her time. The fullness of her dress brushed me when she got up, then she passed me from the front.

I smelled her.

Soft chocolate wafted in the air. Like a Wonka chocolate river I wanted to drown in. The holiday peppermint that chased it only had me scenting the air like a fiend, but I honored our time.

I even counted.

I did in my head, and I gave her every second of her five minutes before I got up. Before I chased.

She'd chosen a bedroom.

I didn't know if this was purposeful, or if she was just as sex-drunk as me at that point, but that was where she was. She hadn't made my search easy. I'd had to look in the library and what looked like a drawing room before I realized this particular room was filled with Snowflake's glorious scent.

She stood in the middle of the room, an angel in white, a temptress. Her hair was down, and the sleeves of her dress had fallen below her shoulders. She looked like a fairy in the woods, and as soon as I took a step in her direction, she ran again. I chased her around the bedroom, making her laugh when we both got caught in the thick curtains.

I laughed too, adrenaline charging through me, and in the

end, I didn't even use the bed to take her down. We'd started this thing on the floor, and I pulled her easily beneath me.

"Caught you," I said, her laughter fading away with me on top of her. I thought she'd kick or punch me like last time, and I was game for any shit she wanted to toss. I pushed her arms above her head. "What next?"

I think we both knew, and her wriggle let me know she wanted to drag this out. I got her wrists in one hand, physically forcing her to part her legs for me.

Christ, this shit was so fucking hot.

I bit her lip, making her cry out, and she bucked when I forced my hand beneath her dress.

"Fuck!" Her hips bucked, my hand invading that space between her legs. I got her underwear, and she was moving so much I decided to rip them off. Immediately, I forced two digits inside her, and she sucked in a breath. "Thatcher, fuck!"

Fuck was right, and I was so goddamn hard. I pressed my mouth to hers, then took my cock out. "You wanted this, baby. Now, you're going to take it. Open up for me."

She didn't make it easy, her hips corkscrewing, evading. But not once did I hear our safe word. I nearly dropped the condom she was wriggling so much, but as soon as that shit was on, I forced her dress up, then pressed her knees down as far as they could go. I thrust in right away, burying myself and tunneling in her sweet heat.

And holy fucking shit.

The sensation was euphoric, hypnotic. The noise that escaped my chest was carnal, and Aspen's soft cries had me fucking more out of her.

"Louder, snow." I pumped, slapping my hips against the inside of hers. She was lying in a sea of white and moonlight. We hadn't even turned the lights on before I got her on the floor. I squeezed her wrists. "Fucking. Louder. For. *Me.*"

I thrust between each word, each syllable, and her sharp

cries shot through the room. They were almost as loud as my groans, and I covered her loudest with my mouth.

I wanted to taste them.

Something was happening between this girl and me. Something beyond hate or even history. I wasn't sure if she hated me anymore, and I wasn't sure what the realization did for me. I just knew the very thought of not being buried between this girl's legs was ending me.

"Thatcher…"

That and when she said my name. She hooked an arm around me, gripping me. Her mouth touched my ear. "Don't stop."

I'd die if I did, telling her that when I bit her neck. "Come for me, snow. Come for me beautifully."

She couldn't come any other way, and when her hips rocked, picking up with mine, I was right there with her.

"Holy fuck," I ground out, then roared when every inch of me exploded at once. I filled the condom like a fucking teen, and it took everything I had not to collapse on top of her. It physically took restraint and energy, and after, I gathered the skirt of her dress.

I cleaned her with my mouth, soothed her, and the ache escaped her lips again. Her knees pulled in, like she was trying to push me away, but I wasn't having it. I needed her taste, needed her essence.

"Thatcher," she gasped, her thick hips lifting, trembling. She didn't need to tell me she was close to coming again so soon. "Thatcher, I can't," she said, but she could.

And she was going to.

"Don't fight it, baby," I said, kissing her snatch. I dragged my tongue through her folds. "Let me taste you. Let yourself come like a good girl."

The praise seemed to be just what she needed for a second time, and I tweaked her nipple through her dress to take her over the edge. She came for a second time with my face between her thighs, and I licked every drop of what she gave me.

I worshiped it.

It was like a warm gift, and I pulled her languid body to me. Her arms draped around my neck limply, her body spent, exhausted.

"More," she said, finally pushing off my mask. She wanted to see me, and she did when her mouth touched my temple. "Make love to me."

Make love.

I wasn't sure I knew how to do that for her. I'd never been in love before.

But I was going to try.

I picked her up like a damsel, placing her on the bed. I immediately went to take my jacket off, but her hands came up.

They touched me.

I froze, flinching with her hands on me, my chest, and she stopped too. Her mouth parted. "What?"

I didn't know, but my instinct was to control. I was the one who did the directing, the guiding.

Then why was I letting her undress me?

Her hands were hesitant. I assumed because I froze, flinched, and I wondered if she remembered that first time I'd fucked her. I hadn't let her touch me, nor had I in the woods or the motel. Not really.

She was touching me now, and she got up on her knees. The material of her dress was above her brown thighs, and again, I'd never seen a girl so beautiful. She was flushed from her shoulders to her thighs. She was thoroughly fucked but ready for me.

She wanted more from me.

I remained incredibly still as she pushed my long jacket off, and my heart kicked up a beat when she started to unbutton my ruffled shirt. She smiled. "You look nervous."

Did I? Her fingers brushed my chest, exposing it. I took over then, guiding her to her back.

I guess everything was a little much, overwhelming.

I pushed myself out of my head when I sealed our lips, and when my hand slid beneath her gown, I forgot about everything else. My fingers played with her sex, and she gasped.

Her hips rose. "Thatcher…"

The most beautiful fucking sound, my name in this girl's mouth. "That's it, snow. Open up for me."

Her legs parted on instinct, so wide as she gripped her dress and let me begin to fuck her with my fingers. I started with one, but it easily turned into three. She was already primed and ready.

"Take this off." She'd realized now, I was still very much dressed. Her hands went to my shirt again, and I closed my eyes.

Because she kissed me.

It was right on my shoulder, my shirt partially off, and I'd been kissed before. I'd been kissed a lot of fucking places, but never did I let a girl just fucking do that. I was the one who directed the kissing. I was the one who directed the sex.

I kept my eyes closed, allowing her lips to drag across my skin. I didn't move, scared to. I didn't know what I'd do, and I didn't want to hurt her.

So I stayed calm. I made myself, and I opened my eyes when her hands pushed into my shirt. She pushed it down my arms.

And it felt so fucking good.

It felt like heaven, and I didn't fight when she guided it off me, exposed me. I also didn't fight when she made me go to my back. She'd told me to make love to her, but here I was being the submissive.

I was in awe that I was. I was in awe *of her*. She directed this thing when she guided her dress off, the costume gone.

She was in nothing but a white lace bra, and I thought I was in a goddamn fever dream. No way had I pulled this girl who was in my bed. I'd been with models. Heiresses…

But apparently, they weren't Aspen Davis.

Groaning, I forced her down to me, our mouths a hungry dance of licks, nips, and bites. I did the biting, and she cried out every time.

"Thatcher," she husked out, my teeth biting her nipple through her bra. I removed her bra, then sucked on her tit. She yipped out an adorable sound, surprised.

I laved her dark nipple after. I did a long drag down her flesh before it popped out of my mouth, and I groaned because she was the one who took it from me. She pushed her hands on my chest. "Lie back."

I let her do that, push me back, and I didn't let girls… people do that. I hadn't in a long time, and I promised myself I never would again. Never again would I be weak and in a position for someone to take power over me.

Perhaps, that was why I loved what Aspen and I had. I'd been the one doing the chasing, the one doing the overpowering. *I'd always* been in control.

But I wasn't now.

My eyes closed again when she kissed my chest, and I didn't fight her when she dragged a leg over my waist. I even helped her straddle me, the condom in my hand next.

She took care of that too, tearing the thing with a cute little smirk, and why was that the hottest fucking thing in the world? I just may marry this girl after this…

The thoughts were weird, foreign, but something about them hungered me. I didn't take the condom out of her hands. Instead, I let her hold it as I eased out of my pants. It was an interesting little dance getting down to my boxer briefs. I had to remove my shoes and tights first, and the latter made her laugh.

I loved it.

Aspen's own shoes were long gone. They were somewhere in this room no doubt, but I didn't know. Didn't care.

I kissed her laughter away in the end, distracting her, and I got her hands. I helped her ease me out of my boxers.

We both sucked in a breath.

Her hands massaged my cock, the fucker steel under her hands. I almost didn't have the stamina to guide her to roll the condom on because as soon as she touched me…

"Snow…" My head rolled back into the sheets, her hands gliding down the length of me. Her eyes were large, radiating with lust, and when she played with my balls, I nearly came beneath her.

"Does the Punisher like that?" she teased before kissing me. She kept playing with me, stroking me, and even though she was on top, I let her know who owned her. I let her know who she bowed to when I lifted her and angled hard inside her.

She ground out a moan so loud I thought she'd shatter above me, and gripping her hips, I fucked her hard from below. This was so different for me. She was essentially fucking me as much as I was fucking her.

And how much I liked it.

I liked letting her own me. I liked letting her…

"I love this," she whispered, my skin radiating under her hands, sizzling. It felt so goddamn good when she touched me, my shoulders, my chest. She kissed my ear. "I love what you do to me."

I loved what she did to me. I loved how I didn't think and how everything felt free when I was with her. I always said she was like a healing agent.

"You have no idea," I said, feeling myself physically holding back words. I thought I'd never been in love before, but somehow it may have snuck up on me.

She wasn't ready for that, for me to say that, and I knew I wasn't. Whatever this was couldn't get a label right now, and if I gave one, I feared it'd take us out of everything. It'd complicate things, and I didn't want complications.

I just wanted her.

I wanted her so bad, and when I rolled her on her back, I knew I was gone. I knew I was *lost*. Aspen Davis had somehow taken me under her spell, and I fucked her so hard on her back. My thrusts labored, my chest rolling with sweat. I pinned her down and was slick above her, my body gliding along hers, warm and hot with hers.

She bit my shoulder as she came, and that charged me. I roared with angry thrusts until I was coming so hard I thought I'd break the condom between us.

"Snowflake." I pushed the word over her dark nipples, my hands squeezing her thighs and loving their heat, their feel. "My pretty girl."

"My pretty boy," she said back, her hand on my face and her kisses deep. I let her do that too, kiss me. Again, I loved it. She smiled. "Who fucks me like a devil."

"A god, baby, and don't you forget it," I returned, crowding her with my arms and pressing her into the sheets. If I wasn't careful, I might just fall in love with her.

I may already be there.

CHAPTER
TWENTY-THREE

Thatcher

I woke up differently from the last time Aspen and I had been together. There were no screams from fucked-up music, or being ripped from dreams that were even more fucked up. I'd let my past get in my head that night, but that wasn't tonight.

It was nice.

It was normal waking up in a bed surrounded by the scent of Aspen Davis. Chocolate and Christmas surrounded me early. In fact, I wasn't even sure it was morning yet, still dark through the chateau's window.

I shifted, on my stomach. Aspen had been under my arm most of the night. I remembered that, remembered her. She was gone, and rather than look for my phone to see what time it was, I rooted around for my boxers. I didn't know if she'd dipped because we had sex again or what, but whatever the reason, I had to find her.

We'd had a good time last night.

I thought we'd had a great time, so I moved in quick time.

She'd friend-zoned me before, and I didn't know if this was her being scared or what. Honestly, I'd never chased after a girl before. I never had to, but Aspen Davis had me putting my boxers and pants on at the speed of light.

"Snowflake?" I slowed down, a light on once I slowed down enough to see it. It was in the bathroom in the corner. I stood. "Hey, snow?"

I kept my voice light, not wanting to scare her. It was still dark outside, and why did relief hit me realizing that and the fact that the bathroom light was on.

She's still here. She didn't leave.

I blocked out of my head how relieved I was by that. If I didn't, I'd have to think about the fact that she had me so swept up last night. I'd been thinking some crazy shit buried between her legs, shit I probably shouldn't think or feel. I wasn't my best self right now, for anyone, and though things had been getting better…

You'd been getting better because of her.

I didn't know how, but I knew my life had completely changed since she'd dropped into it. I wasn't partying anymore or numbing myself. I put my hand on the bathroom door. "Aspen?"

Aspen didn't answer, but I heard some sloshing in the bathroom, water. Was she taking a bath?

I probably shouldn't invade her privacy, but she had the door cracked, and the moment I realized she might be naked behind this door… Well, that woke the fucker up in my pants hard. She might have wanted me to find her in the middle of the night like this.

Thoughts to get my mask hit me, but I let that go at the sight of her naked back, her glorious brown skin on display. Bubbles surrounded Aspen's tiny form, her body hugged up on the side of an old-school clawed tub. The room was warm and smelled wonderful like her.

A sound hummed in my chest. "Aspen?"

She shifted, and the urge to strip off my pants and join her hit me heavy…

That was until I saw her cringe.

It was just slight, but her face had definitely screwed up a bit. She had her hair in the bath, and it passed over her shoulder when she looked at me. She held her body. "Thatcher?"

An ache hit her face, and when that cringe on her face deepened, I left that door so fucking quick. I got by her side. "What's wrong?"

Aspen shuddered, and the race in my chest doubled, quadrupled. She was basically in the fetal position, hugging herself. Did her stomach hurt or something?

"What is it?" I urged, my hand hovering over her. All she did was shift, and the movement ripped a flash of pain across her beautiful face. My fingers brushed her cheek. "Snowflake, what's wrong? Is it your stomach?"

Alarm bells hit that I may have hurt her or something tonight too. We had gotten rough after a few more rounds last night, and though I'd kissed her, cleaned her up, and massaged her before we'd both fallen asleep, I was new to the aftercare thing. That was me being an asshole with my previous partners, but I was used to normally quick fucks and moving on.

Aspen wasn't a quick fuck, and the thought that I'd hurt her… or seriously injured her really rattled me when she did try to get up. She moved just a bit in the water and fell back in, sliding under the bubbles a little. Immediately, I went to reach for her, but she winced so goddamn hard, I recoiled instantly.

I hadn't even touched her.

I'd put not one hand on her, but that didn't seem to matter with the visible pain that lanced her face. She bit her lip, and when tears pressed through her dark lashes, I thought I'd physically throw up.

"Thatcher," she gasped, her voice strained, pained. She gripped her arms. "Thatcher, I think I need to go to the hospital."

Thatcher

I ended up driving Aspen to the campus hospital. We were in Winchester, but that was only a town over from campus. They also didn't have a hospital in the country town, so I had no fucking choice but to drive her all the way back to campus.

I had to carry her. She couldn't even *walk* let alone make it out of the chateau to my car. I also had to put her in my shirt because we couldn't even get her dress on. It'd been bad.

She'd been in so much pain.

I didn't know in what way. I just knew everywhere I touched her even trying to *pick her up* resulted in a wince or cringe. I felt like my touch burned her, but I didn't have a choice considering she couldn't walk.

I tried to ask her what was going on in the car, my hands clammy and my own voice strained, but she was so uncomfortable I didn't want to make things worse. I ended up keeping things deathly silent, nothing but my heavy breathing in the car and Aspen's occasional soft pants and moans through her pain. Hadn't I been drawing out her soft sounds only hours before? Loving them…

"Can we get some fucking help!" I shouted the moment we were in the hospital. Aspen was in my arms like a damsel, and I cradled her. "Someone!"

People weren't moving fast enough for me, and *fucking finally* someone got to us. They questioned Aspen on a bunch of stuff she could barely answer since she was in so much physical pain, and eventually, I had to bark at someone to stop asking so many fucking questions and just help her.

They put her in a wheelchair.

Seeing that nearly broke me. That she couldn't even move enough to make her way anywhere on her own. I wanted to carry her wherever she needed to go, but once the hospital staff found out I wasn't family, they were removing her from my arms and taking her. I'd gotten lots of looks considering I was only in my costume jacket, pants, and no shirt. They were lucky I managed to get that on and my shoes. Aspen still had my ruffled shirt on, but I didn't give a shit about everyone's *looks*.

I just wanted to know what was going on.

They kept me waiting in the emergency room, pacing. I felt like I was there for hours before someone said my name.

"Thatch?"

It wasn't the someone I expected to see. I thought I'd see a doctor first who was there to finally tell me something.

But if it wasn't a doctor, I was glad to see a friend.

I hadn't expected to feel gratitude upon seeing Wells, but the moment he waltzed through the emergency doors, I was up and feeling not as panicked. Maybe it was seeing a familiar face… I didn't know, but I was happy to see him.

"What are you doing here?" I asked, more than fucking shocked. I mean, I put in my friends' group text thread I was taking Aspen to the hospital, but I hadn't done it to get any of them to come. I'd left the chateau out of nowhere and just wanted them to know where I was. I'd been gone hours before that, but they also knew I was with Aspen.

I told them.

The text message thread had been silent after that. I figured none of them knew what to say.

Wells looked just as goofy as I was in his Regency shit, but at least he wasn't wearing goddamn tights like I'd been before. He strode over in his Pilgrim shoes with gold buckles.

"You texted the group," he said, and even though I had, I still twitched. He scanned the ER. "Where's Aspen? She all right?"

Color me more shocked that he was concerned about her. Dorian and Wolf didn't care so much now that I was hanging with Aspen. They knew I was going to do what I was going to do and had never believed her responsible for anything in my past anyway. They were worried about the effect she would have in my life at first, but they never ever deemed her responsible for anything. They even apologized later for backing Wells initially, which I appreciated.

Aspen wasn't responsible, and though Wells knew that too, he was a little more jaded. The two of us were real fucking close, so I got him wanting to be protective and shit.

Which was why his concern definitely shocked me. I swallowed. "I don't know. They took her back." I felt like I was wavering again, rattled and panicky and shit. I pushed my hands through my hair. "They won't tell me anything. She was in so much pain, man. I don't know what to do."

I felt so vulnerable here, and I normally didn't share shit. I wasn't completely in control of my emotions right now, though…

And my friend saw that.

Almost instantly, he left my side, demanding to see someone, and I let him. Again, I had no control over my emotions, but I followed him. Wells went right up to the front desk, and where I lacked control, he had it.

"We'll get a doctor over to see you guys, and sorry about that, Mr. Reed," the nurse said. "We would have gotten you answers right away if we'd known you needed them."

The nurse saying that didn't shock me before she left. My family and all my friends' families had a lot of power on campus, and if I were in my right mind, I would have used my name to get more answers.

Once more, I panicked, and after Wells got someone to listen to me, he had me sit. He got me a Gatorade and himself a water.

"Thanks," I said, accepting it, but my gaze stayed on the ground. It was the only thing I could do to keep myself focused and not wanting to punch someone.

"Thatcher, I think I need to go to the hospital…"

The look on her face. The *pain.* I physically felt it now like she were here, and I gripped my Gatorade bottle.

"The others were right behind me, but fucking traffic," Wells said, cursing while his thumbs tapped on his phone. "It seemed like everyone at the event was leaving that bitch at the same time this morning."

It was okay, and they didn't all have to come. I guess I wasn't surprised they would. We were all friends, brothers. The girls were a part of that too, and I wasn't just talking about my sister. Being in Legacy was some deep shit. It wasn't about titles or even clout.

It was family.

My family sat beside me now, texting with our other friends and holding down the fort until they came. Wells and I had been at odds, but he was the first one to show up. The first one here, and he didn't know what that meant.

"You're almost out. Do you need another?" he asked me, noticing my Gatorade bottle. The two of us hadn't been waiting long, but I already drank that shit.

"No, I'm good," I returned, now noticing how disheveled he looked. I didn't have a shirt on, but his was completely open beneath his jacket. His dyed hair was also all over the place, and I wouldn't have put it past my friend that he was getting pussy and or dick tonight. Hell, he might have been doing both at the same time. Wells loved to share his partners. It gave him options and being open about that kept people from getting attached and catching feelings.

Wells and I both tended to love them, then leave them. At least, that was how I was until Aspen.

I gripped my bottle, then used it to gesture toward my friend. "You seem like you were busy tonight."

I.e., his ass was getting laid, and he smirked a little. He pointed to my lack of shirt. "Seems I wasn't the only one."

He was right, but like hell was I going to kiss and tell. I might have in the past, but things were different now. They just were.

I felt that difference in our awkward silence. Wells and I never communicated on a deep level. None of us guys did really, but whereas some of the others were by choice, Wells and I didn't because we didn't need to. We were just in tune with the other. The pair of us got one another, and it'd always just been like that. We had our own weird dude language or some shit, and it was nice to smile, to laugh after what he said, which I did.

"I saw you playing piano with her earlier," he said, and I hadn't noticed him when I was up there. I supposed I'd been focused on Aspen and helping her. He smiled. "Haven't heard you do that in a long time."

I shrugged. "Reminds me of Gram, I guess, and better times." It did. She'd connected with me over music since she loved it so much.

"Yeah," Wells stated, looking kind of awkward when he stole a drink from his bottle. He swallowed it down. "It was nice of you to help her."

"She needed me." I faced him. "No big."

It wasn't one, and I'd do that awkward shit again a million times over.

Wells nodded, his blond hair flopping. "I'm sorry I gave you a hard time about her before. You're right. She has been helping you. And you're obviously helping her. I saw that tonight."

I didn't realize I had too until he'd said something, and I smiled a little.

Would you look at that?

Maybe the pair of us weren't so toxic for each other. I spun the empty bottle in my hand. "Thank you for saying that and apologizing."

"I think you and I both know it was long overdue," he stated, sitting back, and though I knew that, I didn't rub it in his face. That would be an asshole move, and I was sure it was hard for him to admit he'd fucked up. It would be for me. We were all some prideful bastards. His shoulders lifted. "I think maybe I felt a little powerless when it came to you."

"Powerless?"

He leaned forward. "Things have been fucked for you lately. They've been fucked for a while, and I've been watching you spiral not knowing what to do or how to help you. I've been giving you space but... Yeah, I felt powerless. I feel like I'm always able to help, but with everything with your grandma, I wasn't. I couldn't help, but Aspen was helping you... Yeah, I felt powerless."

I thought about that, shaking my head. "I'm sorry."

"Don't be." He put his hand on my arm. "And honestly, I don't care anymore who fucking helps you as long as it's helping. It seems like she is."

He was right about that, so fucking right, and that shit had snuck up on me. Suddenly, I just wasn't doing stupid shit. I was having fun again and just having a good time. I was doing that in really simple ways too. Just walking with a girl every morning to class. Lunches and hanging out.

"I'm sure everything with her will be okay," Wells continued. "And I'm sorry again. I owe her an apology too, which I'll give when I see her. I was an asshole."

"Yeah, you were."

Wells shoved me before calling *me* an asshole. Maybe I didn't need to give him a hard time, but that was what brothers did.

The rest of my brothers eventually came. My sister and the other girls were with them, and how fucking hilarious we all looked in our old-school costume shit. My friends and I certainly got a lot of attention, and Bru, Sloane and Wolf's brother, was there too. Once again, I was the only one who'd chosen to wear fucking tights to the event. Bru had worn long boots with his outfit, and he had the same questions everyone had once they got here. He wanted to know how Aspen was doing, and I still didn't have any answers to give.

"What exactly happened?" Sloane, Dorian's girlfriend, asked, and my sister was a worried mess beside her. That didn't surprise me. If I was an empath, my sister was an emotional lightning rod. She couldn't help but feel for others when they were in pain. She had my mom's kind heart like that. Sloane frowned. "You said she was in pain?"

I hadn't expanded on my text to the group about Aspen's condition. Just that I'd been taking her to the hospital because she complained of physical pain. I rubbed my neck. "Yeah. I found her in the bathroom, and she was cowering. I don't really know from what. I didn't want to push her. She was…"

"Hey. I'm sure we'll get some answers." Dorian was holding Sloane's hand, but he used the other to squeeze my shoulder. He tended to take the leadership role in our group, so I wasn't surprised to see him stepping up here.

It was kind of crazy how they were all here for me, but not really. I would have been doing the same, and even though my relationship with Aspen was complicated (something both my friends and I knew from previous occurrences between her and me), they didn't question me being here for her.

And that was family.

My friends and I eventually would have set this place on fire if someone hadn't literally come moments after my family did. *I* would have lit this place up, tired of waiting and being dismissed, but gratefully, a doctor came. She had a clipboard and a warm smile considering the hour.

"Thatcher Reed?" she stated to the room filled with people wearing Regency costumes. If that'd thrown her, she failed to express it. I was sure she'd seen some shit in the ER.

"That's me." I left my friends, and more than one of them started to come too. The first was Wells. The guy was right at my side, but I held him off.

I got this, my eyes said to him, and he nodded. If the doctor called me, it needed to just be me. I didn't want any more complications because none of us were family.

Wells tapped my arm before drawing back with the rest of our friends. I was so glad to have his support again, and I had this handled.

"How's she doing?" I asked the doctor. She'd obviously come for me, and I assumed to give me an update.

The doctor waved me off to the side with her clipboard. The name *Dr. Kearns* was embroidered with blue thread on her white jacket.

"I'm Dr. Kearns, the attending physician tonight," she stated, and though my friends peered on from the waiting room, I kept the majority of my focus on Dr. Kearns. "I'm told you'd like an update, and as Aspen gave me permission to speak to you about her condition, I'd like to inform you about what's going on. She told me to come out and see you as soon as we had her stable."

She had? And she was…

Stable.

I didn't know what that meant as far as her condition. I

didn't know she had a condition at all, so it was good that she was okay.

Stable.

I pocketed my hands, waiting.

The doctor started using all kinds of words, but things were simplified when she used words like immune system and others.

"Aspen has an autoimmune disease," she explained, but her expression didn't appear grave. "She's had it since she was a teen. It's something she takes medication for, but she tells me she got behind on it. It affects her joints and makes it hard for her to move sometimes. It's also very painful if she gets behind on her medication, as her body essentially attacks itself. She had what's called a flare, but we have her on a lot of pain medication. She's already turning around and asking for you."

She'd said a lot, but what kept the alarm from rising was the last bit.

She's asking for you.

I nodded, and after I gave a quick update to my friends, I followed the doctor back into the ER. They hadn't kept Aspen far away, and she was in a hospital bed wearing a hospital gown. She was hooked up to an IV, and the minute she saw me, her shoulders visibly relaxed and her expression brightened.

And why did that shit hit me in the chest?

It was like a full-on hit during a football game, the wind knocked out of me, but only in the best way. I left Dr. Kearns's side and went to Snowflake's. "Hey, you."

"Hey." Her hand lifted from the bed, like she wanted mine, and I didn't resist.

I even laced them.

I didn't know what this thing going on between us was, but the way my big-ass hand ate hers up sent me through clouds of open air. I was turning into a little bitch because of this girl.

Aspen started to rise up, but when she cringed a little, I helped her.

"Don't get ahead of yourself, snow," I said, touching her delicately and adjusting her pillow behind her.

She cringed again. "God, I'm so fucking embarrassed. I'm normally so good about my medications." Her lips turned down. "I'm sure I freaked you out, and I'm sorry."

She had freaked me out, but she appeared to be doing much better now. I mean, she could move, so there was that. "It's okay, and you don't have to be embarrassed."

"It's not, and I am." She huffed. "It's something I've dealt with a long time, so I should know better." She chewed her lip. "Anyway, once I realized what was happening, I got in the bath. Usually, the warm water helps."

That made sense. My grandmother had a form of arthritis, and that was what the doctor said Aspen had. Gram always used heat for hers.

"I fucked up." Aspen studied our hands, and even though I helped her adjust, I hadn't let go. "Thank God my mom's not here. She would have gone straight momanager and swiftly lost it on me for being absentminded, careless." She shook her head. "She's really protective."

It sounded like it, considering what she'd told me before. They were all each other had, so I got it.

Aspen faced-palmed herself. "I'm so sorry—"

"Hey, don't be." I wouldn't let her cover her face, holding her other hand. I guided her locs away from her cheek. "And you're handling it. Your mom doesn't need to worry."

"Yeah, I'm really handling it, seeing as how I ended up in the hospital."

"Your thoughts were probably on other things," I said, my hand loose in hers now, but I didn't allow myself to let go. I glanced up. "And I'm sure I didn't help."

I'd caused her all kinds of stress and shit since she'd been here at Pembroke.

This probably was your fault.

The thought this might actually all be because of me caused my hand to leave hers, but she reached and tugged at my jacket. A smile replaced her previous frown, and the way that shit lit up her dark eyes sent me to those clouds again. It made me feel warm and light, and I was a big motherfucker.

"You know, I actually think it was your fault," she said, and when I started to move away, her fingers gripped my sleeve weakly. She clearly wanted me to stay, but might not have the strength to pull me back.

Wanting to make things easy for her, I came back. "Well, I'm sorry about that."

"Don't be." Her smile got bigger, brighter. She wet her full lips. "For the first time, I wasn't thinking about being perfect. I was just having fun and…" Her head tilted. "You make things fun, Thatcher Reed."

I make things fun.

I hadn't expected this, nor the effect her words had on my insides. My soul. I glanced at her hand, my smile teasing. "So you're saying I made you careless."

"Fuck, yeah, you did, and thank God for that." She sat back, her smile teasing now. "I think you and I both know I'm way too high-strung."

I started to agree with her. I liked getting in her head and messing with her, but she moved and a little pain lanced across her lovely face.

"You should probably get your rest," I said, adjusting her pillow again. Her eyes creased warmly in the corners, and that told me she appreciated it. I smiled. "I should probably give everyone another update on how you're doing."

"Everyone?" she asked while adjusting her position in the bed.

I nodded. "All my buddies are out in the waiting room

with their girls," I said, and Aspen's mouth fell open. I laughed. "Yeah, and you got my sister worried sick."

"They..." she started. Her head shook. "They all came? Why?"

I wasn't surprised she asked. I touched her bed. "They're my family, and they probably knew I needed them even though I didn't ask." I shrugged. "Wells came first."

Aspen blinked once, then twice. He hadn't been her biggest fan, so she probably really was surprised about that.

"They knew you needed them?" she questioned, and even though I'd taken a step away, I returned. I didn't say anything, but I took her hand once more. It felt good in my hands. We felt good together. I did need my family...

But I also needed this.

"I'm glad you're doing okay," I said, and I glanced up to see rose color her brown cheeks. "I'll let you go, though, so you can sleep. I'll keep my phone on me, though, in case you need something."

I'd probably crash in the waiting room or something. It was still kind of the middle of the night, but I wanted to be nearby.

"Thatcher?"

She said my name as I got to the door. She was completely up in her bed, her hands in her lap. "Can you stay? I'll talk to the staff. Um..."

I came back, picking up a chair along the way. I placed it next to her bed, and when she put her hand out, I took it again.

"If I must," I stated, feigning exasperation. It made her laugh, which was the point. "Night, snowflake."

"Night."

I put my head to the wall after sending a text off to my friends. Someone probably would come in here asking me to leave. I wasn't family or anything, but I wasn't going anywhere. Not if she wanted me here.

Aspen closed her eyes eventually, and when she did, I leaned down. My hand still in hers, I crossed my arms on her bed and rested my chin on them. I just looked at her and did that until my own eyes got heavy, closed. I thought she was asleep, but she wasn't.

Her hand in my hair told me that.

It startled me at first, being touched, but then I settled into it. I drank her touch in like a dying man in need of water. She hit every electrode in my scalp, and I felt that shit down to my shoes.

"Snowflake?" I questioned, my eyes still closed. I couldn't open them even if I wanted to. Her touch just hit different, was perfect.

"Yeah?"

"What would you say if I told you I'm having feelings for you?"

Her hand hesitated for the briefest of moments before she continued playing in my hair, and my heart stopped with it, believing I'd said the wrong thing.

"I'd say you weren't the only one," she said, her voice dreamy, light. I knew when she finally fell asleep because, after that, I didn't. I just lay there with her hand in my hair.

And wondered how in the hell I'd fallen in love with this girl so hard and so damn fast.

Aspen

I think I was in love with Thatcher Reed.

I didn't know when it had happened, but the how…

Damn.

Seeing him last night had only solidified it, and I wasn't talking about how he'd made my body sing, which he had. What we created together sexually was freaking amazing and only added to how I'd felt earlier that night about him. I'd been sick even thinking about picking up my cello after what had happened at Carnegie Hall, but not only had I done it…

I'd loved it.

I truly loved my craft, and he had helped me see that. He brought the passion out of me again. I hadn't even known he played piano, but he'd stepped up for me in my hour of need.

And then there was the hospital.

I was truly embarrassed by that, and my mom's voice had certainly been in my head when it'd all been going down. How I couldn't take care of myself and I needed her, but Thatcher was right that I had this handled. I could take care of myself, and I didn't need to play weak to make my mother happy. I truly had this, and he helped me see that.

I was smiling when the sun hit my face that morning despite still being in the hospital. I think that was because I knew I'd see him.

"What would you say if I told you I'm having feelings for you?"

I wasn't sure how deep Thatcher's feelings went, but he'd admitted them.

One thing at a time.

I was hopeful… for whatever this was happening between us, and I did plan to tell him how deep my own feelings had gotten. Maybe this guy was making me brave.

I sat up that morning, a lot easier to do now that I wasn't in so much physical pain. I was still aching in my shoulder joints and my hips, but they weren't locked like they had been last night. Dr. Kearns had said I just needed to take it easy while I got caught up on my medications. With some movement exercises, heat, and of course, my meds, I'd be right back to where I was. I just had to give it time, and though that made me sad since I did want to play my cello now, I'd give it all the time I needed for my joints to heal.

Flowers.

Something floral hit my nose, and when I turned, my eyes flashed wide. I wasn't the only one in the room, but the other person wasn't Thatcher.

"Mom?" I blinked once, then twice. A woman with braided-back locs in a peony-colored suit arranged a huge bouquet of flowers by the window. For a second, I hoped she was a nurse who'd just decided to forgo her scrubs for something more fashionable that morning, but the moment the woman angled around, I knew my wishes fell on deaf ears. I gasped. "Mom…"

What in the entire… *fuck* was my mother doing here? I didn't know, and I definitely one hundred percent hadn't called her. I wasn't exactly talking to her after she'd set up for me to play at a charity event I hadn't wanted to play at. That charity event had turned out to be for a fraternity, and though I hadn't known it was Thatcher's, I'd quickly found out when I discovered him there last night. All the frat guys had worn pins on their lapels.

Everything had turned out okay in the end obviously, but still.

Mom glided over, her expression a mix of concern and frustration. I knew the look well. She never enjoyed pushing me as much as she did. She loved me, cared about me, but she also wanted me to be the best. She put her hand on the bed, then me. "How are you doing? Damnit, Aspen, you should have called me the moment your flare happened."

So she knew about it? How? I started to adjust but stopped, still stiff. "You know?"

"Of course I know. Despite the fact *my daughter* didn't call me about it." Her frustrations rang now, and she didn't bother to hide them. She huffed. "The hospital called me. I'm your emergency contact here on campus, you know, and you *should* have called me."

Maybe I should have, but I hadn't. I didn't need to. I was okay.

She smoothed out my bedding. "I imagine this happened because you weren't taking care of yourself. You got behind on your medications, didn't you? I knew I should have called you every day to remind you. Jesus, Aspen, what were you thinking?"

I wasn't, and that'd been the point. I was so goddamn *tired* of thinking so much, of being perfect.

Where's Thatcher?

I needed him, but not for strength. I just wanted him here, and I didn't want my mom.

Alarm bells hit me that he wasn't here but Mom was. Mom wouldn't be happy that he was around. She had a vendetta against him and his family after what had happened when we were kids since he'd gotten off so easily after taking me. It was a vendetta I had as well, but things had changed.

While my mom huffed around the room scolding me about how I managed to do what I had to myself, I eased my phone out from beneath me.

Me: Hey, my mom is here, and you should probably make yourself scarce. I still don't think she's your biggest fan, so I'd be on standby wherever you're at until you hear from me.

He was probably in the hospital somewhere, but he shouldn't be here in this room right now. I didn't know what my mother would do honestly, but freaking out was a given. She was already on one hundred right now.

"God, this is the day from hell. Between your flare and finding that crazy boy poking around the hospital…"

My head jerked up. "What?"

Eugena Davis swiveled around. She'd obviously lost her composure, but she'd gotten it back when she settled her hands. "I don't know if you remember Thatcher Reed. Of course you do since he terrorized you."

It was like my lungs went tight, locked in my fucking chest. "Thatcher?" It came out more in a gasp than a voice, and my mom glided over again.

"Yes, and I don't want you to be scared, honey, but…" She placed her hand on mine. "I caught him coming out of your room this morning. I didn't recognize him at first. He's obviously gotten older, but with your threats and us not knowing who did them still, I instinctually called the authorities. I mean, a strange man coming out of my daughter's room…"

My lungs squeezed harder. "You had him arrested?"

"I did, and with the previous history between you two, that was easy. I recognized who he was after I followed him, and they caught him in the cafeteria. He was getting food or something."

Probably for me. In fact, *I knew* what he was doing was for me. It was just something he would do. Something he had done. He used to bring me breakfast every day.

Short breaths left my lips. "Mom…"

"But he's gone now. So you shouldn't—"

"Mom, it was bullshit!"

She twitched after what I said, and I was frantic, spiraling. Thatcher had been *arrested*? What the fuck? Mom frowned. "Honey—"

"Thatcher did not threaten me. He did nothing wrong, and you're going to fix this."

"What are you talking about, baby?"

She wasn't listening to me, and I wasn't in a place where I could properly explain. I threw my bedding off, a big mistake since I was still stiff. The pain lassoed the entirety of my tender joints, but I didn't care.

Thatcher…

I had to get to him, but my body was betraying me. On top of that, my mom started to fight me, and I screamed.

Mom's hand shot off my arm. "Sweetheart…"

"Thatcher didn't stalk me. I never had a stalker." My head hit the pillow, tears of frustration falling from my eyes. My body had betrayed me, yes, but I'd also betrayed myself.

"I think your best, snowflake, isn't having a quarter-life crisis at twenty-one… You hate what you're doing, and it'll eventually make you hate everyone who's making you do it."

Thatcher's words played in my head, but I didn't hate my mom. I *hated me* for what I'd done to both of us. I'd become complacent and let her think what she was doing was okay. I'd allowed her to hurt me, and though that didn't justify her treatment at all, I'd made it easy for her.

Mom put her hand on my arm. "Baby girl, what do you mean?"

"I mean, you're making me hate everything that I used to love. The things that gave me life…"

"Aspen—"

"You're making me hate cello, Mom!" I yelled, and she distanced. I swallowed. "I hate the schedules. I hate the diet. I hate the *fucking hustle*, and I do want to be the best. I do, but you're making what I love work for me, and that's making me hate it."

And maybe it was also making me hate her too, and it definitely would if we continued the way things were. Thatcher was right.

Mom's throat jumped too. Her mouth parted, but no sound came out. Like she wasn't sure what to say.

"I froze at Carnegie Hall, but it wasn't because I received threatening letters," I said, blinking down tears. My fingers gripped the bed. "I made up the letters."

The shame hit me. That I'd gone to such lengths to put a pause on my life. That I was hating everything so much that I had to escape.

Mom's expression fell. "You made them up?"

I nodded. "I just didn't want to do this anymore."

The letters had gotten me off tour. The threats had gotten all this to *stop*.

It had gotten my mom to stop.

She'd prioritized my safety, and I knew she would. Me being physically threatened was the only thing that would force her to take action. I'd suggested lying low by going to college. It was something I'd always wanted to do anyway.

"Why did you freeze, then, honey? You..." She touched my arm. "You hated it that much? This life?"

I didn't use to, and it took playing with Thatcher for me to realize I did still love playing cello. I just didn't love the hustle of it. It sucked all the passion out of it, and I just wanted to *play*.

"It was because of me... You froze because of me, right? Because I pushed you?" My mother had come to her own conclusions, but they weren't far off. Actually, they weren't far off at all. She put her hand over her mouth. "I made you hate it."

The words were to herself, and I never saw my mom cry. She was always so strong, but her eyes glassed a little.

Her lashes flashed. "It was because of me."

But it wasn't just because of her. I shook my head. "I need to do things differently, and I never let you know that. I'm sorry…"

"Honey." Her arms came around me, so tender, so gentle. She was trying not to hurt me. "Honey, I'm so sorry. I got lost. I thought this was what you wanted."

It was but not at this price.

"What can I do?" she asked, pulling away. She placed her hand on my cheek. "What can I do to fix this?"

I handed her my phone. She needed to make a call, and maybe after that, we could fix this, us.

We'd do it together.

CHAPTER
TWENTY-SIX

Thatcher

The call came to get me out of jail before I could make my own. My dad could have gotten me out of here in seconds, and my name even faster than that. The latter would have eventually gotten back to him, though, me being in here, and I didn't know how to explain what had happened.

It wasn't my secret to tell.

I knew Aspen's mom had had me arrested, and after I got my cell phone back from the cops, I put the rest of the pieces together. Aspen tried to warn me to keep my distance, but her mother had obviously seen me at the hospital. I'd been downstairs trying to get us some breakfast.

Damn.

The charges had been weak at best, but I'd been accused of stalking and making threats against Aspen herself. These were the accusations, and Aspen's mother obviously had a little power. Her daughter was essentially a celebrity, so that made sense. Once I found out the charges (and who had accused me), I hadn't fought the arrest. I hadn't known *how*.

The threats on Aspen's life had obviously been bullshit, but her mother didn't know that.

I'd simply been in the wrong place at the wrong time, and calling my dad to get me out would have made things more complicated. I would have had to tell him something, and I wasn't about to out Aspen. I couldn't and didn't want to.

"I'd say you weren't the only one…"

Fucking hell, that girl… She obviously had me gone because never in my life would I have fallen on the sword for anyone but my family. I had for her, though.

Fuck, I really am in love.

I must have been, and now I kind of got how crazy my friends got when they initially got with their girls. Dorian had been *fucked* when he met Sloane. He'd literally lost his fucking mind, and Wolf had proposed to Fawn in the end. Out of all of us, I think my buddies had seen me getting engaged before that dude. *Me* who was the ultimate fuckboy.

Yeah, love had made my brothers crazy, and I supposed me too because I never did call my dad or use my name to get me out of my cell. Again, that call came from somewhere else, and I think I got an indicator when the police escorted me out. There was a woman filling out paperwork at the front desk, and I froze upon seeing her.

She did too when she glanced up. Aspen's mom did a double take and was a colorful sight in this dingy-ass precinct. She wore a full-on pink suit and black pumps, the things clacking when she ultimately cut me off. I'd planned to pass her.

She didn't allow me, but she stayed her place, kept her distance. She held her purse like I'd steal it, and I certainly didn't blame her for her reservations about me.

I mean, I'd kidnapped her daughter once upon a time.

She also eyed my interesting state of dress, her dark eyes peering down the length of me and flashing at my bare chest.

I was still wearing my costume from last night sans shirt. Aspen still had it.

She made no mention of any of it, though, standing there in silence. I swallowed. "Ms. Davis."

Even *my voice* put her off. She gripped that purse in a vise grip, and that was a big reason I'd tried to sneak around her initially. Aspen had told me to avoid her mom, and that was for good reason with our history.

"Thatcher Reed," she stated, clipped. She put her purse higher up on her arm. "They treat you well back there?"

I blinked, surprised she asked. I nodded. "Yes, ma'am."

Her jaw moved a little. "Well, you didn't do anything wrong, so… in this instance, so…" She shook her head. "I had to make things right. My daughter told me the truth about everything. How there were no threats, and she's been spending time with you."

Whoa.

"I don't understand that. Her hanging out with you." Ms. Davis shifted in her heels. "But you've obviously reconciled."

We had, and I started to say something, but the woman locked up. I thought because I moved when I started to speak. I put my hands in my pockets, keeping my place. "I'm sorry for the confusion."

A curt nod in my direction, but she didn't loosen up. "I'm down here filling out a statement, which is why I'm at the precinct. I dropped all the charges, and I wanted to let you know that, I suppose."

"I appreciate that, Ms. Davis."

Another curt nod. "Anyway, I have, but I just also want to let you know I don't agree with… whatever you and my daughter are doing. I don't know how it is you both have come to be in each other's lives, but I think you know, Thatcher, how inappropriate that is. Or maybe you don't or you don't care, but it is. What you did to my daughter was sick when you were kids. It was cruel and damaging, and she spent years trying to get past you and what you did to her."

My stomach locked, not wanting that. I hadn't wanted to hurt her, the opposite.

Ms. Davis's head lifted. "So there's that. If I had things my way, she'd have nothing to do with you, but my daughter is grown, so…"

The conversation was ended by the older black woman. She passed me, and I simply should have let her.

"All due respect, Ms. Davis," I said, not able to hold my tongue for some reason. I should have but I didn't. I glanced over to her. "There was a lot more going on back then… during that time than you knew."

I really shouldn't have said shit, and the moment I did, my stomach tightened again. Ms. Davis's lips parted, but before she could say anything, I walked away. I nearly clipped a few cops, though, and a cluster of them made me stop. They all rushed to the door, and Ms. Davis had to move too as more rushed from behind her.

"What's going on?" she asked a cop at the front desk, and I was curious too. That was a lot of fucking cops moving out of this place at once. Ms. Davis frowned. "Is something happening? Should I be concerned?"

The woman sounded like a concerned citizen, but it was bold of an ask. Aspen was bold too, so I wasn't surprised.

The cop behind the desk was a lady cop, and her mouth turned down. "I'd avoid Queenstown Hospital and the surrounding areas, ma'am. There's unfortunately a hostage situation going on there right now."

"A hostage situation…" Ms. Davis's voice faded into a heavy breath, and almost instantly, her dark eyes flashed in my direction. She rushed in the same direction the cops went, but I ended up ahead of her. Queenstown Hospital was where we'd both left Aspen.

It was where I'd left Aspen.

CHAPTER
TWENTY-SEVEN

Aspen

"Please… Tell me what it is you *want*."

I'd seen some things. Some wild things, but a guy coming into my hospital room with a gun was topping the charts. The fact that he had a costume on only added to the crazy situation that was happening here. Honestly, the costume wasn't the weirdest part. He wore a Regency outfit like Thatcher and I had last night.

I shifted in my bed, the guy circling me. He didn't have the gun on me, but he had one. It was at his side, the man middle-aged, a redhead. At least, I believed him to be. His hair was cropped short, but he had a trim layer of stubble on his face. He also had bags under his eyes like he hadn't slept.

I shifted again as he came closer, something weirdly familiar about him. I'd never seen him before. I think I'd remember.

Honestly, I was too busy thinking about how this whole situation had happened. The man had run in here like a bat out of hell as I'd been dozing off. Of course, that had startled me, but before I could ask him who he was, *he had a gun* on me. The irony of that wasn't lost on me. I'd made up threats in the past.

This was a real one. Tried and true, it was real, and I couldn't back up against the bed far enough. His Regency costume wasn't quite like Thatcher's and mine had been. With his long blue jacket and ruffled ensemble, he looked more like a servant in the period. Not a guest.

The man was beside my bed now, my gaze following him. I twitched when he grabbed the phone at the side of my bed, my phone.

My mouth parted. "What are you—"

He placed it at the foot of my bed, then backed away. He nudged toward my phone with the gun. "Pick it up."

I did even though I was still stiff, my chest fucking locked. My hands fumbled with it. I was still sore and panicked, and the guy shook his head like he was about to shoot me for the fumble.

"Stop freaking the fuck out. Just pick it fucking *up*," he said, starting to assist me, but I got the phone. There were missed calls on it, texts…

Thatcher.

He actually started to call me while I had my phone in hand, and on instinct, I went to answer it.

That was a mistake. The guy with the gun noticed and put the gun in my face.

I raised my hands.

"You don't do shit until I tell you," he stated, his voice clipped, serious. His Adam's apple bobbed. "Now, listen really carefully. This will be easy, and I don't want any trouble."

He didn't want any trouble? Again, the irony. I swallowed. "Look, if you want money—"

"I want fucking *justice*, and you're going to use that phone." He paused, using his gun again to nudge toward the air. "To call your fucking boyfriend and get him to admit what he did."

Okay, so there really were some weird fucking things happening in this room right now. "My… boyfriend—"

The guy was moving fast again, and it freaked me out so much I dropped my phone. It landed in my lap about the time the man put his own phone in my face. He had a picture on it. My picture.

I was with Thatcher.

It was a stolen moment between us, one I thought was stolen, and though others were around while we danced at the time, I hadn't seen them. I'd been lost in the moment. I'd been with Thatcher and it was easy.

My lashes flashed up, the picture of Thatcher and me dancing on the man's phone.

"You're going to call him," the man said, backing away. "Get him on the phone. Now."

This was crazy he wanted me to call Thatcher. Especially since Thatcher had just tried to call me. My throat jumped. "Why do you want me to—"

"Just." He pressed the gun to my head, and I shrieked. The whimper that hit my throat was more of a terrified groan, but the instant it sounded, he shook it out of me. He growled. "Stop fucking *crying*. You didn't do anything wrong, but he did, and you're going to get him to set it right. You will or there will be trouble. You hear me?"

I didn't understand…

And I was crying.

A steady stream of tears fell down my face, but I couldn't stop them. I was panicked, terrified. I got my phone, using steadiness I didn't have in me to scroll to my missed calls. I touched Thatcher's name and the phone dialed.

"You calling him?"

I nodded and even showed him my phone. "Look. It's ringing."

He no doubt could hear the ring just as I could. Even still, I put the phone on speaker mode.

I sat with bated breath waiting for Thatcher to answer. I didn't know what he'd done to this man. I didn't know what this was, and I wanted Thatcher to pick up just as much as I didn't. If Thatcher was in trouble with this man, truly, then I didn't want him anywhere near this situation. I didn't want him involved, and the fear suffocated me then. I may be on my own in this in the end…

Because no way would I let this man hurt him.

TWENTY-EIGHT

Thatcher

The moment Aspen's face flashed on my phone screen, I answered. It was a candid picture of her I'd taken during one of our campus lunches. She hated it, her face full of salad, but I loved it. She was calling me via video call, and I couldn't have answered the phone fast enough.

"Thatcher..."

She said my name before I could say hers, and I started to respond, but then the camera shifted.

She wasn't alone.

A dude was with her, a grizzly-looking motherfucker with a buzz cut and five o'clock shadow. He was also wearing a Regency costume, but before I could question anything... do anything at all, the camera shifted again. It honed in on the gun pressed to my girl's temple.

Ice hit my veins, cold, frigid-as-fuck ice, and Aspen's image went away completely when the man filled my phone screen.

"Wherever you are, get yourself alone," he said, his voice

clipped, serious. His eyes narrowed. "Don't speak until you do and don't draw attention to yourself."

That'd be hard to do at the present. I wasn't the focus of attention where I was. Not when literally there was a hold-up at the local hospital. Everyone in this entire precinct was buzzing about it, and the only reason I was here was because being at the hospital had been pointless...

They weren't letting anyone in.

I called my father after I'd been turned away. I didn't know what he could do, but I needed to either get inside that hospital or know what the fuck was going on. I told him Aspen was in there, and the moment he knew, he started making calls from home. I hadn't heard back from him yet or any new updates from my friends. I called them to let them know what was going on, and they started making their own calls to help. Their parents had connections just like mine and were apparently helping my dad in whatever way they could once my friends had called them.

I loved my family, my friends there for me. After I'd been turned away from the hospital, they had all offered to come to the police precinct to wait things out with me. I figured being there listening in on conversations was better than nothing, but I let my friends know it was best they stay away from the place. It was chaos here and wouldn't help.

I waited here for news from both my friends or my dad, Aspen's mom with me. She too had been turned away despite the fact her daughter was in that hospital. She told the cops that, but she'd been informed a lot of people were in there, and she needed to wait to hear news like everyone else. The police weren't letting anyone in or out via the directions of the guy inside holding up the place.

He said he'd start filling bodies with bullets if anyone left.

Apparently, he was watching news coverage of this whole hold-up on his phone. He'd know if someone left, so the cops were playing things safe.

Ms. Davis and I hadn't known what that meant for Aspen, but I think we both hoped (and prayed) she would remain out of all this. This was a big-ass hospital, so odds were, the fucker doing all this was nowhere near her.

This obviously wasn't the case, and my blood managed to run even colder. Aspen hadn't been answering her phone when both her mom and I had tried to call, but Ms. Davis also said Aspen had been sleeping when she'd left the hospital.

I lifted a hand so the guy on my phone could see, then made an exit. Again, everyone in the police station was buzzing, and Ms. Davis wasn't paying me any attention. She was still on her phone, probably still trying to call Aspen.

I ended up taking the call outside around the building, and the moment I was alone…

"I don't know who you are, but if you hurt her, I'll dig your grave myself," I said, gazing around. There was no one out here, but I kept my voice low.

The guy on the phone said nothing, shaking his head. "I'm sure you would," he said, his response to what I said curious, but I gave no reaction. His head tilted. "It really is you, isn't it?"

I unfortunately couldn't hide my reaction to that. I blinked. "I don't know you, man."

I'd never seen this fucker in my entire life, but something seemed oddly familiar about him. His buzzed hair was red, and I didn't know a lot of redheads but something about him…

Like stated, something familiar was there, but I couldn't put my finger on it.

"You don't," he said, and my chest got all caved at a sudden flash of Aspen on my screen. Soon enough, it wasn't just a flash. The fucker leaned against the wall beside her bed, and the way she winced had me gripping my goddamn phone. The man's nostrils flared. "But I know you. You look different, but it is you. Actually, it's because of her I figured it out."

The camera moved, and Aspen filled most of my screen again. Her eyes closed when the gun touched her neck, and my stomach churned. My throat filled with bile instantly, but I got control of my shit. I had to for her.

I held up a hand again. "Look, man…"

"Nah, I'm talking, kid," he said, and he was older than me, well older. He looked to be pushing fifty considering the dull color in his eyebrows and the age lines around his eyes and mouth. He may have been younger. He had bags and shit under his eyes, which made him appear older. Fuck if I knew how old this dude was. I didn't care considering he had a gun pointed at my girlfriend.

Aspen was *mine* whether I'd put that out there between us or not, and if I never got to officially ask her to be my girl, *I would* put this guy in a fucking grave.

"She looks the most like she did when you guys were kids," he said, staring at her, and Aspen's gaze zoomed over to him. Her dark eyes narrowed, clearly confused, and I was too. This fucker knew us? The guy's jaw clenched. "I saw her playing cello and the name matched, her name. I was a bartender at the party you both were at last night."

"And that's supposed to mean something to us?" I questioned, wondering how this fucker *knew us* when we were kids. If anything, that just raised this fucker's ick factor ten points.

"It will," the guy said, and his focus didn't leave Aspen. "I saw you come in and play with her, then later, dance with her. Then later…"

What the fuck?

Aspen's head darted back, a horror ringing her brown eyes, and that didn't shock me. We both knew what had happened after we'd danced. We'd fucked *a lot*.

And that dude had been there?

How much had he seen? I'd waited to get her naked until we were in a room, but had he followed us in there. Watched us...

"Who the fuck are you, man?" I asked, getting both parties' attention. "What the fuck do you want?"

The seconds in which this guy didn't talk had me ill, nauseous.

"I want you to admit the truth," he said, then sniffed before rubbing his nose with the hand holding his gun. Aspen closed her eyes, whimpering at the gun so close to her face, and it took all I had not to lose my shit.

The guy kept us in silence while he peered at his phone for a second. I didn't know what he was watching, but I assumed the news coverage since I'd heard about his threats.

Aspen's attention focused on me. Her full lips parted. "Thatcher—"

"Don't talk to him." The guy pointed his finger at her, and I cursed. I bit the inside of my cheek after, and I clamped down so hard I drew blood. Right away, my mouth filled with the taste of metal, but I didn't say shit about it.

I was too afraid. I was too goddamn afraid he'd hurt her, and I felt powerless like how Wells had admitted the same to me yesterday. Aspen was there at the hospital, and I was here. I was and couldn't do anything.

"You killed my brother, you shithead," the guy continued, sniffling again, and I realized now it was emotion that was overcoming him. He was visibly fighting down an emotional response, his face filled with red color, and Aspen blanched beside him after what he said.

I did too. I didn't know what the fuck this dude was talking about. My hand patted the air. "Look. I don't know—"

"Don't you fucking," he started, biting down whatever initial thing he was going to say. He directed the gun toward the phone. "I saw you. You were different, *younger*, but it was you. You left my brother's house, but not before setting that shit on fire, so don't lie to me, motherfucker!"

Aspen's eyes expanded in width, huge but mine hadn't matched. I didn't even need a mirror to confirm that because I had no visible response to what he said. I didn't because I wasn't surprised by what he said. Not like her, and most definitely not in the same way.

The fact I had no outward physical response hadn't stopped my insides from contorting, though, restricting. The bile choked my throat in a new way now. It was sharp, *violent*, and I nearly lost control of the angry sea going on inside my gut.

The red hair, grizzly…

"It was you," the guy continued, his voice somehow reaching me through the screen. It was like I had left my body and was now watching myself watch this guy on the phone. He got closer to it. "You killed my brother. You burned his house down while he was inside it."

While he was inside it…

"I watched you leave. I watched you—" The guy cut himself off again, rubbing his face. Meanwhile, Aspen lay there horrified. Her mouth gaped open like she was watching the most gruesome part of a horror film. Her gaze shifted between me and the guy, and she really couldn't do anything. She was trapped in that bed whether she had an aliment or not and forced to listen to this guy. He looked at her. "Did you know about it? What he did? You were obviously his friend back then."

Aspen said nothing. I mean, what could she say? She was obviously rendered speechless, and when her focus veered over to me, I avoided eye contact like I could through a goddamn phone.

"Thatcher, what is he talking about?" she asked me, and I turned back just in time to see surprise register on her captor's face. It read there, just briefly before his head tipped back.

"You didn't tell her," he stated, but there was no question in his voice. He rubbed the shadow on his face. "You murdered my brother… the man who was going to be her stepfather, and you never told her."

The horror on Aspen's face elevated. Her cheeks filled with so much red, and I lost it. I gripped my phone. "Stop, man—"

"What kind of sick fucked-up kid does some shit like that," the guy gritted, and the blood pounded all up in my head. It made me dizzy, nauseous, and I had to use the wall of the precinct to stay upright. The fucker did look familiar to me. So goddamn familiar. The guy's eyes narrowed. "I never did find you. I didn't, and even though I told the cops about some snot-nose kid leaving the scene, they didn't believe me. I had no proof. Told me I was fucked up after everything that happened to Joe and seeing shit."

Joe…

Even the *name* made my world tilt, spin like I was on some fucked-up Ferris wheel and couldn't get off.

I was holding on to the wall now, and from some far-off place, I could hear Aspen.

She was pleading.

"Thatcher, what's he—" Her voice broke, and I dared to glance up. Something that made my nausea shift into overdrive was the expression that had overtaken her beautiful face.

A labored swallow passed through the column of Aspen's throat, and when her eyes crinkled, cringing, I thought I'd vomit. The way she looked at me… so much uncertainty in her eyes. Terror backed it, and that was what made the sickness swirl. Terror was only a click away from something else. It was so close to *fear*, and that was a way I never wanted to see her look at me again. When Aspen came back into my life,

I hadn't given a shit about that. But now was different. *Now,* the way she looked at me had me gripping the wall to the point of breaking the skin on my hands.

Aspen cringed again. "Thatcher, what is he talking about? Joe? My mom's fiancé, *Joe?*"

He had been her mom's fiancé, but he'd also been my coach. He'd coached my friends and me for three summers at football camp. Three before he'd died and left this world just a little bit better. His absence from this earth had left the planet purer.

Cleansed.

There was nothing bad about the fact that that man was gone. There were absolutely zero things bad about that, but how did I say that to the girl looking at me through a phone screen? The one waiting to hear something, anything from me that would stamp out this guy's accusations. I saw Aspen and her mother back then. They'd visited Coach for part of the summer and stayed with him, a new almost family. The guy had brightened their world, and anyone could have seen that.

Anyone could have seen the lie.

Coach had been real good at creating bullshit, a persona that he was a good person, and so many people had believed that shit. He'd been good at that shit. My throat jumped. "Aspen..."

I couldn't finish. Once more, I didn't know what to say, and Aspen blinked. She did just once before that terror on her face clicked over to the next level. That fear finally danced in her brown eyes.

"Thatcher, tell me what he's saying isn't true. Thatcher..." Her lip trembled, quivering. "Thatcher, tell me he's lying. You were nowhere near that fire Joe died in. You weren't."

Each word she said was cracked, fractured, and honestly, the sentence was hard to make out. Each word she said was so light. It was timid when she wasn't. Aspen Davis was the girl who told me off. My girl.

She wasn't looking like that girl when I finally managed to make eye contact with her again. I'd been looking at the ground and trying to do anything but upchuck my lack of breakfast. I hadn't eaten anything this morning, but I felt like I'd had a goddamn buffet with the way my stomach lurched.

Aspen shook her head. "Thatcher—"

"He can't tell you that." The man beside her, the one with the gun, stared at me coldly through the screen. He spoke to her, but he only looked at me. "He can't because he did it, and now, he's going to tell the world what he did. I found you now, boy, and you're going to own up to what you did to my brother."

He hadn't been looking for me that well. After all, I was the kid who'd taken Aspen for most of that summer. I'd held her captive, but he obviously didn't know about that or didn't know it was me who'd done that. The fire had happened later that year, but not much later.

I'd made sure of that.

"Thatcher..."

My eyes closed, Aspen's voice too much for me. I could literally hear the emotion in it. Like she was on the cusp of crying and doing everything she could to hold it back.

"Thatcher, please tell me it's not true," she continued, her voice strained. "Thatcher, you didn't have anything to do with that fire. Tell me."

Like Coach's brother said, I couldn't. I gazed up. "Sorry, snowflake."

It was real fear now, real horror on her lovely face. The back of her head touched the bed. She looked like she was going to spiral, and my apology, well, that was only for her. It was for this reaction *only* because I couldn't apologize for what I'd done. Not really.

Not ever.

"So here's what's going to happen," her kidnapper said, but I was only looking at Aspen.

She hugged her little body. Like she was trying to fuse herself into the bed, and I lifted my hand like I could touch her, hold her, and make whatever she was feeling go away.

I'm so sorry, snow. I'm sorry.

"You're going to hold a press conference. Get the news. Get the cops. *Get everyone* and tell the world what you did to Joe," the guy with the gun continued, but I was haunted, hollow. "You got two hours, kid. I'll be watching, and you better do that shit right. You will or your girlfriend gets a bullet in her brain."

It was like something clicked for me then. Especially when he ended the call and took Aspen from me. He took her away, and I was walking, running. I was going to see my girlfriend again.

Even if she had to know the darkest parts of my soul.

CHAPTER
TWENTY-NINE

Aspen

I was *shaking*. Thatcher was a killer? A murderer…

This didn't make sense. No, it didn't at all, and I refused to believe it. I…

"Sorry, snowflake."

I gasped in the bed, not even bothering to hide the tears in my eyes. I ended up pressing my face into my pillow to mute my sobs. If I audibly wailed, I didn't know what this guy with the gun would do.

"I guess it's nice to know that you really didn't know."

I lifted my head, but only silently. The gunman's expression was grave after what he said, but not cold. He didn't look the way he had when Thatcher had been on the phone or even when the man had initially threatened me.

He gazed out the window. "Though, it doesn't really help. My brother is still dead."

And I didn't get that. It made absolutely zero sense. Thatcher had been what? *Twelve* back then? Twelve like me, and what kind of twelve-year-old was capable of killing a man?

My thoughts sobered me, as I realized exactly what kind of kid would do that. One who had done terrible things before and had held another kid against her will. That kid had been me.

No. No. No.

Another wail came out from my throat then, and it was hard to hide it. My current kidnapper didn't give much of a reaction to it, but he gazed down.

"Sorry, kid," he said, and him saying that surprised the hell out of me. He shook his head. "Your boyfriend's obviously sick."

I gasped again, my sobs in my hand. The guy with the gun had moved to watch his phone, and I didn't know what he was looking at. He might have been looking for news articles regarding Thatcher's press conference or the hold-up. I didn't know. I was too busy focused on the ache in my chest.

"Sorry, snowflake."

Still shaking, I curled up on my side, numb. I didn't even feel my aching joints anymore. Thinking about Thatcher and all the conversations we'd had made things even more chilling for me. I'd talked about Joe's death with him and how it'd affected my family, my mom. Her fiancé's death had changed everything, and Thatcher had just listened to it, completely unaffected. I didn't know if he was a sociopath or what, but I wanted to get sick in my hospital gown. I'd given him my body.

I'd given him my heart.

I didn't know how long I lay curled in that bed, but it felt like hours, days. It couldn't have been because the guy with the gun made no moves to hurt me. He said he'd kill me if Thatcher didn't come through, and if all this was true about Joe, then a part of me just might die.

If I'd had anything in my stomach, it would have come

up. I knew it would, and I flinched when the guy with the gun approached. He darted in my direction, and I moved sharply into the bed. I quickly realized he wasn't coming at me but to me. He stayed at the side of the bed with his focus on the door. He had his gun pointed toward it, and I easily discerned why.

The door opened.

The movement was timid, cautious, but it was moving, and the guy gripped his gun. He sneered. "Whoever the fuck you are, stop, or I'm literally going to shoot this girl—"

"Please." The door stopped, but not before a hand eased through, a voice… "*Please*. It's me. Don't hurt her. I just want to talk. I'm not armed."

I gasped again, and the man beside me did too. Shaking, the gunman kept his focus on the door. His gun was shaking too, and I wondered if he'd ever shot anything before. Or maybe he was just scared. He sniffed. "This is a stupid move, kid. I gave you simple instructions."

I shrieked when that cold gun touched my temple, and I thought he would shoot me when the door swung open. It'd been quick after I screamed, and Thatcher filled the door. He had his hands up, and he was still in his Regency costume without the shirt. Thatcher knuckled his hands. "Please, don't shoot her. I swear to fuck, I just want to talk. I don't have any weapons. It's just me here."

"I don't want to fucking talk, kid, and you're *killing her*," the gunman gritted, and tears squeezed out of my eyes when that gun dug into my temple.

I couldn't help but think, was this it? Was this how I'd die? Like this, and with a broken fucking heart. It certainly felt that way, and I closed my eyes.

The guy grabbed my head, making me open my eyes. He shook me. "I don't want to do this, kid. I don't want to hurt her."

I looked at the man upon hearing the crack in his voice.

Pain lanced his face in the same way it had as when he'd been talking about his brother. He probably didn't want to shoot me, but in my heart, I knew he would.

"Don't make me," the man threatened, and though Thatcher stayed in his place, he appeared horrified. Like he did care. Like he was affected when he stared at me, then the gun.

Thatcher wet his lips. "Like I said, I don't have any weapons. I don't have anything. You can check me. I legit just came to talk to you. I'll do whatever you want after that. I just... Just let me say what I have to say, then I'll do whatever you want. No one knows I'm here, and I brought no one. I swear to God, I just want to talk."

It was rare I saw true fear on Thatcher Reed. He was so big and all-encompassing, but this situation had his large body shaking and his hands clenching. It had his expression tight and a cringe on his lovely face. He was so beautiful, handsome.

Thatcher's throat flicked, the bright light in the hospital room reflecting off his earrings. "Please. Check me. I have no weapons."

The man with the gun seemed to be debating, and something told me he really didn't want to shoot me when the gun lifted off my temple. I released a breath, and Thatcher's broad shoulders sagged when he did the same.

"You move, I shoot you both," the guy said, coming over to Thatcher. Thatcher nodded, and after he did, the man put a hand out. He patted Thatcher down *cautiously*, and the expression Thatcher made while he searched him knotted my stomach. His jaw locked as well as his body. He even closed his eyes, and his hands knuckled so tight whenever the guy touched him.

His reaction had me gripping the bed. Especially when Thatcher started shaking. There was a quake to his big body every time the guy touched him, and at one point, he was breathing through it. Like he was two seconds away from punching the guy in the face and the opposite of logic made me want him to give in to the urge. I didn't want that man touching him. Making him look that way…

Eventually, the pat-down was over, and I gripped the bed more when the guy pressed his gun to Thatcher's head. "Go over by the window. You talk over there."

Thatcher nodded again, and his body finally relaxed with a decent proximity between them. Actually, he appeared entirely more calm despite a gun being on him. Like he was more bothered by the man touching him than putting a gun on him.

I might have misread the situation. I didn't know, but at the present, I was more so focused on the fact that a gun was on him. I didn't know it was possible for me to feel more scared, but I did in that moment.

I loved him.

I did despite the gunman's accusations and even Thatcher admitting them. I didn't know what that made me. I just knew someone I cared about was in danger, and I couldn't do anything to help.

"This was really stupid of you, coming here…" the gunman said. He was by my side again. "I mean, how the fuck did you even get in here?"

"A window on the first floor. No one saw me." Thatcher's focus stayed on me, his expression calm but haunted. He was clearly trying to reach me from across the room, and I was here, but my mind was in a whirl.

Thatcher…

How was it possible he'd done the things he was accused of? He was so kind and sweet. True, he was a big guy, but he was such a teddy bear when he let his guard down. None of this made sense.

"I wanted to say you don't know the whole story," Thatcher continued again, only keeping his attention on me. His face screwed up. "You don't know shit."

His voice cracked, and my heart tattered at the sound. He looked to be in physical pain. Like someone was cutting him with a dull knife.

"There's nothing you can possibly say that could excuse what you did to my brother, you sick fuck," the man said, and Thatcher winced. I did too. The man cringed. "Nothing you can fucking say."

His voice cracked too, but Thatcher gave no reaction to that. If anything, the man wasn't there anymore. It was like just Thatcher and I were in the room then. His eyes narrowed at me like he was almost pleading...

Snowflake...

I could almost hear his voice in my head, and the next thing I knew, he wasn't looking at me anymore. It was like *I* wasn't in the room, Thatcher's blue eyes only on the gunman now.

"Nothing, huh?" Thatcher questioned, and the gunman shook his head.

The gunman sneered. "Absolutely nothing. You—"

"How about the fact that your brother raped me for two summers."

My blood ran cold. It *chilled* especially when Thatcher continued.

His jaw moved. "It started when I was ten, and it would have continued if I'd let it..." His attention stayed on the man, his voice even, empty. "If I hadn't stopped it."

If he hadn't stopped it...

I heard screams then, and they must have been inside my head because no one appeared affected by them but me. No one wailed internally but me.

He was raped. He was...

The gunman froze after what Thatcher admitted, his eyes wide, but he didn't lower his gun. "I… I don't believe you."

I blinked over to Thatcher, and I wasn't just crying on the inside now. I physically had to hold my sobs back with my hands, actual tears flowing over my fingers. Thatcher wasn't looking at me, though. He still had his focus on the man, calm. My insides called for him to look at me, to lean on me.

He wouldn't.

He kept his focus ahead. He stood sturdy by the window, solid. He nodded toward me. "She's why I stopped it. I was scared for her. I was scared of what he'd do to her." He gazed away. "She was my same age, and I saw her for the first time when he brought her and her mom to camp one year. He was my football coach. It was football camp and Aspen and her mom were visiting."

I was shaking now, blinking down so many tears.

"I didn't want him hurting her too," he said before glancing up. He still didn't look at me. I didn't know if he couldn't or… He dampened his lips. "She wouldn't have me if he married her mom. She wouldn't have me like my friends did. Coach took that sick shit out on me, and I took it *for years* so my friends wouldn't have to."

I bent over in the midst of my sobs. I gripped the bed, and that was when Thatcher finally peered over at me. His stance was still sturdy, but a pain I'd never seen before rimmed his blue eyes. He'd hidden it so well, hadn't he? So well from me…

Thatcher…

"I took her from him," Thatcher continued, speaking to the gunman but talking to me. He cringed. "I panicked, and I took her the summer I saw her. I didn't want Coach to hurt her, and I thought I could figure out a way to prove what he was doing to me. What *he'd done* to me. The abuse didn't happen that third summer, but I figured it was because he'd moved on, and that scared the ever-loving shit out of me. That he moved on to something else. Someone else..."

He was still focused on me, and I made sure to shake my head. I wanted him to know the truth. I hadn't been abused, but I might have been...

If not for him.

Almost instantly, Thatcher's eyes closed. Like relief hit him in a *whoosh*, and my heart ached. He took a step toward me. Like he wanted to hold me and how I wanted him to.

He saved my life.

I hadn't understood back then. He hadn't told me. Why hadn't he told me?

As soon as Thatcher took the step, he thought better. He stayed his place, facing the gunman, and it was a good thing he did. The gunman rushed over to him and put the gun directly in Thatcher's face, and I screamed.

Thatcher closed his eyes as the gun touched the middle of his forehead, and I couldn't breathe.

Please, God, no.

I'd never been really religious. I believed in God, but I didn't go to church on the regular. In that moment, though, I pleaded to a higher power. To save him. Save the man I loved, please. He'd been through so much. He'd saved me.

"You're lying," the gunman gritted, and I forced myself to open my eyes during my prayers. The guy was shaking, and though Thatcher's eyes were closed, he wasn't. He still stood there, calm, composed. The gunman shook. "You're lying, dude. *Fucking* lying."

"Why would I make this shit up, man?" Thatcher questioned, then slowly placed a hand on his chest. "Why. Would. I. Make. This. Shit. Up!"

Each word radiated in the room. Like they hit all the walls and amplified. They shot through me like a dagger, but the man with the gun didn't lower it.

"He used to play this old record while he did it. I don't

know if it got him through it or…" Thatcher's jaw clenched, still calm, still focused. "It was this old shit from like the sixties. A guy singer—"

"A record?" the guy asked, and Thatcher nodded. The man squeezed the gun. "We had this record. Our dad gave it to us, and we used to play it all the time before he died."

The two referring to music had me thinking about it. Especially when Thatcher referenced how old it was. I didn't really listen to old music, but the last time I'd heard an old song by a male singer, I definitely remembered.

I chillingly remembered.

I hadn't understood that night. I hadn't *gotten it,* but I think I started to now. Thatcher had had such a strong reaction the night we'd hooked up at that motel, that old music playing next door…

Oh, God, Thatcher.

I really wanted to be sick now, and Thatcher's reaction to what the man said only hardened his expression. His nostrils flared. "Well, Coach used to play a record all the time. Every single fucking time."

I gripped the bed. "Thatcher…"

He wouldn't look at me again, staying focused on the gunman and the situation.

"Joe played it a lot after we got our niece," the gunman said, backing away a little. Actually, he backed completely away, and it was as if he was talking to himself. His own musings. His jaw moved. "Our niece came to live with us after our sister passed. Our sister was in an accident at this power plant she worked at. It was bad."

The room was silent other than what he said, deathly silent, eerily silent.

The man rubbed his mouth. "Kimi… our niece, couldn't have been any older than nine." His gun lowered to his side, his head shaking. "And Joe used to always play that record for her. I got Kimi in a home now. She's not well. She's…" The guy started shaking. He stared at the ground. "She's troubled and self-harms a lot. I thought that was just because she lost her mom. That she was sad because she—"

The man pressed a fist to his mouth, the same fist that had the gun.

"He used to play that record. All the time he used to play that record for her..." The guy's voice broke, and the only movement in the room was Thatcher when he faced me. The gun wasn't on him anymore. It wasn't on anyone. It was angled toward the ground, forgotten.

Thatcher said nothing in response to what the man said, but he didn't need to. I didn't think he needed to try to convince this guy of anything else, that his brother was a pedophile, a monster.

The man swallowed, and his sight shifted from Thatcher to me. He went back and forth, back and forth so many times.

"I'm sorry," was all he said, and then, he was leaving the room. I didn't focus on him because Thatcher finally made his way to me.

And how quickly I fell into his arms.

It was like home there. Wonderful. Solid *home*, and I whimpered so hard into his chest. "Thatcher..."

The tears racked my body, his bare chest drenched beneath his costume's jacket. I couldn't stop crying, but it wasn't for myself.

Not by a long shot.

Thatcher said nothing during my sobs. He just held me, his big hands warming my back and holding on to me so tight. He was consoling me, and that made my tears fall more. That he felt the need to do that for me when I should be doing that for him.

"Snowflake, I was so scared," he said, the words a whisper in my hair. "I was so fucking scared he'd hurt you. I thought I'd fucking die, snow. I would die if he..."

I pinched out more tears, but again, none of those were for

me. He really was only thinking about me right now, my safety and well-being. He was doing that just like he had for me the summer when we were twelve. It was the same thing he'd done for his friends before that. Thatcher Reed took abuse for *all* of us, and here he was trying to protect me again.

Here he was trying to save me again.

Thatcher - age 12

"Holy shit, she's cute."

I glanced up from the lunch line, Wells ahead of me. Dorian and Ares were ahead of him, and they turned too after what Wells said. My friends and I focused on a girl across the mess hall, and she stood out since she was the only girl here. This wasn't a boys' football camp, but girls never came. Probably because they didn't really play too much.

The girl Wells was talking about was cute. She was a black girl with long hair that looked like braids but weren't quite. They were thick, and she had them in a braid over her shoulder. She was with a woman who had her arms around her and was grinning. They were both speaking to Coach Barlowe, and that was when I looked away. I didn't care who that dude was talking to.

Wells continued to say stuff about the girl, but I wasn't listening anymore. That wasn't good because my friends knew when I was quiet since I wasn't usually. I wasn't quiet. Except for when we came to camp. I was quiet, and I played ball, and that was it. Dorian and Ares called me focused when I was here. Yeah, I was focused.

I nibbled on my chicken strips, kind of in and out of the conversation when my friends and I sat at our table. Everyone wanted to sit with us since we were popular, but this was just our time. No one else got to sit with us during lunch.

"Yeah, I heard Coach is marrying her mom," Dorian said, and the chicken got weird in my mouth, tasted weird. Dorian shrugged. "Maybe he'll lay off working us so hard this summer if he's getting some."

Dorian nudged Ares, who smirked, but Ares was more focused on his sketchbook. Ares's lunch tray was full, but he barely ate when he was really getting into his sketching. He was an artist. Wells was howling, though, after what Dorian said, but I wasn't. I looked at the girl again, focused.

"Her mom's getting married to Coach?" I asked, casual, and Dorian nodded. I frowned. "You sure? How'd you hear about that?"

"I overhead some of the assistant coaches talking," Dorian stated, then glanced over at the girl and the woman who I now assumed was her mom. They were still with Coach. Dorian dropped an arm on his chair. "She is cute. Maybe I'll talk to her."

"I think this one may be Thatch's," Wells stated, and when Dorian asked why, Wells shoved me. Wells threw an arm around me before directing a finger at the girl. "I mean, look how he's looking at her."

I was looking at her, but I was thinking harder. I couldn't taste the chicken in my mouth at this point, and rather than try, I pushed my tray away.

"I'm going to go do some suicides," I said to my friends, and they were used to me just leaving sometimes. At camp, I was always moving, always training.

It was the only thing I could do to curb the nightmares.

Tiring myself out, exhausting myself let me sleep, but I

didn't that night. I couldn't. I tossed and turned thinking about a cute girl and the fact that this summer hadn't been like the last two so far. There hadn't been any late nights in Coach's cabin, music… There hadn't been any of that, and I saw that pretty girl's face when I woke up in a cold sweat. I ended up in the bathroom half the night, and after I was done vomiting up the little bit of chicken I'd eaten, I sat by the lake. I thought there. I thought there for hours, and when I was done, I had a plan.

I just hoped I could actually do it.

Knight

The call came from my wife. Our son was a hero. He'd gone into that hospital and done something I hadn't even had a chance to do, nor the authorities. He'd done that.

He'd done that.

He'd been holding Aspen Davis when his mother and I finally got to him. Greer, my wife, had been in tears and our daughter, Bow, the same. I hadn't wanted Bow anywhere near the hospital yet, but she fought us. She was a Reed, and she got her way. I didn't regret her coming when I saw my family together, my wife holding on to our son and our daughter crying in between them. Aspen Davis was nearby with her own mother, who was crying and holding her. I'd seen the two in a similar state years ago. I had no idea what had compelled Thatcher to take her back then, but he had and the mother's and daughter's tears had been from that day. They'd been because of my son.

Now, Aspen's mother's tears were for her daughter *and*

my son. At one point, she held on to Thatcher too. She squeezed his hand, saying, "Thank you."

Thank you.

Greer, Bow, and even Aspen gazed on while Aspen's mom shared a moment with my son. The nightmare today was over. The gunman had turned himself in to the authorities.

I had no thoughts about him at the present. If I did, I'd wrap myself up in that. I'd want to kill something and not be present with my family. I needed to be here. I needed to be strong here.

"Dad?"

My son's voice brought me over to where he stood by Aspen's hospital bed. I'd waited, wanting his mom and his sister to have their time with him. It was hard for me to express emotion outwardly. It came from years of Reed men and their tough edges. I'd lost my dad too young, and he'd never had problems with emotion from what I remembered. He hadn't despite having been raised by my stern grandfather. I loved my grandpa despite all his sins, but he hadn't been the best caretaker after my dad had passed.

I folded a hand behind Thatcher's neck. "You're okay?"

"I am, sir," he said, nodding, and I did too. I should have hugged him in that moment. The fact that he was okay and the heavy possibility that today could have gone the opposite of how it had made me want to pull my son to my chest and never let go.

But then... the moment passed. I waited too long, too goddamn long, and others sought my son's attention. His sister did when she hugged him again, and their mother did when she embraced them both.

Thatcher gazed over their shoulders as they did, his hand leaving mine. Apparently, I'd taken his hand or maybe he'd taken mine. Regardless, we both let go at the same time, and I stepped back again.

I always stepped back.

The evening was long, and I spent much of it caring for my family. I received calls from everyone, my brothers and their families. Royal Prinze, Lance Johnson, and Jaxen Ambrose may have started as friends, but they were my brothers, my family. Ramses Mallick was a part of that too. We'd all gone to high school together and, later, raised our children together. They all wanted to stop by the house and visit with Thatcher, them and their kids. My friends' sons and daughters had created their own family unit with my own kids, but I kept everyone at bay for the evening. The Reeds ended up spending that first night as a family along with the Davises. I invited Aspen and her mother over, and our household staff made everyone dinner. I'd been told Aspen had a pain disorder, but she was doing well, so she and her mom were both able to get her out of that hospital that was swarming with media and onlookers. That was the last thing any of us needed tonight. Tomorrow it'd be there.

Tonight, I made sure it was a safe night for the Reeds and the Davises. It was a calm night and keeping myself busy with that allowed me to feel like I had some semblance of control. Like I was doing something for my son and my family. We'd had so much chaos in our home lately. So much pain.

A Reed man stayed busy. A Reed man stayed calm, and that was what I did for my family that night. We all had a nice dinner and fine conversation. It was over pretty late, but that was what we'd all needed.

"Let me take you home," came my son's voice later that evening, stopping me.

I'd stumbled across my son on the terrace of our property. I'd been taking a walk, a calming one, and caught him and Aspen Davis out there. He had his hands on her shoulders after having spoken to her.

She smiled at him. "I need to go with my mom."

"Let me take you both home, then," Thatcher said, a smile

overtaking his own mouth. My son smiled a lot, but not usually in front of me. It gut-punched me that that was the same way I'd been with my grandpa. Smiles left when the father figure entered the room. The climate of the room changed, serious, always so serious.

Aspen shook her head with a grin. She denied him again probably knowing how silly the request was. Aspen and her mom had driven here, and they obviously didn't need a ride.

That didn't stop my son from asking, but his smile didn't leave despite the denial. He simply put his arms around her, and a visible ease settled over him when Aspen touched her forehead to his. I didn't know what was going on between the two of them, but they'd been inseparable since the hospital. Thatcher was only a breath away from her at all times.

Her hands settled on his chest. "I love you," she said before lifting her head. She stared deeply into his eyes, and he did the same before his hands covered her cheeks. He wasn't smiling anymore. In fact, he appeared nothing but awed before scanning her eyes.

"I love you too," he said, and I backed away after that moment, seconds before he leaned in and the two were going to share an obviously more intimate moment. My son was going to kiss a girl who he was in love with.

My son was in love.

I made rounds through the house in thought after I left. I hadn't done tonight very well in regards to Thatcher. I'd reacted toward him and the situation he and Aspen had been in in the typical Reed way. I'd been sturdy, unmovable, but inside a war was there. It was one my wife had seen on many occasions. At one point, Greer had even taken me upstairs after Aspen and her mom had arrived.

"It's okay," my wife had said to me, the two of us sharing our own stolen kiss. "It's okay. He's safe."

I didn't know what I'd do if our son wasn't. If I lost him too...

I'd kissed my wife back then, and I didn't make it brief. Actually, it was only because we had people downstairs that I'd allowed her warm body to leave from within the confines of my embrace. I took those moments. I got calm again, and I stayed that sturdy rock. I'd done good and maintained composure.

I was about to go upstairs but stopped upon hearing a noise. It was in the kitchen, but the staff should have cleared things by now.

As I got closer, I knew who was in there before I even entered, her smell unique, warm. It reminded me of my childhood and the few moments I had before she was stolen from me. My mother had been in a coma a good part of my life and woken up when I was in college.

"Hello there," she said, the woman aged and so beautiful. My mother was a showstopper, a performer in her day. Her eyes went warm from across the kitchen. "You're up late."

I was up late, but so was she. I entered the room. "I could say the same about you, Mrs. Reed." She was still a *Mrs.* despite my father passing.

My mother wasn't confined to any part of the house, but we did like to know where she was. I supposed with all the people in and out of our home today, she'd decided to roam a little.

That was fine, and I took the barstool at the kitchen island in front of her. I simply watched her, her hands moving as she prepared pie of all things at close to midnight. She'd taken one out of the fridge, one she'd made, and I couldn't deny her when she offered me a slice.

"I haven't seen Knight, but it is late," she said, taking so much care preparing my slice. She even rubbed the plate when some crumbs escaped. She glanced up. "Were you guys up working late? He studies so hard, my boy."

Knight, aka me, was my son, Thatcher, to her. We looked so much alike, and that confused her. I forced on a smile. "We were, and he's gone to bed. He's such a hard worker, and you're right about that."

She believed I was his live-in tutor. That was easier for her to understand my constant presence in the house and something I'd come up with to help the situation. A Reed was always sturdy. A Reed was always strong.

I picked at my pie, then ate it quickly in two bites. My mother watched as I did and beamed so bright suddenly.

"My son eats like that. No fork. Just wolfs it down," she said, actually getting me to laugh. Imagine. She shook her head. "You remind me so much of him. I'm glad he has you. You're so kind to him. Good with him."

"Thank you, ma'am," I said, then took her hand when she reached for mine. If she engaged, I did too. Sometimes she'd even embrace me, but that wasn't tonight. Maybe another day. Another time.

I made sure my mother got up to her room, then mentioned to Greer that she was there. Greer was her nurse for all intents and purposes, and of course, my wife knew where my mother was. She admitted she'd even watched us in the kitchen for a beat before going back to bed. She said she'd wanted us to have our moment.

I didn't know how I was so blessed to have that woman in my life. She kept me from self-destructing when things got the hardest, when my mother started to forget me and leave for the second time in my life. Greer kept this whole family fucking strong and was way stronger than me.

I didn't go to bed right away. I peeked in on Bow, happy my family was all in one place tonight. She and Thatcher lived on campus, but they were staying home tonight after everything.

Bow slept soundly in her room, and after I knew she was okay, I started to go to Thatcher's room to check on him. I didn't make it there because I heard another sound downstairs, voices.

Janet, our live-in housekeeper, was in the foyer, and she wasn't alone.

"Thank you," I heard Aspen Davis say before accepting a black jacket from Janet. I'd been striding down the staircase from the second floor, and both Janet and Aspen glanced my way when I made it downstairs.

"Mr. Reed," Janet said, nodding, and I gave her a curt nod in return. "Miss Davis forgot her jacket."

Already having noticed the exchange, I tipped a nod in Aspen's direction too. She held her jacket, a small smile on her face, and Janet ended up excusing herself. Perhaps, she noticed I lingered, and I did want to speak to Aspen.

"How are you doing?" I asked her, but not just because she'd hired my company in the past. I was human and asked on a human level. She and my son had been through hell today.

"Doing as well as I can," she said, and I could only imagine. She bunched her jacket in her hands. "I wouldn't be here at all if it wasn't for Thatcher."

Her statement sobered me to the fact that he'd been there, *that my son* had been in the line of fire, and of course, I knew that. I did, and every time I thought about it, the man who threatened him...

"You don't know how grateful I am that you're both okay. That you're both safe..." I said and realized when I felt my insides coiling that I needed to excuse myself. My usual walk of the property should do it to calm this down a bit, my insides. I'd already done my rounds, but I'd do it again. I'd do it a dozen times if I had to.

I wished Aspen good evening, but she called me.

"Mr. Reed, I," she started, bunching her jacket again. She braced it so hard before looking at me. "I can't tell you how much your son means to me. What he did for me..."

I lost her voice in the evening air, and suddenly, she touched her eyes. There was a shine there that she didn't bother squeezing out. Not everyone hid their emotions. Not like me, and I admired people who didn't. It was another kind of bravery I didn't always have.

"He's done so much, and I—" She paused, then finally glanced up. "But you know, don't you? What he did back then? Everything with the cabin and everything…"

"The cabin?" I questioned, curious about her bringing that up, the past, and she blinked, gasped. She backed up, and when tears started to leave her eyes, I stepped forward. "Aspen, what do you mean? The cabin? What about it?"

"I just meant that…" She pressed her jacket to her mouth, shaking her head. She gasped again before blinking down more tears. She swallowed. "I just want you to know your son is the best person I've ever known."

She left me with those words before she scooted off. The door breezed open, and I followed just long enough to see her dash down to her waiting ride. Her mother was in the front seat, and after Aspen was inside the car, the window went down.

Ms. Davis lifted her hand. "Good night, Mr. Reed. Thank you so much for this evening. I'll never be able to thank your son for what he did. Truly, I'm so grateful."

She squeezed her daughter's shoulder, but Aspen only gave a small smile at me before gazing ahead. She took in a harsh breath, and soon, her mother was driving her off.

They were both right about my son, about his character. My son was also one of the best people I'd ever known. He was better than me. Stronger.

And it was time he knew that.

CHAPTER
THIRTY-TWO

Thatcher

A creak in the floorboards caused me to turn on my grandma's piano bench.

I sat up as my father entered the room. I didn't know how I'd ended up in the parlor of my parents' house that night, my hands on piano keys. I hadn't started to play anything yet, even though I knew this room was soundproof and wouldn't bother anyone with it being so late. I put my hands in my lap. "Dad?"

He said nothing as he came over, still dressed from dinner in a sweater and dress pants. I guessed he hadn't gone to bed yet, and I hadn't either, still in my hoodie and jeans.

I remained silent when he took the space beside me on Gram's piano bench. There was surprisingly enough room considering how large we both were. Dad lifted his hands, placing them on the keys, and my breath stopped when he started to play.

I hadn't heard him play in years.

Gram had taught us both, of course. She'd taught the

whole house outside of my mom. Music wasn't really Mom's thing, but my sister and I knew how to play and, of course, my dad. He played a familiar duet, and since I knew it, I joined in. He'd motioned for me to do so.

It was easy.

My fingers touched the keys lightly, complementing his. We both could have played louder, and the song called for it, but we stayed timid on the keys. Maybe because the hour was late, but I kind of loved that we were. It was like we were both here in this confined space of the music we played. I wasn't much of a musician, not like Snowflake. It was something I'd done to bond with my gram, and I bet my dad would make the same claim, but in that moment, I got why Aspen did what she did for a living. Why music was her chosen field. It made you feel some kind of way and doing this with my dad...

At one point, he smiled, and I did too. It was nice to smile after today. So much had happened today.

The air emptied of sound after the final note my dad and I played, the moment over. I sat back after, kind of awkward.

"Not bad," Dad said, and I laughed, chuckling lightly.

"Not bad yourself," I returned. I placed my hands in my lap. "Never hear you play anymore. It was cool."

I think, like me, it hurt him to do so. My grandmother (his mother) loved her music so much, and I think the only reason we did do it was for her. It was hurtful for both of us. In different ways, but yeah.

Dad's hands stayed on the keys for a second, his expression tight, his smile tight. It didn't look like what I said bothered him, but I wasn't sure he knew how to respond. I knew the feeling. I loved my pop, but we didn't talk a whole lot, both of us awkward, I guess. I usually talked to my mom about things like tonight. She'd pulled me aside at the hospital, done her mom thing and fawned all over me. That was just what she did, and I was never hard up for that part of my life when it came to her. It was like she overcompensated for Dad, but she didn't need to. My dad may not be very open with his emotions, but I knew it wasn't because he didn't love me or anything. That was just his way, and I got that. I respected and loved my dad. I loved him so much.

"I'm glad I caught you," he said in the evening air. The dim light from the wall sconces softly illuminated his broad frame. Especially when it rose with breath. He faced me. "What you did… for Aspen was so brave, son."

I had to release a breath hearing him say that. I wasn't sure how his reaction would be to what had clearly been a desperate and dangerous move. It was one I didn't regret, but I could see him being angry. Things could have gone completely different than how they'd gone. I messed with my hands. "I know I probably shouldn't have gone into the hospital."

I'd had to, though. There hadn't been an option. That fucker had had Snowflake and…

My dad's hand coming onto my arm caused me to gaze up. He squeezed once, then moved it to the back of my neck, and I fell into a state as calm as when my mom and sister had hugged me today. When it was all over and I got to see them again. When I knew everything was okay. It was the same feeling I had when I'd hugged Snowflake after everything was over as well as another time tonight. It was after I'd asked if I could take her home.

"I love you." Aspen had said that, and it was like the world had started singing. Like every cliché thing that could have happened in that moment actually happened to me. Like feeling like you could dance and sing when I wasn't the best at the first and couldn't do the latter for shit. I would have sung a fucking opera tune, though, after she said what she had.

And how quickly I'd said it back.

It was how I felt, so that was what I'd done, and so much

comfort and calm came with that. It was crazy because I'd felt so vulnerable earlier that day and still had, but she'd done something so amazing for me in that moment. She made me feel calm and okay, and though this was a different feeling of comfort, I felt it again here with Dad. I'd been so happy to see him after it was all over.

Dad squeezed my neck again, and his face flashed with something. Whatever it was made his face so red, and my heart thudded. "Dad?"

"You are amazing, Thatcher," Dad stated, nodding. My mouth parted, but no words came out. Not one. His eyes crinkled in the corners. "Sometimes I find it hard to believe you're my son. You're so strong. So... so much better in so many ways than I've ever been and probably could ever be."

I didn't understand him saying this. In two seconds, he could have been in that hospital too. He would have done that for my mom, me, my sister, or anyone he cared about. I swallowed. "You would have gone into that hospital too, Dad."

"I'm not just talking about that." He gazed down. "You have handled your life with such grace. With such strength. Everything with your grandmother has been hard. I know it's hard for you, but you show up every day. You're there for her. You're there for this family and..." He braced my neck. "You're there for me. I look to you as the example. A way to be better. Your heart is so big, son, and I know you get that from your mom."

He looked... to me? I blinked, my face hot. "I look to you, Dad."

He let go, waving me off. I'd never seen my dad like this. We didn't really talk much. Not unless it was about business really or more neutral topics. I got that, though. Everything we were all going through with Gram was so hard.

Dad shook his head. "I admire *you*, son. Your heart is so big. So open. You let people in, and you're not afraid to show what you feel. I see you with your friends. You're the life of the party, and you definitely get that from your mother too. That likability and the ability to make people feel good. To just have a good time and be joyful, vulnerable." His head cocked at me. "You're not afraid to just be yourself, and I admire that so much about you."

My breath stammered now, my chest fucking locked. I didn't know what to say or how to be. I actually did all I could *not* to be that way around my dad. He'd never say it, but I always thought he saw that side of me as weak. Soft. It was something I couldn't always easily put away, and I wanted to be like him. *He* was always so strong, and I wanted to be like him.

"You're not afraid to love and to be loved," Dad continued, his smile small. "Your mom had to fight hard to get through to me, but you make that easy for people. You're so open, and you trust people. You don't shut the world out like I do. You step up. You're visible, and you don't disappear when you're going through something."

But didn't I? I mean, no one knew about everything at camp all those years ago. No one but my friends, my brothers…

Even they hadn't found out about things until after the fire. I'd done all that shit on my own, taken care of shit, but after, it'd taken a part of me. It didn't matter if I'd killed a monster. I'd still killed someone, taken a life.

I'd literally spilled everything to my friends after it all happened. I couldn't keep what I'd done in, and I'd felt weak then. I felt *soft.* I should have been able to take care of my shit, but I'd run to my friends like a little bitch. I'd vomited so much that night. Especially when I'd told them about Coach, what he'd done to me…

I just kept thinking back then, and even now, that my dad wouldn't have broken down like that. He would have been able to handle things and keep a lock on his shit. He would have handled his business *like a Reed* and not gone to his friends for emotional support. It'd been bad when I'd told my friends. They'd been angry, but not at me. They'd wanted to go back and set another fire. They'd wanted to burn Coach's entire world down, even though he no longer existed in it, and it had taken goddamn everything to keep their mouths shut about everything. They'd urged me to tell my parents, but I...

They'd been the only ones who knew about my past until I had to say something today. I had to protect Snowflake above *everything*, and it was one of the hardest things I'd ever done in my goddamn life. I'd kept thinking she'd look at me differently after she knew. That she'd see me as something weaker, lesser... I couldn't be that way in front of her, and especially in front of my dad. He was so strong.

"You don't disappear like I did," Dad said, rubbing my shoulder. "I have faded away after everything going on with your grandmother, and I'm sorry about that, son. I'm so sorry."

He didn't have to apologize, and he was *breaking me* right now. My chest hurt, so fucking tight.

"The way you've handled everything teaches me something," he continued, nodding. "You've taught me how things should be. I wasn't raised to express what I'm feeling, and I'm going to do better. I left you alone in this, Thatcher, and I'm so sorry about that."

It was too much at that point. This shit *killed* my insides. I had to look away, and my dad got closer.

"Son?" he questioned, and I gazed up. Dad's mouth parted upon seeing me, and I wasn't surprised. I couldn't fucking see him my eyes were so cloudy. He squeezed my arm. "Thatcher..."

It came out then. It *all* came out, and it was just like that day when I was twelve. I'd taken two buses to get back to my hometown that night after the fire. Coach had lived downstate, so I'd booked a ticket, a round-trip ticket. I'd handled my business and then come back, but I'd broken on the way. I held shit in, but the moment I got back into town, I called my friends. I'd broken down with my buddies around me, wailing, *crying* like a weak little shit. They hadn't judged me. They were just there for me, my brothers.

I never cried in front of my father. In fact, only my brothers had ever seen me shed a fucking tear, but they were there now just like that day when I was twelve. I squeezed them out, but that didn't stop the words from flying. I told my dad everything. The real reason that gunman had come to the hospital, how he was actually there for me, and how I'd ultimately gotten him to stop, turn himself in. The guy with the gun knew I'd told the truth about what had been done to me. He believed me.

And my dad did too.

I never questioned if my father would believe me regarding the abuse. His eyes on me, he held on to me during each and every word I said. His hold got stronger after every dark truth I shared, and it wasn't his lack of belief that kept me quiet for all these years. I was just so scared of not being able to be like him. Not being able to be strong, and I didn't want him to look at me like I wasn't. Like I was lesser. I'd let someone hurt me for *years*.

I hadn't been strong.

That wasn't how he looked at me, though, as I admitted things. It wasn't even how he looked at me after I explained the fire situation, then gone running to my friends. When I told him I'd cried and vomited, he only had one response.

"Thatcher..." I'd never seen my father cry, and I rarely saw emotion. He was a Reed and so strong, but when he blinked, I knew his eyes were just as cloudy as mine. He didn't even bother to squeeze them before a tear blinked out. He let it fall, a single tear hitting his chest. He grabbed both of my shoulders. "Son..."

His voice cracked. I saw *my old man* crack, and I broke too. It was like that day when I was twelve, and like my friends had back then, my dad's arms came around me. He hugged me so hard, fusing himself into me. He was shaking.

"Dad…" I felt my voice shake, my body shaking too. "Dad, I'm…"

"Son, I'm so sorry," he said, apologizing when I'd been about to do the same thing. I didn't know what my apology was for. Maybe because I wasn't who he thought I was. I was a fraud and not all those things he said. I wasn't open. I wasn't vulnerable. His hand gripped my hair. "I'm so sorry, my son. Thatch… My boy…"

I didn't know what my father was apologizing for, and maybe like me, he didn't know. Maybe we just needed to be like this. Maybe we just needed to break together. Maybe it was high time. Maybe it was past time.

Maybe it was *finally* time.

CHAPTER
THIRTY-THREE

Greer

The stands of Pembroke University's Memorial Field roared, the football game in full swing. Things were close. Terribly close.

"I'm not sure we're going to make it," I said, my boy out there on the field. He and his friends were, and they made their mothers and fathers watch one of the closest games of the season. In fact, this was the closest, and I was kind of shitting bricks.

"They got this. They got this." The whispers came from Aspen beside me, my son's girlfriend. The pair of us watched together from a private suite at the stadium. My son and his friends had gotten it for their families to watch whenever any of us came to Pembroke's football games. With our various schedules, it was rare the parents and families got to all be here at one time, but one person who always made the trek was my husband, Knight. He dropped everything for a game and didn't work nearly as much anymore. He was here and always at the same table with his mom when she was well enough to come.

Today was a good day.

I gauged my attention from studying my husband and his mom to the monitors in the suite, and Knight did too. He helped his mom stay current on what was going on, pointing things out to her, helping her. Did it hurt him that she wasn't always there and didn't really know who he was? I was sure it did, but it didn't stop him from showing up. He took every opportunity he could to be with her while she was on this earth. He loved on her while he could.

He always had so much love.

His love was there for me too. It was there for our son and daughter. It was there for our family and not every day was easy. There were still some nights I cried myself to sleep. It couldn't be helped after discovering the full brevity of what had happened to our son so many years ago.

"Greer, I failed him. I failed him…" My husband's voice had broken the night he'd told me. It'd been the same night we'd almost lost our son to a gunman. Knight had shaken his head. *"I didn't protect him, baby."*

My husband had taken the full weight of what had happened. He blamed it on his busyness, or various other things. Of course, what happened wasn't his fault. *It was a monster's* and a man our family put our trust in, and to find out that Thatcher had said nothing for years… had allowed this to happen to protect his friends from the same fate… Our son had thought he was protecting everyone, and we'd found all that out through family therapy. He'd told us.

Our son was so much like his dad.

There were so many similarities, that fierce protector who'd rather hurt than allow others to be caused pain.

I made myself the rock in our family after that. The beautiful men in my life needed it. I created a safe space for them to lay down their swords, to heal, and we told Bow once Thatcher was ready. The news had nearly broken his sister just like the rest of us. It had nearly shattered all of us, and there were still very hard days. Sometimes, I woke up to my husband sitting in the moonlight, so many thoughts behind his eyes as he stared outside. I held him close during those times just like he held me whenever I cried. We felt everything together, and after, we rose up for our family. Come to find out, Thatcher had been seeing his own counselors and therapist over the years. He'd wanted to handle everything on his own emotionally, he said, but he wasn't alone, and Knight and I would never let him feel that way again. He didn't have to be so strong. He could just be our kid, our boy.

I held Aspen's hand, being there for my son in another way now. His girlfriend was a nervous wreck just like I was, and I couldn't help but grin seeing what she wore around her neck. Thatcher had given her the ring he always wore. He'd put it on a chain just like his father had when he'd given me his ring so many years ago.

His girlfriend never took it off, squeezing the chunky gorilla ring in her hand. The ring represented community, and many in our small town, Maywood Heights, wore them. The rings and what they represented meant so much to the town, so it was a big deal that Thatcher had given his to Aspen. These two seemed destined, and of course, Knight and I knew what he'd done for her all those years ago with that monster. It all made sense now really. He was protecting her just like his friends when he took her.

I brought Aspen in, and we hunkered down. I think we both held our breaths, gazing from the monitors to the actual football field. All my friends' boys were out there too, their parents in here with me and Knight. At one point, Knight came over and put his arm around me. I noticed his mother by his side, like she felt safe there even with their distance.

I held Knight's hand too, and even Bow looked up from her books. She didn't always come to the games, and this one clearly had her engaged like the rest of us. Dorian, one of my son's friends, sprinted down the field with the ball, and though I didn't always know what was going on (I wasn't a huge football nut), I knew what it meant when the crowd roared. When Dorian cheered and his friends gathered around him. When our son found him and picked Dorian up.

The whole suite exploded, parents, friends. Aspen's mom had come to this game too, and even she was up out of her chair, cheering and applauding. We'd all come together through trauma, but somehow, someway, we'd stayed together and developed close friendships.

It was our kids, of course, to do that, our miracle kids, and the monitors flashed to a different image than the boys celebrating on the field. They suddenly filled with Aspen's face and mine beside her. This happened quite a bit actually. Aspen was a celebrity, and her and my son's relationship was apparently buzz-worthy. The camera man got Aspen cheering, then panned to Thatcher who was still on the football field with his friends. They put the camera right in his face and got the clear shot of him pointing to the stands. He kissed the necklace he wore around his neck while he did. He used to wear a cross during all his games, but somewhere along the way that had changed. He wore a gold snowflake now, something he said Aspen had given to him.

I didn't know what the snowflake meant to the pair of them, but him kissing it was meant for her. Of course, that made the stadium lose their freaking minds, and Aspen kissed her hands before blowing a kiss toward the stadium. The gesture was obviously meant for my son.

I smiled as Knight rubbed my shoulders. He kissed the top of my head before we both stared warmly at Aspen, who herself stared warmly at the monitors. I didn't think I was getting ahead of myself by predicting something wonderful in the future for the two of them. I mean, my son was still young yet, but I'd always wanted grandchildren.

"Baby..." Knight eyed me, as if knowing my thoughts. The subject of grandchildren and weddings had certainly come up when I'd realized how deep the two had gotten in with each other. Knight wrapped his big arms around me. "Let them be kids for a little longer."

He definitely knew my thoughts, didn't he? How I loved my husband, my protector.

We swayed together, a perfect harmony around us. Beautiful friends, both new and old, surrounded us. Family.

Like stated, harmony.

CHAPTER
THIRTY-FOUR

Thatcher

Wells scooted past me in the front row, fashionably late, but that was just how this dude was. I eyed him, his seat next to mine. "Nice of you to show up."

Dorian, Sloane, Wolf, and Fawn had gotten here over a half hour ago. They were up in the box seats, preferring to be out of the fray, but I was good right here in the front row. I wanted to be as close as I could for tonight's show.

Wells's eyes lifted, wearing a sports coat and no tie like me. I'd told my friends to dress nice, but tuxes and ballgowns weren't necessary. Not for Snowflake's concert. It may be at Carnegie Hall, her dream venue, but she wanted her patrons comfortable.

I was proud of her.

She'd worked really hard to get back here, but that had nothing to do with booking the actual venue. These people were greedy for her, everyone was, but I knew it had taken a lot for her to go back to the place where she'd frozen so many months ago. She'd finished the semester at Pembroke, but right after, she'd decided to have her first concert here. She was conquering her fears.

Again, I was so proud of her.

Her mom was here too somewhere and probably in her own box like my friends. She'd offered me a seat, but I had to be right here up front where Aspen could see me. I'd told her I got her and would be there for her.

"Dude, I got on a plane as soon as I could," Wells stated, settling into his red chair. None of my friends had to be here today, but of course, they wanted to be. They wanted to support Snowflake, and how good she fit into my friend group. They loved her just as much as I did and maybe even more. The guys had all apologized to her for how they'd acted when she first came to campus, and Wells had been the first in line. Shit, the two even bantered more in our group text than I did with them. Mostly to poke fun at me or give me a hard time.

And I didn't hate it.

I loved that all my friends were friends with her.

Wells nudged me. "Relax. She's going to be fine."

He knew me, so he knew I was nervous, but not because I didn't believe in Aspen. She just had to be so tense right now. I mean, how could she *not* be, and I didn't like being away from her if she was. I'd seen her before the show, and she'd seemed okay but...

"Seriously, she's got this," Wells said, and though he could have been up in the box too, he was down here with me. That was something I knew, so I decided to let go of the fact that he was almost late.

I tried to do what he said, *relax*, and I released a breath before flipping through tonight's program. Snowflake was performing the show all on her own tonight, with the exception of a well-known pop singer coming to join her for the final song. Apparently, Aspen had had quite a few people reach out when they'd heard she was going to play Carnegie

Hall again. They wanted to be there for her too. My snowflake had a lot of good people in her life, a lot of good friends. Two of which were my gram and sister. Gram would have loved to be here, but my parents thought it best that she watch the show from home. That was why they weren't here. They'd stayed home with her. My sister was tied up too, and when I mentioned that, Wells shook his head.

"If she and the kid could stay out of the library…" he grunted, and I had to roll my fucking eyes.

I faced him. "Well, who the fuck's fault is that?" We were basically the reason my sister had no social life. At least not outside of Legacy and whatever we were doing. Because she didn't do a whole lot, she filled her time with her studies, classes. She'd started a winter class today, and she probably was in the library.

Bru had taken one too, which was why he hadn't flown over to be here. They both were staying on campus during winter break with the exception of the days surrounding the holidays, and I think Bru mostly took a class so my sister wasn't alone. He was a good guy, the kid.

Wells just sat back, bunching his arms like I hadn't said anything. We were the reason my sister had no social life. We were because Dorian, Wolf, and myself were complacent with shit *Wells* started. He had a beef with my sister from years back, one that was still following her to this day. It had pretty much made her a pariah in high school and followed her into college since most people who went to our high school went to Pembroke. The only reason I was still letting that shit continue was because it made my job protecting her easy. Guys didn't mess with her because of her pariah status, and that meant I didn't have to break any faces of dudes trying to get into her pants. She was my baby sister, and I had to protect her.

Even still, it was kind of getting old, Bow and Wells's beef, but tell that to Wells. Maybe one day he'd come around, but my thoughts let go of that when the lights dimmed...

And my snowflake came out on the stage.

She wore a black dress with a slit that went so high it touched her hip. It made my cock twitch that I'd get to peel that shit off her later, her brown skin glowing when her thigh peeked with every stride she made across the stage. She had her cello in hand, her locs gathered in two intricate braids over her beautiful tits that pillowed in the tight fight of her dress. Her lips painted red, my girl was a goddess, and I was the first to applaud her entrance. The room erupted in clapping and cheers, but she heard me.

I made sure she did.

I was the loudest motherfucker in this place and would have stood if I didn't think that would embarrass her. That was the only reason I stayed in my seat, and right away, Snowflake's dark eyes connected with mine. She smiled slightly, those painted lips fighting a full-on grin. I knew that because I knew her.

My applause got louder, her head shaking at me before her gaze connected with the crowd. She nodded before taking her seat, and I thought I'd have to wait a second after the crowd silenced. I worried I'd have to wait a second. When she'd performed for my frat, it had taken a minute for her to get going, and that'd been with my help. I worried she wouldn't release her fears and hesitate.

But then I wondered why.

Her music filled the air, precision in each note, and I sat there with little breath. My girl fucking stole it, and she did that for the whole crowd. No one was breathing in that room as she played.

Absolutely no one.

I'd heard Aspen play before. She did sometimes back at school in the dorm. I'd catch her practicing sometimes, but that wasn't anything like this. She commanded this entire audience, the whole room just like she did whenever she played in front of just me. With this girl's music around me… nothing and no one else was getting in.

Nothing at all.

I had to look like a goofy kid, my grin on my face while I watched her. She was magnificent, and it kind of reminded me of how she looked whenever she came to my football games. The season had, of course, wrapped, but nothing was like knowing my girl was in Legacy's private suite. She didn't come to all of my games, but she came to most of them. She supported me, the pair of us a team.

"Fuck, yeah!" I couldn't help shouting after the final note my girl played that night. The pop star who'd performed the final song with her heard me. The girl's eyes flashed in my direction, but Snowflake's didn't. Aspen just laughed and pressed her hand on her dress. She did that as she bowed, and I was sure I was the only one who noticed she had a chain around her neck. It was the chain she wore with the ring I'd given her, and though that ring was tucked into her beautiful dress, she put her hand right over it. She had me with her the whole performance just like I had her with me whenever I was on the football field.

I pulled out my gold snowflake she'd given me, kissing it, and she beamed at me from the stage. There were a gazillion people here, but in that moment, it felt like we were the only ones.

We were the only ones.

Aspen and I ditched my friends and her mom after dinner that night. I loved my family and appreciated them for making the trip to NYC, but yeah. I was spending the rest of the night with my girlfriend. Aspen must have felt the same because she parted with her mom after dinner as well.

I will say my friends understood the dismissal. They all had partners, with the exception of Wells, but that dude never found issues trying to find folks to spend his time with. In fact, he was probably balls deep in someone right now, so I was never concerned about him.

My concerns lay with a certain snowflake and how I couldn't get her clothes off fast enough when we were finally alone back at my hotel. The night consisted of hard fucking, and after? Time in the bath. I made sure to soothe and kiss every visible part of her, spending extra time massaging her joints and hands. She didn't have too many issues with her autoimmune disease since her flare during the semester. She was on top of her meds, but I knew playing still took a toll on her. It was something she never publicly advertised, but I'd see the days where she'd need a heat pack or had to take some pain meds. It wasn't often, but it happened, and I figured massages and extra care didn't hurt. I liked taking care of her. Loved it.

"Thatcher!" She laughed, giggling like a schoolgirl in my arms. I had her embraced deep in my arms, my mouth on her neck, my teeth biting her skin. I loved breaking down this girl's walls, and she did when she unleashed the most child-like laughter. I didn't let her take herself too seriously and sometimes she serioused my ass up. We were a perfect combination. She touched my arms. "Thatcher..."

Oh, yeah. I definitely liked when she said my name like that. I also liked when she touched me, and she knew my boundaries. Some days it was still hard, but she got it now. She took care in knowing my limits, and what was nice was, I never felt ashamed about them. I never felt judged or weak with her.

I just felt.

I felt safe with Aspen Davis, and I knew she felt the same with me. The two of us were great, fucking magic.

I sucked hard on Aspen's skin in the bath. I didn't do it

hard enough to leave a mark but the brown tone of her skin definitely had a nice shade of rose coloring the surface. I pressed my mouth softly where I'd bitten. "Snowflake?"

She'd done so good at her performance tonight, and I was so fucking in love with this girl. Everyone knew of that love, my friends, my family and hers, including our parents. I caught all three of them looking at us sometimes whenever we were all together, her mom and my mom and dad. We'd all spent a lot of time together before the semester had wrapped.

It'd been nice.

I saw a visible change in Snowflake, her and her mom's relationship so different than how she'd explained to me before. Don't get me wrong. Her mom still put off that hard-ass energy, and I knew she pushed Aspen creatively, but those pushes were only on Snowflake's terms. Aspen had set boundaries, and her mom not only respected them but embraced them. Also, her mom fucking loved me, but then again, who didn't? Needless to say, whenever her mom came to town during the semester, I was asked to join her and Snowflake for dinner. Her mom was pretty cool behind her hard exterior, and I was used to a little tough love in my life. My dad had always been a hard-ass, and though that hadn't changed, our relationship had. It too had transformed. It was different.

And different wasn't necessarily a bad thing.

Once upon a time, I'd thought telling my father everything in my past may allow him to see me as weak. Like he'd look down on me. I'd wanted to handle things in my past on my own, and I hadn't wanted him to see how many of my choices I still carried on my shoulders. It was something I'd probably be working through the rest of my life, but I now understood I didn't need to go through things alone.

"Allowing people to be there for you makes you strong, son, and you're showing me that every day."

Dad had actually said that to me during family therapy, and he and my mom were still working through everything too. We all were with my sister. Our family had done therapy together and communicated. Our whole family dynamic had changed. *We'd* changed.

I'd changed.

There were some things that stayed closer to home. Things like the fire and the real reason I'd kept Aspen in that cabin. My parents wanted to protect me, and my mom had made the calls to make sure all that in the past stayed there. Normally, my dad would have taken the reins on that, but Mom wouldn't let him. She turned into Mama Bear and took care of her boys. I was sure that was hard for my dad, and though it was hard for me too, we let her. Sometimes, it was okay to let yourself get taken care of. Mom kept what I'd done to Coach within the confines of the Reed family. Aspen and my friends knew about it, of course, but Aspen's mom was still in the dark. That had been Aspen's request. She wanted to protect her mom from more pain, yes, but she wanted to protect me too. She didn't want to risk any potential fallout for me.

Fuck, how I loved this girl.

How different I'd become in such a small amount of time. How different *I'd allowed* myself to become, and I knew a big part of that had to do with this girl in my arms. There was no keeping myself locked up around her. It was like I wanted to tell her my secrets, my desires. Currently, those desires involved bringing out more of her little sounds in the bathtub, and she smiled after the last one I got her to make. She sounded so beautiful when aroused.

"What's up?" I asked her at one point. She'd gotten kind of quiet after the water settled and we just sat in the bubbles for a while. Actually, the bubbles were nearly gone. "I feel like you've been quiet."

She had with the exception of the noises I was physically making her make, and really, she'd kind of been like that all night since the performance. It was something I'd noticed. She'd allowed everyone else to talk, and I figured that was just because she was the star tonight and wanted to drink it all in.

I might have been wrong about that, her lips turning down after what I said. I pinched her chin, tipping it up. "Something going on?"

She knew she'd done amazing tonight, right? A fucking badass. She hadn't frozen, and she'd commanded the whole damn room. It'd been amazing to watch and inspiring.

Her eyes lifted, her expression warm. "Can't you just... I don't know, not know when I'm in my head about something?"

She was in her head about something? Fuck. I arranged her in my lap, making her look at me dead-on, and she laughed.

Her hands smoothed over my shoulders, feeling so fucking good, and my cock rose beneath the water under her. How quickly she could get me hard... distract me, but I wasn't getting fucking distracted if something was wrong with her.

"As you know, I'm going on a winter tour," she said, her arms wrapping around me, and I did know that. This concert today was pretty much the kickoff to that, and though she'd finished her semester at Pembroke, she planned to go back to work. She wanted to because she truly loved what she did and the music she made. She did, and I loved that for her. Though, I would miss her. She was going to do online classes while she was on the road, though. She wanted her degree too. Her head tilted. "Multiple dates. Dozens of cities."

She'd be busy throughout Christmas and the New Year. I would see her on Christmas, though. We'd already worked out that time. I braced her hip. "Okay?"

Her head dipped, suddenly looking shy in my lap, and

Aspen Davis wasn't fucking shy. She shook her head before facing the ceiling. "You know what? I'm just going to ask..."

"Snowflake, you're kind of fucking scaring me," I said, but my unease left a bit when a smile lifted her full lips.

Her thumb touched my mouth. "I wanted to know if you wanted to go on tour with me. We'd be back for Christmas still, and you'd be back for school in the spring. None of it would interfere with that." She shifted in my lap. "It's a lot of dates. A lot of travel, and you probably want to spend that time with your family, but—"

I pressed two fingers to her lips. "You were nervous to ask me to come with you? Seriously?" Did this girl not know I'd literally do anything for her? I felt like I'd proven that, and honestly, I'd been debating stowing away in her luggage, hard-pressed to let her leave without me. I'd like to say that was just for her, but this girl had made me completely dependent on her ass. What could I say? I was in fucking love and didn't fucking care who knew that.

Her smile went sheepish, shy. She shrugged. "I just feel like you'd get sick of it."

"Of what? You?"

"Maybe." Her arms settled around me. "I have no right to ask anything from you. Not a damn thing, Thatcher Reed. Not ever."

She'd never ever asked anything of me, and she'd never have to. I touched my forehead to hers. "Do you want me to go on tour with you? If so, I'd be fucking honored. Honest to shit, I wasn't sure how I'd let you leave me for weeks. I need to be with you."

"You do?"

I smiled. "I do, and that's a choice. It's one I'd make every time."

Something about what I said put tears in her eyes. She was so strong, but I had to remember sometimes, that was a front. This girl needed to have her walls broken down sometimes, and I had no problem bringing the hammer. She helped me with that too.

I fucked my girlfriend again that night. I fucked her a couple of times until I proved to her every word I'd said. The bubbles were gone by the time we finally got out, our hands and toes prunes, and she showed me something too that night. That it was okay to ask for what you wanted and accept when someone wanted to be there for you. That was hard for me sometimes too. Some of my nightmares had come back after I started going hard again with therapy, but Aspen was always there. Sometimes she never even said anything. She was just *there* allowing me to be in that safe space with her, and she didn't know how much that fucking meant to me. She was a rock I hadn't known I needed, a lifeline who had casually worked her way into my soul, and I'd forever be grateful for that.

I was eternally fucking grateful for that.

EPILOGUE

Aspen

I stared into the wide arena from the stands. This was by far the largest venue I'd ever performed in.

And I'd sold it out.

My entire winter tour had sold out, which still blew my mind. I'd been performing for years and on countless stages, but it still shocked me people came to see me. I was grateful, honored.

The arena was pretty dark now. My concert had been over for hours. This was my first date of my winter tour, so now it was typically time to relax.

Typically.

When large hands moved around my rib cage, I jumped but only on instinct. There was a reason the arena was dark, and I smiled, then gasped when those same hands gathered my breasts. They massaged my nipples through my glittery bustier. He'd told me to wear it.

"You remember the rules, snow?" Thatcher hummed into my hair from behind, and I just about melted on the concrete floor. My knees weakened, my breathing husky. "You don't leave this arena. No one sees you but me."

The material over his mouth brushed my ear, which let me know he'd covered it. That had been *my* rule. I'd let him chase me, hunt me, but only if he wore his Punisher mask.

My eyes closed, I placed my hands over his. He let my fingers glide over them, then move to his large forearms. My fingers teased the soft hairs, and even though he always let me, I still moved delicately and with intention. I wanted him to know he was safe, and I wouldn't ever do anything he didn't want.

I'd come to find out later Thatcher had issues with touch. It was something he hadn't allowed me to see at first, but once he'd admitted it, I completely understood. I *finally* understood, and I did everything I could to make him feel safe every day.

For so long, I hadn't understood, but now that I did, he'd never feel anything but safe and secure with me.

He made me feel the same way, this arena so dark, but I would still be exposed here. Thatcher had made sure everyone was cleared out, and my mom had had so much wine at dinner she was definitely busy tonight. She'd started seeing someone recently. Someone good and kind. He'd been the one to actually make sure she lay back on the wine tonight. She wanted to celebrate my opening date with me. Eugena Davis was finally letting down her hair and just having a good time.

We both were.

"No one sees what belongs to me, snow," Thatcher continued, his voice gruff. He dipped a hand into my bustier, part of my final outfit during the performance tonight, and as soon as his big hand gathered my breast, I forced out a breath. "I mean it, snowflake. Test me and see what happens."

Being a brat, I moved a hand over his cock, and he growled so deep in my ear. The grizzly sound traveled into my back, and I ran before he could tell me anything else. He didn't let me get far, his hands around my neck. He grabbed that and my ass.

"Dirty impatient girl," he crooned, pressing his dick between my ass cheeks. I was wearing faux leather but felt everything he had packing back there. He chuckled. "You wait. You wait for me. I'll give you ten minutes before I find you, but that's all you get."

He then proceeded to count, his hands slowly releasing my body. I could get pretty far in ten minutes, but this was Thatcher. I'd seen him play countless times on the football field with large dudes who were way faster than me.

Even still, I gave him a run for his money. I took the stairwell to the floor level, but all the while I felt his presence in pursuit of me, stalking me. Thatcher wasn't light on his feet, but he was quick.

"Snowflake," he taunted, teasing, and in the arena, his voice traveled. I'd seen nothing but darkness before his voice got closer. "At least make this hard for me."

Shit, I was *dripping*. He'd chased me a few times since we'd started dating, and it always got me wet.

I panted. "Fuck off."

His boisterous chuckle came from somewhere in the arena, and I cursed, knowing I'd probably given my location away. It probably didn't matter anyway, but I tried to make these chases hard for him.

"I'm taking your ass today," he said from somewhere, and I tightened below, in both places. Fuck. "I'm taking it hard for that."

I was sure he would. I never had been into anal sex, but something about when Thatcher was back there... He was unrelenting, vicious, and so fucking hot.

I really did try to make things hard for him. I ran away every time I heard him, but he still caught me barely into my run on the main floor. He was dramatic about it too, picking me up, and tossing me over his shoulder.

"You fucker!" I slapped at his back, my locs swaying, and his hand cracked down on my ass so hard I nearly came on his shoulder. I wriggled as the pain faded, and he chuckled.

"Oh, snowflake," he said, and I wasn't sure where he was taking me until we ended up on stage. Thatcher had watched the show from backstage with my mom, but nothing was like seeing him in the front row at Carnegie Hall. I'd told him I was fine that day, but I had still been nervous. I mean, I'd frozen the last time I'd played there, but seeing him in the front row… rooting me on…

It'd meant so much to me and made performing so easy. Some of his family had been there too, and it meant a lot that Wells had showed up. Obviously, we hadn't gotten off to a great start, but he had later apologized for that. All of Thatcher's friends had for giving me the cold shoulder at first.

Wells and I were super cool now, and he'd explained to me he had just wanted to protect his friend back then. I understood that now too. Thatcher Reed was a unicorn, a beautiful, intense being who needed to be protected at all costs. He *took care of me*, protected me.

And let's not even start on what he did for my body.

My pants were stripped away quick on the stage floor, and it wasn't dark on the stage. Here, the spotlight was still on from my final performance. Thatcher had me on my knees, my boots and pants stripped away.

"*Fuck*, your ass…" Thatcher bit it easily, nothing but a lace thong back there, and I bucked, mewing. He gripped my ass cheeks. "This shit's so fucking beautiful."

He kissed my bottom like it was, his mask rough on my skin. He forced me to my back, but I fought him, kicking. He had on nothing but his jeans and mask, his cutoff tee tossed somewhere.

Goddamn was this man beautiful, his dark hair curling

over his electric-blue eyes, his sharp earrings flicking back and forth. He was like an erotic dream, and his breath got husky when he forced my wrists to the stage. We'd made such beautiful music out here earlier tonight, and I meant *we*. It'd taken a lot of convincing, but I'd gotten Thatcher to play piano with me again during one of the softer numbers. I thought it would be a great tribute to his gram, and she'd loved it when I'd played the footage of our performance for her through FaceTime earlier. Thatcher had gotten her on the phone, and we'd played it for her. She'd loved it, and I was so glad we had gotten to share that with her.

Thatcher and I had created beautiful music, which made what we were doing now on this stage that much dirtier, depraved. Thatcher forced my legs apart, but that left my hands free. I went for his face, but he gathered both of my wrists in one hand.

"Watch the goods, lovely," he said, arrogant as fuck. He was such a pretty boy and spent more time at the mirror than me. He brought his masked face close, smelling like sea and so very male. "Otherwise, I won't stop even after you beg me."

He probably wouldn't. Not unless I used my safe word. I wriggled, and he brought one of my arms behind me, his abs clenching and dick so hard. The outline surged at the fly of his dark jeans, and he rubbed it as if to give himself relief before moving himself against me.

My hips corkscrewed, but that didn't stop his pursuit. He ended up getting me on my knees again, my panties ripped away when he shoved his hand down my bustier. He gathered my tits in one large grip before shoving his fingers inside me.

"Fuck!" I called out, trying not to enjoy this… to make him fight for this, but it felt so good. He flicked my clit while he did, and the next thing I knew, his mouth was on me from behind.

His fucking mouth.

He didn't even have to hold me down now. I was gripping the stage as he feasted, tasted. He got me so wet, and he'd obviously taken his neck gaiter down.

"So fucking sweet, snow. So goddamn sweet," he crooned, and I gazed back to see him reaching into his pants. He had his cock out, fisting himself, and the fact that this got him off as much as it did me did something for me.

I fought my orgasm. I fought it so hard. I was on the cusp of it, and it was like he knew. His mouth left my sex, and the next thing I knew, he was reaching into his pocket.

It wasn't for a condom.

A large squirt and he had his hand filled with lube. Apparently, he'd come prepared. He forced it all over his large cock, then used even more to push into my tiny hole.

"I said I was taking your ass, snow," he said, putting the lube bottle down on the stage. He kissed one of my cheeks. "This beautiful… gorgeous fucking ass."

He bit at it like it was. Like he really meant it, and we didn't use condoms anymore. Not since we'd both gotten tested. I hadn't had any recent partners before him, but I wanted him to feel safe too.

Again, he'd always be safe with me.

I made sure he felt that whenever I could, and like him eating me out, I didn't fight when he pushed my ass cheeks apart, then later eased himself inside. I made it so easy for him, always did whenever he fucked my ass, and the invasion had us both groaning, bowing. I curled, and he embraced me so tight, his bear hugs the epitome of his own version of safety and security.

"Fuck, I love you," he said, his hips thrusting, slapping. "I love you so much, Aspen."

I was close to coming before, but then he said that. It was like I could physically feel his love in the words. I did feel it, loved it.

Taking his hands, I brought him closer, meeting every thrust until my walls vibrated below. I came so hard and fast, always did. "I love you too."

Thatcher's high was right behind mine. He roared as he filled my ass with so much cum I felt it drip from my ass to my sex. It even went down my thighs and Lord knew we'd have to clean up this stage once we were done.

"God, I love you." He said the words while hugging me, kissing my back, my neck. He squeezed my breasts. "I'm so fucking lucky. I'm so goddamn lucky, snow."

Oh my God.

If I hadn't already come once, I would have again. This guy was literally a fucking unicorn.

And he'd chosen me.

I'd chosen him too, of course. We'd chosen each other, and I noticed his ring around my neck when I finally came out of my emotions a bit. It glided above the stage via a long chain and had been something he'd given to me.

I'd given him something too, and I studied the gold snowflake when we later lay on the stage together. He kissed my brow, holding me there. He'd told me he was lucky to be with me, but I considered myself the lucky one. The guy had been looking out for me longer than I'd even known. He'd shown me love even before he knew me.

And he said he was the lucky one.

The end.

ACKNOWLEDGMENTS

I want to take a moment to thank all my patrons on Patreon for all their support! I appreciate each and every one of you. Thank you so much for supporting me and my work <3

My Lovely Patrons:

abbycadabby	Daisy G	Kaitryn S	Michelle M	Taylor G
Aiden	Daisy_66	Kara G	Michelle T	Taylour K
Ajia B	Danielle	Karina R	Mike L	Tiffani
Alex J	Danielle B	Katelin	Mona B	Tiffany S
Alex M	Delayne	Katherine	Ms. Diamond	Torri L
Alexis C	Destiny H	Katherine M	Naomi	Trinity S
Alondra A	Devon O	Katie	neli	TurtlezBooktok
Alyssa G	Devonne H	Katie H	Nichole T	Valorie B
Amanda B	Dixie	Katie J	Nikki S	Victoria P
Amanda C	Elissa C	Kay	Nikki W	Vieve
Amanda M	Elissa C	Kaylea G	Nusrath C	Violeta W
Amanda S	Emi B	Keathe S	Oyatunde A	Whitney C
Amandha K	Emilee R	Kelley M	Paige L	Xen G
Amber M	Emily D	Kelly S	Peggy S	
Amber O	Emily C	Kenda L	Pippa S	
Amie N	Emily K	Kimberly	Rachel	
Angelica	Erika ~ eat.read.lift	kimiy	Rachel M	
Annalisse G	Fanny L	Kirsty A	rae	
Aria B	Frances G	Kittycat	Rebecca C	
Ashley H	gaige	Konstantina S	Ressa	
Ashley P	Gemma	Kristina	Rhi Rhi	
Ashley R	Gi	Kristina M	Rosa M	
Aubrie O	Gigi M	Kylie N	Rose C	
Becky B	Grace	Lauren L	Rose-Mari	
Bibiana	Haley R	Leah A	Ruby H	
Blair H	Heather L	Leah C	Ruth Y	
Breanna	Hissa A	Leah R	Ruthy	
Breanne T	Imara	Leanne	Samantha	
Bree B	Jacquelynn R	Leighton G	Samantha	
Breister Family	Jamiese	Lindsey W	Samantha M	
Brianne	Jasmin W	Lis	Sara S	
Brittany	Jasmine J	lizbit1979	Sarah J	
Brittany V	Jenascia L	MacKenzie	Schella D	
Bryn M	Jenna B	Madison G	Shaunna D	
Caitlin R	Jennifer	Malaika M	Shekinah K	
Candias K	Jess M	Maria D	Sophia A	
Carrie	Jessica B	Marie C	Sophie	
Christina	Jessica R	Marissa P	Sophie B	
Christine M	Jessica W	Melissa	Stevie B	
Ciara C	Josephine M	Melissa P	Sunni	
Cici K	Justice	Michaela P	Tabitha O	
Coffee Break with Books	Kaci L	Michele S	Tammi H	
Cynthia	Kaely C	Michelle	Tawnya M	

If you'd like to join me on Patreon (and be listed in the acknowledgements page in my next book!) You can join me at the link below:

https://www.patreon.com/edenoneillwrites